"You're my adventure," Meg murmured

Ridiculous woman. Adam tightened his grasp on her shoulders and heard her suck in her breath. He pulled her closer to him, so that they were touching. She didn't resist; instead she looped her arms around his neck.

"Are you trying to frighten me?" she asked softly, her breath hot against his cheek.

With one hand he cupped a breast, waiting for her to push away. Instead her eyes widened and her mouth opened with a sigh. That's when he lost it. He covered her parted lips with his. Kissed her hard and deep and lost himself in her.

She was so sweet. He angled his mouth to take the kiss further. She filled all of his senses—she was all he could think of, all he could imagine. His hands explored her body—the sweet fullness of her breasts, the lush curve of her hips. Her body fit him so perfectly, he could easily imagine them together naked.

He wanted to make love to her.

He wanted to make love to Meg more than he'd wanted to make love to any woman in a long time.

Instead he pulled away from her. This was insane. He was *not* going to become involved with Megan Cooper.

Meg smiled at him and he felt a reluctant tug.

"That's twice," she said. "If you kiss me once more, we'll be lovers."

Molly Liholm loved her visit to Sedona, Arizona, and did indeed spend time communing with the vortexes—she figured it couldn't hurt! The Arizona landscape is breathtakingly beautiful. The town is populated by interesting characters. Morever, the positive power of the place must have helped, because she had a lot of fun writing about an abandoned bride searching for her own happy ending. *The Adventurous Bride* is a delightful spinoff to Molly's February Temptation novel, *The Getaway Groom*, where we first met the heroine Meg.

Molly lives in Toronto, Canada, where she longs for the nice weather of Sedona!

Books by Molly Liholm

HARLEQUIN TEMPTATION
552—TEMPTING JAKE
643—BOARDROOM BABY
672—THE GETAWAY GROOM

THE ADVENTUROUS BRIDE
Molly Liholm

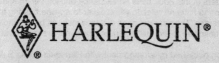

TORONTO • NEW YORK • LONDON
AMSTERDAM • PARIS • SYDNEY • HAMBURG
STOCKHOLM • ATHENS • TOKYO • MILAN • MADRID
PRAGUE • WARSAW • BUDAPEST • AUCKLAND

For Maggie Strawbridge
a good friend who knows how to tell
a really funny story

ISBN 0-373-25806-2

THE ADVENTUROUS BRIDE

1

SHE NEEDED A MAN.

Megan Elizabeth Cooper had considered the idea all day long as she rang up her customers' purchases. Meg's feet hurt, her neck was stiff and she was tired, but she couldn't get the thought out of her head. She would have closed the shop a few minutes early if Gloria Logan hadn't arrived just as she was thinking of locking the door and turning over the sign to read Closed. Then she could slip upstairs and enjoy her Saturday night ritual of a long bubble bath, followed by pizza and a video. But Gloria was a frequent client at the bookstore, coming in every two weeks and always buying a substantial selection of novels, so there was no way Meg could ask her to hurry up.

Especially not for pizza and a video. Beautiful Gloria with her choice of men would never understand. Meg sighed. How had she ended up like this?

Once again Meg studied the virile, barely dressed, extremely broad shouldered heroes on the covers of the dozen romance novels that Gloria had chosen, and decided she needed a man exactly like one of those romantic characters. He would certainly liven up her Saturday night routine.

A romance novel hero? She was definitely losing it, Meg thought. Sure, she needed more adventure in her life, but get real. Had the last fourteen months really led to this? To Saturday night all alone, dreaming of paperback hunks? All that was missing from the classic spinster image was the cat.

No, her little voice argued. A strong, virile hero was exactly what she wanted. A man who stood up for his beliefs. A man who valued women. Who wouldn't be afraid to commit. Unlike her fiancé. No, she was wrong once again. Her fiancé had been perfectly willing to commit, only not to her. She wasn't really sorry that Max had decided to marry Emma instead of her. It was just that after fourteen months of looking, Meg thought she would have figured out what she was looking *for*.

Gloria noticed Meg eyeing her selections. "Gorgeous, aren't they?" She sighed dreamily, tracing the bronzed pectoral muscles of the open-shirted pirate on one of the covers with a well-manicured fingernail. Gloria's pink lips curved in a soft smile. "If I ever met a man like that, I'd keep him."

Meg was surprised. "You must meet a lot of different types of men on the ranch." Indeed, with Gloria's angelic blond curls and wide blue eyes, petite yet curvaceous figure, men fell all over themselves trying to get to her. There might have been something that bothered Meg about Gloria, but there was no denying that she was gorgeous. While Meg considered herself attractive, she'd never had the knockout effect Gloria had on men. The best Meg had ever done was perhaps a mild concussion.

Gloria frowned. "All city slickers looking for a little adventure." She shook her head, her curls framing her face. "Corporate guys in suits aren't my idea of heroic."

Heroic. Meg tested that word. Did she really want a hero?

"No cowboys?" she asked Gloria instead. The books Gloria had chosen featured a pirate, a dashing knight and several clones of the Antonio Banderas desperado type, but Meg knew the romance rack also featured a plethora of cowboys. She rather liked cowboys.

Gloria wrinkled her perfectly pert nose in disgust. "I want an ideal fantasy man. Not some stinky old cowboy I can find around here anytime." She studied Meg, and Meg hoped she wasn't blushing. She'd sought adventure in Sedona, Arizona, because she liked cowboys. All her life, she'd been fascinated by Western TV shows, Zane Grey novels and Clint Eastwood. But Gloria didn't ask about Meg's preferences. Instead, she said, "My brother asked me to invite you to dinner on Thursday."

Now Meg knew she was blushing. Reid Logan was a cowboy and a very successful rancher. Moreover he was a really good-looking cowboy. He had one of the largest cattle-raising properties in the state. Reid had invited her to the Liberty L once, and Meg had enjoyed visiting a real ranch and riding the range with a real cowboy. A very sexy cowboy.

As well as being a cattle ranch, the Liberty L hosted a very exclusive dude ranch operation. Gloria was the apparent brains behind the fantasy vacation, handling small groups of high-paying guests looking for the Western "experience." Reid hadn't thought much of Gloria's operation, he'd admitted when Meg questioned him, but he'd said it gave Gloria something to do. Reid's clear affection for his sister, his willingness to let his younger sibling find some sort of career for herself were traits that Meg found appealing. She believed in family loyalty.

And Reid was appealing himself, with broad shoulders, sun-bronzed hair and a mischievous smile. His "aw shucks, ma'am" demeanor didn't hide his quick intelligence or the sudden flare of interest she'd spied in his blue eyes more than once when he'd looked at her.

Maybe she should take Reid Logan up on his unspoken offer.

After all, she'd always liked cowboys.

In her other life, the one that Max tore apart, some of her favorite books she'd edited for her family's publishing company had featured rugged Western mavericks. Meg wondered if fate was trying to tell her something. Kismet. The forces of the universe bringing her to the Southwest to live out her dreams. Then she wouldn't be the dumped bride anymore. Instead she'd be the adventurous bride, a wild, daring woman who found the man of her dreams in cowboy country.

No, she had simply been living in Sedona for too long. Its mystical beliefs were beginning to sink in. Soon she, too, would be believing in the power of the vortexes, in crystals and magic. She shook herself. She was a hard-headed and hard-hearted New Yorker. Still…it would be nice to believe that fate was taking care of her life for her. That she didn't have to.

That adventure would just come barging through her door.

Meg noticed she was unconsciously tapping her finger against the cash desk. She thought she'd stopped that bad habit once she'd arrived in Sedona. Clearly, she needed to do something different with her life. "I'd be happy to come to dinner," she announced, deciding that Reid Logan might indeed be the man for her. Ever since her aborted nuptials she'd been man-shy. Perhaps it was past time to get back in the saddle. She'd encourage Reid's interest and find out. After all, she and Reid did have a lot in common. They were both the responsible ones in their families, the ones who struggled on despite the odds. Plus, sex with a handsome cowboy had always been one of her favorite fantasies.

Sex had been the mistake she'd made with Max. They had agreed to wait until their honeymoon to consummate their relationship. And what had happened? He'd married someone else—the bridal consultant!

Yet Meg had to admit that her hard-hearted, hard-headed New York self seemed to have mellowed. Nothing was so important that she had to rush through her days. Before, deadlines and the competition had had her racing to simply keep up. The need to sign up the next bestselling author before another editor could had always driven her. Now, however, she had time to look around, to enjoy the sunsets and the spectacular scenery of the red rock country. Driving through the desert, she could stop and spend hours looking at its changing colors; the wondrous reds varied in richness and brilliance according to the sun and clouds. She was thrilled by every change and nuance.

Moreover, she positively enjoyed working at the store, gossiping with the customers. She'd never had time for that in New York. There all her days had been filled with thoughts about Scorpion Books. How her books, the books that she had acquired and edited, would sell. How she could steal away a top-name author from another publishing house. Her job had been her life. She'd worried more about the company and loved it more than she'd loved Max. Max hadn't made a mistake marrying Emma Delaney.

As Gloria paid, took her bag of romance novels and waved as she sashayed out the door, Meg considered yet again what it was that she really wanted. She wandered over to the romance section of the shop and studied all the heroic bare chests displayed on the racks in front of her.

What in the world was wrong with her? Why couldn't she ever be satisfied? She'd spent the last fourteen months searching within herself for what she truly wanted in life, yet she still didn't know what she was seeking. In Sedona, however, for the first time, she'd been happy. The last four months felt good. Sedona and this shop, The Gateway, felt like where she was supposed to be. Meg smiled at her own thoughts; she really was turning into a New Ager.

But she'd also found herself falling into old habits. She'd agreed to manage The Gateway for Abigail Milton, so that Abby could spend more time on her search for spirituality—and have more time to play with her state-of-the-art computers, which Meg sometimes thought gave Abby more pleasure than the search for inner peace. When she'd taken over, the New Age store had specialized in crystals, angels and natural medicines. The book section had consisted of one small rack holding bestsellers that were long out-of-date according to New York publishing standards. Meg made some changes. The book section now filled half the shop and sold briskly.

Meg was a little surprised at how instinctively she understood public taste, but then it wasn't so different from her old job. Even though both the tourists and residents of Sedona were there for the mystical properties of the place, to experience the powers of the vortexes, they still liked to read the latest legal thriller or romance novel.

Rubbing a knot in her neck, Meg cast one last look at the glistening, alluring covers. She was going to give Reid Logan a chance. And if he wasn't what she was looking for, well then, maybe it was time to go back to New York, to go back home.

Maybe she should just accept the fact that she wasn't going to find adventure here.

She needed to lock the front door before she emptied the till and deposited the cash in the wall safe. While Sedona was a quiet, peaceful town, Meg was glad she didn't have to walk alone in the dark to the bank to make a night deposit. There was too much of the Manhattanite in her to trust even a friendly little town like this.

But not so much of the old Manhattanite anymore. No Donna Karan power suits for her in Sedona. Her well-faded jeans and feminine pink blouse were a far cry from her professional-urban-career-woman look. She sighed, fingering the ruffles. She liked her new look. It was a lot softer, reflecting a side of herself that she had previously ignored. Maybe she should stay. But in the last letter she'd received from her father, he'd begged her to return. Was she really willing to give up the career that she had prepared for so carefully and thoroughly, a profession she'd centered her whole life around, a job she had truly loved? She'd still be sitting in her corner office of Scorpion Books if it hadn't been for her abruptly canceled wedding. Would she have been happy if she'd stayed? If Max hadn't abandoned her, would she just have continued as always? No, even before the debacle with Max, she'd begun to fear that her career had become her life. And that a life centered around work wasn't enough.

She missed her father and her brother, however. Wasn't

it immature of her to be afraid to return? Was she really jealous of their happiness? Her brother had recently eloped with Sarah Tepper, and Meg suspected her father would be making his own wedding announcement soon.

Everyone in her family had found true love, except her. No wonder she was spending too much time staring at romance novel covers!

Meg turned her back on the books and straightened her shoulders. She had to finish closing the shop before she could retreat upstairs and enjoy her Saturday night. *Alone and loving it*, she thought with a weak grimace. At the door, Meg turned over the Closed sign and had begun to twist the lock—it was tricky and needed jiggling—when she was thrust backward by the force of the door swinging in. She stumbled, caught herself and opened her mouth to tell the rude customer that the store was closed. The words died away and her mouth gaped open as she stared.

She was staring at a gun. A Smith & Wesson .45, she realized, having edited a very successful police-procedural series. Refusing to give in to the panic threatening her, she let her thoughts drift to wondering how the police procedural writer, Doug Hatfield, a homicide lieutenant, was doing. She'd write to him tomorrow. He'd get a kick out of hearing about her radically different new life.

If she was alive.

Back to reality. This was one time when she wished her propensity for daydreaming could take her far, far away from the gun pointing at her. Back to her nice safe office in Manhattan. A nice corner office with a view of Central Park. What had ever made her give it up for adventure?

She tried to take a deep breath but couldn't get air into her lungs. Her legs began to shake, and she could hear the blood pounding in her head. *Pull yourself together, Cooper*, she told herself angrily. *You're faced with a dangerous situation. This is not the time to faint.* She had to think. She was proud of how she could always reason her way through any situation.

Her powers of reason fled at the sight of the dangerous man holding the dangerous gun.

He looked ruthless, his hard face not handsome but compelling. Stubble covered his chin and Meg could see several bruises along his jaw. Dressed in dusty jeans, a T-shirt and dark leather jacket, he could have stepped off the covers of one of the romance novels that Gloria Logan had bought.

Meg felt an incredible urge to run her fingers along his battered face, to soothe him.

She gasped, raising her traitorous hands to her mouth to cover her reaction. Her palms were sweaty.

"Quiet," the man ordered, his voice low and gravelly. Meg felt a bead of sweat trickle down her spine, and she kept her hands over her mouth to stop herself from saying something foolish.

Her shocked gaze locked with his. Green eyes. She'd always been partial to green eyes.

"Move," he ordered again, waving his gun toward the center of the shop, indicating she should stand there, far away from the front door. She did as he asked, keeping her eyes away from the cash register. What was she doing, trying to distract attention away from the money? She should be pointing him toward it and away from herself. Another bead of sweat trickled down her spine and she shivered. Surely this man wasn't an ordinary thief? No, he couldn't be. For some reason she was convinced that he wasn't.

She heard the door lock snap shut—naturally he didn't have to jiggle it like she did—and her stomach leaped. She was alone with this gun-wielding desperado, no one would look for her until Monday morning—thirty-six hours from now—and her heart was pounding fast and furiously. But it was no longer from fear.

Meg turned around to face him and as unobtrusively as possible pinched herself. The man didn't disappear and Meg was irrationally happy.

He stood at about six feet, Meg noted. A taut and muscled six feet. For a moment she lost herself admiring his broad shoulders. She'd always been a sucker for broad shoulders—that had been part of Max's allure.

The man limped toward her. Meg stood perfectly still and raised her chin, telling her crazy libido to rein itself in. She'd read that fear could be a powerful aphrodisiac, but she was behaving ridiculously! Her pulse pounded furiously. "There's over three hundred dollars in the cash register," she tried to say calmly, but heard a quaver in her voice.

The man turned those hard cold eyes on her, and she was afraid again. She remained frozen to the spot as he assessed her from head to toe in a calculating, derogatory way. She locked her knees together to remain upright.

"I'm not here for your money."

Oh God, Meg prayed silently. "Don't hurt me, please."

He advanced toward her until he stood only inches away. Meg could smell him, a mixture of leather, sweat and male. Her knees threatened to buckle but she held herself upright. She wasn't going to let him see her fear.

He pressed the gun nozzle between her breasts and Meg screamed. To hell with not showing her fear. She stepped back to run—as fast and as far as she could—but his hands grabbed her, one like a steel vise around her waist, holding her against him, the other over her mouth, stifling her scream.

Her pleasant little Antonio Banderas fantasy shattered at being held captive by this potential rapist. She bit him. Hard.

"Dammit!" the man shouted in pain, the arm pinning her to him loosening enough for her to break away and run.

She heard him curse again, and hadn't taken more than half a dozen steps when a hand on her shoulder pulled her back and spun her around to face him. She used the momentum of his movement to swing her arm back and punch him in the stomach.

This time he made an extremely peculiar noise, dropped

the gun and fell back. Meg dove for the weapon, grabbed it and pointed it at him with shaking arms.

He got to his knees and while clutching his middle— surely she couldn't have broken a rib with only one punch—raised himself to his feet. He'd looked dangerous before, but as he glared at her, she became even more frightened—which was ridiculous because she was the one holding the gun, she reminded herself. The piece of practical advice didn't cheer her the slightest, however.

On his feet he took a menacing step toward her. "Stop or I'll shoot," she said, not nearly loudly enough, her voice again quavering.

"I don't think so." He took another step forward and stopped.

How did he do that? she wondered. How could he scare her silly with just his tone? Now he was calmly assessing her while the gun shook in her hands.

He studied the gun and then her. She was imprisoned by the fierceness of his eyes, by the green that was so dark it was almost black. The gun was now bobbing up and down in her clasped hands like a life jacket caught in a storm. She hoped he didn't try to grab for it; she might shoot him by accident.

He took another step forward.

"Stop. I mean it." She held the gun tighter, trying to stop the trembling.

"You've never fired a gun in your life—much less at a person, Abigail Milton," he said with complete confidence.

His arrogance made her mad. He might have twice her strength and be intending to rob her or kill her or whatever, but he didn't need to insult her. "It's a Smith and Wesson .45," she said. "With eight bullets in the magazine, plus one chambered. The design gives it greater accuracy, so that when I release the safety, like this—" she did so "—it's ready to fire. Because it has a hair trigger, the slightest movement could set it off, so I'd suggest you stand very, very still. Because you're right, I'm very nervous, but I am aiming at your chest, the biggest part of you, so I'm bound to hit something.''

The man didn't move, but she could see him ready himself to strike if she lowered her guard even for a second. Meg took a deep breath and then another, wishing she'd paid more attention to Greg's mantra lessons about calming herself. Her new Sedona friend believed in meditation, claiming it could save one even in a life-threatening situation, giving one the calmness needed to analyze the possibilities of one's actions. He'd tried to teach her, believing she would need it on the dangerous streets of New York City, not the quiet sidewalks of Sedona. Unfortunately, she'd found all the deep breathing a little silly, but now wished she'd paid more attention and had some way to lessen her fear.

"Who are you?" she demanded.

"You asked me to come, Abby."

"I'm not Abby," she snapped, before realizing that telling him the truth might be a mistake.

He scowled at her, seeming to take up even more space in the tiny shop without moving a muscle. "Abigail Milton is the owner of The Gateway. She lives in her store. I watched this place all day, and you're the only one here." His words came out in a gasp as he held his middle. How badly had she hurt him? Meg realized abruptly that he'd been injured before he'd walked into her store; the bruises on his face, the way he held himself made it obvious.

Thinking of him watching her and her shop all day made her neck prickle. When she'd stepped outside for a few minutes during lunch, she'd felt something unusual, but thought it was only her growing dissatisfaction with her search for adventure. She really should be careful what she wished for. She wiped a bead of sweat off her face. "I'm Meg Cooper. I work for Abby."

The man shook his head. "Abby said she would be here. She asked me to come."

"She's not here," Meg said almost gladly. Maybe the man would just leave if she told him the truth. "She went on one of her retreats. She's been gone for over a week. I don't know how long before she'll be back."

The man seemed to sag. It was only a slight movement in his shoulders and a lessening of the rigid tension in him, but it was as if he'd just lost a portion of the fight.

Meg realized she was no longer as scared as she'd been a moment before. Now she was more curious and worried. Abby did know a lot of unorthodox people, but why would she be involved with a man like this? Why would she have asked him to come and then not waited for him? No, this story was too suspicious; he was probably trying to trick Meg into letting down her guard. She tightened her hold on the revolver.

"Damn," he muttered. He gave her a funny half smile full of confidence and arrogance, just like Travolta did in all of his films. "Now what do we do?"

Meg ignored the tingle she felt at his smile, ignored the sweat on her hands. "Why did you want to see Abby?"

"She asked me to come," he repeated, his green eyes holding Meg's gaze.

She blinked to break his spell on her. Didn't he know how to say anything else? He certainly wasn't a very creative liar. "Abby didn't tell me about you."

He shrugged, and Meg stiffened, afraid he would strike. "I didn't tell her when I was coming." He studied Meg and then smiled again, a lady-killer smile. Meg's heart raced.

"If it's okay with you, I'll just leave now." He took a slow step backward, his hands raised in the air to show that he was harmless.

He would never be harmless, Meg thought as she watched him take another careful step toward the door, toward freedom, away from her.

He was practically at the door, and Meg could only watch with fascination as one bead of sweat after another trickled down his face. Was she really just going to let him leave?

In this suspended moment in time, where there was

only Meg and this dangerous, sexy man, Meg watched him reach the door. His hand was on the knob. "Wait," she cried, and the man froze.

"It would be better if I just left." The words came out hard and clipped, and Meg could see that sweat was now drenching his black T-shirt.

His fierce eyes came back to her face, burning her, holding her captive. He raised an arm toward her. "I need my gun."

Meg had taken a step toward him before even being aware of deciding to help him. She was too late to catch him as he fell face forward on the floor.

"Oh, no. Let it be nothing awful. Not him," she said, chanting her own personal mantra as she rushed to his collapsed body. He lay very still, and for one moment Meg wondered if he was dead. Or if this was a trick, but she didn't have time to worry. She had to help him; she couldn't explain the compulsion, she just felt it. Kneeling down beside him, she touched his neck and found his pulse erratic. She rolled him over onto his back, frightened by his pale face. His shirt was soaked and she struggled to pull off his leather jacket. Finally she managed to tug it off one shoulder and then the other.

She ran her hand over his chest, stopping when she touched something warm and sticky.

She stared at her hand.

Blood.

She pulled up his T-shirt and saw something of the wound—a slash made by a knife, caked with dried blood and fresh rivers of bright red. She tore off the old bandage it looked like he'd wrapped around himself and stared, her heart pounding in her ears, her eyes clouding over.

She blinked, clearing away some of the nausea. *Stay calm,* she told herself, trying to quell the sickness. It didn't work. She raced to the small bathroom at the back of the shop and threw up.

Once finished, Meg splashed cold water on her face and then glanced in the mirror. Was this wild-eyed woman really calm, collected Megan Elizabeth Cooper? Her brown eyes glittered; her cheeks were flushed. Shaking her head at her reflection, she wondered what she was getting herself into.

She'd asked for an adventure and she seemed to have received her request. In spades.

On legs that wobbled, she walked back through the shop and looked at the unconscious man. "It's okay," she told him. "I'll help you." She felt a little click inside of herself, as if a missing piece had just found its home.

She set to work, picking up a medical book and some of the natural drug therapies. She'd need boiling water and clean towels. After she checked out the deepness of the cut, perhaps put in some sutures and bandaged the wounds, she'd figure out how to get him to the storeroom. Meg thanked fate that a year ago she'd volunteered at a health clinic in Los Angeles. At the free clinic in a desperately poor neighborhood that included gangs, she'd expected to fetch and carry, to hold patients' hands and do some filing, but due to the shortage of staff and funding, Meg had done much more. She'd watched enough nurses and doctors fixing wounds to know what to do now.

On the way to the kitchen she passed the phone and stopped. She should pick up the receiver right now and dial 911. Calling for help was what any calm, sensible, rational person would do. She lifted the receiver, but slammed it back down.

The old Megan Elizabeth Cooper would have called the authorities, but the new Megan Elizabeth Cooper was determined to find out if this man was what she'd been looking for.

She plugged in the kettle and gathered the towels. For herself she added a bottle of whiskey, taking one quick gulp out of the bottle. It burned on the way down, but it gave her confidence.

Returning to the man, Meg touched his proud, hard face. He didn't move. She might be the most susceptible victim of the Stockholm syndrome ever, when hostages began to sympathize with their captors, but she knew she had to help him.

She didn't believe he was a murderer or a rapist or anything awful. She searched his pockets for identification, but found nothing. Maybe he was a private detective. Or a spy. All she really knew was that he was a desperate man and he needed her help.

No matter who he was or what he wanted, Meg wasn't going to let him die. Or turn him over the authorities. Somebody had stabbed him and she was going to save him.

Because he was her adventure.

victim of the Stockholm syndrome even when hostages
began to sympathize with their captors, but she knew she
had to help him.
She didn't believe he was into S&M or a rape, or anything weird. She searched his pockets for identification,
but found nothing. Whoever had beaten him had taken it
away. All she really knew was that he was a desperate
man and he needed her help.
No matter who he was or what he wanted, she wasn't
going to let him bleed and then...

2

HE FELT PAIN.

Everywhere.

He kept his eyes closed, isolating the injuries. His ribs
were definitely broken. They'd been broken before; he'd
survive. The rest of his body felt sore, but nothing else
was broken. He moved carefully and a searing pain in his
right side made him gasp. Fighting to stay conscious, he
searched his memory for what had happened to him ever
since he'd begun this stupid investigation.

He remembered the parking lot at the Phoenix airport,
the Arizona heat scorching him to his bones. Then something hitting him hard. He had faint memories of being
bundled into a car and being driven to what seemed like
an empty warehouse. Two men who kept asking him
who his contact had been. The beating and the knife.
They'd threatened him with it, telling him all the slow,
painful ways they could cut him. He'd thought of his sister, Kelly, and how she'd been hurt and never said a
word. Slowly he'd realized the two men hadn't wanted to
kill him. When they'd heard noise which turned out to be
the janitor unlocking a door, the blond younger man had
panicked and thrust the knife into him. He'd managed to
twist slightly so that the blade made a long cut and he
bled a lot. Feigning unconsciousness, he'd dropped to the
floor and the thugs had run. Their mistake. They should
have made sure he died. Their carelessness, he judged,
meant they weren't professionals.

He opened his eyes. His mistake. The woman was sitting on a chair next to him.

She smiled. "Good, you're awake. I was getting worried. Here—" she raised a glass of water to his lips "—you must be thirsty."

He drank, trying to figure out where he was this time. After the pair of hoodlums had abandoned him, he'd dragged himself to a corner, where the janitor hadn't seen him. The janitor had been a kid, really, more than happy to play his walkman too loud and do only the most perfuntory job.

Then he'd passed in and out of consciousness a couple of times while planning his next move. Somehow the bad guys had known he was after them while he didn't even know what he was investigating. He was following his instincts and his desire for revenge. No one could hurt Kelly as they had and not suffer for it.

Now he used his military training to observe and analyze: the room was small and dark, with no window. Shelves against one wall held an assortment of junk.

"You're in the storeroom," the woman said, answering his unspoken question.

She refilled the glass and he drank the water down. He was thirsty. "What happened?" he asked.

"You passed out from your wound. It looks like you lost a lot of blood. I cleaned out the cut. It didn't look like any major arteries were severed, so I sewed you up."

She looked pleased at her words and he felt even worse. "*You* examined my wound and sewed it up? Are you a doctor?" he demanded.

"Oh, no." She smiled at him and patted his hand. "I read what to do in a book and then followed the steps. Just like Salma Hayak in *Desperado*. Plus I'd volunteered in a clinic where we saw a lot of knife wounds, so I kind of knew what to do."

"What?" Surprise made him try to sit up, which was a mistake. Pain attacked him and he collapsed back on the bed. Immediately, the woman was next to him, helping him settle back, moving the pillows to find him a comfortable position. Her small hands felt surprisingly strong on his shoulders. He noticed how pretty she was now that she wasn't scared of him. Of course, she hadn't been scared of him the entire time he'd pointed his gun at her last night, either. For one wild moment, he'd thought she'd been attracted to him, that she'd been imagining them together. That she'd been thinking about sex.

If she had a brain in that pretty little head of hers she'd still be afraid of him.

He trusted his instincts when it came to people, and his instincts were telling him this woman intended him no harm. But clearly she was a nut. "You could have killed me," he complained sourly. The woman thought she was the heroine of a bad movie. She'd performed surgery on him. Ignoring the fact that he hadn't gotten any help for himself while knowing the wound was a bad one—he'd needed the time to get one step ahead of his opposition— he complained, "Why didn't you call a doctor?"

Her mouth tightened a little. He thought he saw anger in her eyes as she shifted slightly away from him. "I could phone a doctor now if you want. I thought that you might want to avoid the authorities, but if it's all right with you I'll get Dr. Jenkins."

"No." He grabbed her hand to stop her exit, but the woman hadn't moved.

"I didn't think so." She held his hand with both of hers, looking down at his much larger fingers between her soft ones. Then she smiled, the anger gone, replaced by pleasure. Her brown eyes sparkled. She was certifiably insane. "You're just like Harrison Ford in *The Fugitive*, aren't you? A desperate man on the run. I knew I had to help you."

"Help me? Lady, you're nuts. I could do anything."

"Are you going to hurt me?"

"No."

"I didn't think so." Still holding his hand, she smiled again and leaned forward as if sharing a secret. Her brown hair fell against his bare chest. "You see, I wished for you on Saturday night," she confided, as if her words explained her bizarre behavior.

He extricated his hand from hers. Yep, he was dealing with a total nutcase, all right. He needed to get out of here and call in. Get some help. Check in with Kelly and try to make her tell him what had happened to her. "What time is it now?"

"It's Monday morning. I'm about to open the store."

It couldn't be thirty-six hours later! He was losing valuable time. The whole point to his desperate race to Abigail Milton, to risking his life, had been to win time and surprise. He'd managed to drag himself out of the warehouse and, with the money he always kept in his boot, he'd gotten himself back to the airport and the rental car that was still waiting for him. The amateurs had ambushed him at his car and never thought of getting rid of it.

Whoever was after him thought he was dead. He'd made the quick drive to Sedona and then spent the remainder of the day checking out Abigail Milton's store. The fact that he could make contact with her was his only advantage.

But if he didn't get out of here soon, he might as well be dead. "I can't stay. I have to leave."

The crazy, if pretty, woman gently pushed him back down, and he found he was too weak and too tired to resist. He had to fight to keep his eyelids open.

She assessed him calmly and then informed him, "The medical textbook said you needed lots of rest. It also looked like you took quite a beating. As a result, I've kept you sedated."

"I have to leave," he mumbled thickly, wondering what was wrong with him.

She picked up the water pitcher and stood, examining him critically. He wanted to tell her to go away, but he couldn't make his mouth move. "There was a double dose of sedatives in the water. I didn't think you'd take it voluntarily. You might as well relax and enjoy." She smiled at him. "We haven't had any time for the social niceties. My name is Megan Cooper." She raised an eyebrow at him questioningly, but he scowled and closed his eyes.

More sleep might clear his head. It felt thick and jumbled and he couldn't concentrate. When he woke, if he was lucky, he might be back at the Phoenix airport, where he'd been ambushed. And the pretty but crazy woman would be gone, a figment of his fevered brain. Then he'd be safe.

HE WOKE AGAIN.

Opening his eyes, he was glad to see that he was alone. The crazy woman was gone. Megan Cooper, he remembered. It wasn't a name he'd forget anytime soon. The next time he heard it he was going to run as fast and as far as he could. She reminded him too much of his family.

He spent a minute testing the aches and pains in his body before sitting up. The wound in his shoulder was only a dull ache. Once he got his ribs taped, he'd be fine. He'd been hurt a lot worse. The knife wound felt surprisingly good, although the stitches were beginning to itch. His crazy doctor-wannabe had done a good job.

He looked around the storage room. He was lying on a tiny fold-out bed tucked against one wall; the opposite wall held shelves. All kinds of weird junk filled the space: rocks, jewelry, old books, boxes of papers. He shook his head. Neither Abigail Milton nor Meg Cooper were much into organization.

He'd spent more than long enough here, it was time to go.

The door was locked and surprisingly strong, he discovered when a good kick didn't knock it off its hinges. He kicked it again, this time out of frustration, and then had to lean against the wall to gather his strength. The ambush had taken more out of him than he liked to admit.

Someone was unlocking the door. He was too weak to make it across the small space and surprise whoever was on the other side, so he lowered himself to the bed, feigning even greater weakness.

It was the woman. The last ray of sunshine backlit her shiny brown hair, catching the golden highlights. *Be careful,* he warned himself. He'd had experience with her type before.

"What was all that noise? Are you all right?" She moved into the room, bringing a wave of freshness in with her, but that was only because the small storage room had grown stuffy. She knelt by his bed, concern on her face.

Even if her little nurse routine wasn't an act, even if she really was worried about him, she was still trouble, he reminded himself.

Meg touched the bandage covering her surgery, a frown creasing her brow. "Does it hurt?"

He captured her small hand against his bare chest.

"What?" She raised her eyes to his and tried to free her hand. He held it a little tighter and watched her eyes grow wide with fear and something else. Good, he could use fear. He was going to ignore that "something else." He knew how much trouble a woman like Megan Cooper could be for him—his personal Achilles' heel. Instead, he studied the open door, but so far, he hadn't seen or heard anyone else.

"Why did you lock me in here?"

"I didn't want one of my customers stumbling across you by accident."

"You could have closed the store."

She'd stopped trying to pull her hand away. "I have no idea if whoever is after you knows where you were headed. A break in my routine would be suspicious." She looked at him proudly. "I've read a lot of mystery and spy novels."

She had a point. He let go of her and she scrambled away from him, holding her hand against her breast as if it had been branded.

He stood, crowding in on her. She took another quick

step backward. At least she had the sense to be a *little* afraid of him. "Do you have any more medical tape? I need you to bind my chest."

"Your chest." Her eyes darted to his bare chest, up to his eyes and then back to his chest. He watched her blush. So she liked his chest. That was something else he could use. *Carefully.* He knew how easily he could get burned. But first he needed fresh air. "I have some broken ribs. It's easier to move if the injury is bound."

"Oh, of course." She blushed again and blinked. "Come to the kitchen—there's more room." She led the way through the store. It was one of those touchy-feely, in-sync-with-the-universe places that he found so ridiculous. He hated places like this and the kooks who believed in all the mumbo-jumbo. Kelly had probably spent time here and liked it. Ignoring the shop, he watched the sway of Megan Cooper's butt under her flowing skirt.

The kitchen was a regular kitchen decorated in the Santa Fe colors so prevalent throughout the area. The window offered a spectacular view of one of the highpoints, a landscape of red rocks.

"That's Coffeepot." She pointed at the natural monument of red rocks, which didn't look anything like a coffeepot, as far as he could tell. "I couldn't believe how beautiful it was when I got here. It's why I've stayed."

"You're not a lifelong Sedona resident?"

She ignored his tone, which made it clear she fit in just fine with the leftover hippies and mystics that populated the area.

"It's a nice town," she said simply, still sorting through the first-aid kit. She advanced toward him with the Ace bandages and a pair of scissors. He suddenly wondered what she'd done with his gun; he needed to find it before he left.

Meg was flipping the pages in a book, and he saw it was a medical textbook. He was glad he'd been unconscious when she'd performed her beginner surgery on him—though she couldn't be quite as flighty as he'd pegged her for if she'd taken care of him herself.

But was she foolish enough to leave herself alone with him?

"Raise your arms," she commanded, frowning at an illustration in the book. "Okay, I've got it." She placed her arms behind him, securing the Ace bandage and pulling it tight across him. She bit her lip as she concentrated.

She was pretty when she did that. To distract himself, he asked, "How did you get me into the storeroom?"

Meg frowned as she concentrated. "Oh, the bed rolls. Luckily, you regained consciousness near the end of the…procedure and were able to get yourself on the bed. I just rolled you into the storeroom."

So the silly little fool *had* taken care of him by herself. Exactly the kind of woman he had vowed to stay away from, he told himself yet again as he felt her breasts brush his chest, smelled her scent…of roses. Very feminine and lovely. He let himself enjoy it for a few seconds and then clamped down hard on his weakness.

"There." She stepped away from him. "As long as you don't run into any doors you should be fine."

"It wasn't a door that did this." He made his voice gruff, intending to scare some sense into her. She was too much like Kelly, and Kelly had almost died. He needed to scare some sense into Meg so that when he left she'd be smart enough to take care of herself. In spite of himself, he couldn't bear the thought of this sweet, brave fool ever getting hurt.

Her startled gaze flew to his. She exhaled her breath in a soft gasp, color rising under her fair skin. But she wasn't as scared of him as he'd wanted. She was mesmerized by what she saw in his eyes. He knew what she saw and cursed himself for a fool. But he couldn't help himself.

He raised one hand to trace the softness of her cheek. She was so lovely, with that beautiful skin, the golden brown hair framing a perfectly oval face. He liked her neck, long and slim, perfect for a man to trail kisses along to her breasts. Great breasts, great butt. He hadn't seen her legs yet—her long skirt covered them—but he knew he'd like them.

She was breathing faster, her breasts pushing against her blue silk blouse. He lowered a hand and held on to the edge of the kitchen table behind him to stop from reaching out and covering one of her breasts with his palm, just to see how she'd react.

He'd bet Meg was one of those woman who flushed from head to toe during climax. And he'd like nothing better than to make love to her for a long, slow time and watch the color spread over her body. No throwing her across the kitchen table for him; he wanted a soft bed and all night.

He broke the spell first, reminding himself, again, that this impulsive kind of woman was dangerous. He'd learned all about women like her through painful experience.

"You should have phoned the police."

Meg stepped back as if a bucket of cold water had been dumped over her and glared at him. "You are awful," she exclaimed. "I save your life, I keep you hidden and all you do is criticize! Well, that's it. I've had it. I am going to phone the police."

She walked across the room and picked up the phone—actually, she flounced, and he admired the movement very much before he acted. He grabbed the phone out of her hands and hung it up. "I don't think so," he whispered into her ear, realizing he was holding her too close. He let go, but it was too late.

Meg flung her arms around his neck and kissed him. Enthusiastically and passionately. Like she'd been imagining kissing him for days. He felt his equilibrium slip as her soft lips tantalized and her even softer body melded itself to his. God, she smelled like roses and sunshine and woman. He could imagine what it would be like to make love to her: she'd be giving and so damn sexy.

Meg moved seductively against him, but he resolutely

kept his arms down by his sides, hands balled into fists. When she traced the seam of his lips with her tongue, searching for entrance, he pulled her off of him.

She raised bright, sparkling eyes to him. "Do you want some soup?"

SOUP. She couldn't believe she'd asked him if he wanted soup, but she wasn't good at asking for what she really wanted. *Do you want to have sex right now? Fast, hot sex on the kitchen table if necessary.*

When she'd asked for adventure she'd had no idea what she was asking for. No man had ever been able to turn her on with just a look before. Or with a kiss—even if he hadn't kissed her back.

He hadn't kissed her back, she thought as she poured pea soup into two bowls. But he'd wanted to. The look he'd given her earlier had revealed that. He'd wanted a lot more than a kiss then.

He was probably being noble or something, not wanting to involve her in his troubles. What a guy!

Her hands trembled slightly as she passed him the bowl of soup. If he noticed, he didn't comment. He eyed her soup suspiciously, his slash of a mouth turned down. "How do I know it's not drugged?"

She raised a spoonful of her pea soup to her lips and swallowed. "Delicious." Running the shop and checking on her mystery man hadn't left any time for herself, so she was starving. She sneaked a glance at him. He was still frowning and stirring the soup. Finally, he raised the spoon to his lips and tasted. She remembered what those lips had felt like pressed against hers and had to busy herself with her own soup, trying not to drop her spoon due to suddenly clumsy fingers. She'd just thrown herself at him!

He didn't comment on her culinary skills, but she shouldn't really have expected him to notice that she had made the soup from scratch that morning. She might as well have opened a couple of cans.

He helped himself to another bowl. That was good. He needed to build up his strength. So they could catch the men who had tried to kill him, and do whatever else he needed to do.

She hadn't spent half her life reading mysteries and thrillers for no reason. Or watching every Alfred Hitchcock film and every episode of *Columbo*. Meg knew she would be of invaluable help to this stranger. This was what she'd been waiting for her whole life. What she'd been searching for during the past fourteen months.

She was going to have a real-life adventure.

All the other things she'd tried over the last fourteen months—volunteering at the clinic, the stint as a kindergarten teacher's aide, working as a personal assistant to a TV star, bungee jumping and rock climbing to test herself—had really only been leading up to this man. To this moment. To helping him.

As soon as he started talking.

"What?" he finally asked, when he noticed Meg staring at him.

"I want to know everything," she said enthusiastically. He swallowed some more soup. "What's going on? Who tried to kill you? How I can help?"

"You can help by getting me my gun and saying goodbye." He pushed away his empty bowl.

Meg put the teapot on the table in front of him with more force then she'd meant to. "You could at least tell me your name."

"Smith." He paused slightly and his green eyes bored into hers. "John Smith."

Meg thought that one corner of his mouth twitched. Let him laugh at her all he liked; she just had to remember no one had ever said that having an adventure was easy. She also remembered how he could make her sweat with just one look. Calm, cool, collected Megan Cooper turned into a puddle of longing with just a look. She loved it!

Their eyes locked for a second and Meg heard that little

click again. Definitely the right man. Her man. Now all she had to do was convince him.

John Smith, or whatever other absurd name he liked to call himself, could pretend all he wanted, but he felt it, too. By the time he figured it all out, it would be too late. He'd be hers. She was sure of this. How she felt about him wasn't at all how she'd felt about Max.

Meg knew it was silly, but all her life she'd believed that if she just waited long enough she'd find her soul mate. That the other half of herself was out there some- where, searching for her as well, and when she met him she'd know immediately he was the man for her. She'd feel a click as their two souls connected. But she'd spent a lot of time waiting in New York, she'd spent her entire life getting ready and then...nothing. Then she'd met Max and decided her romantic dreams were ridiculous, that she should be mature and marry a man who loved her and was right for her. So what if there weren't any fireworks and or a soul-clicking moment.

After the debacle with Max, she'd decided to find out what else there was in the world for her. But after all these months, she'd grown tired and discouraged. She'd tried all kinds of new things, met all kinds of odd and wonder- ful people, but she still hadn't felt that click.

Not until this man.

Meg smiled as John Smith finished his tea and she poured him some more. "Why are you here? Why are you looking for Abby?" He didn't answer. Instead he leaned back and surveyed her kitchen.

She liked her kitchen. It was in this cozy room that she'd finally made the time to cook, and learned that she liked it. The earth tones of the view outside the window were reflected in the decor. She'd had a good time shop- ping for the dusty rose placemats and matching tea tow- els, for the oversize mugs and brightly colored dishes. This kitchen was the first home of the new Megan Eliza- beth Cooper.

John Smith yawned, then looked surprised.

She bit back her smile. "Maybe you should go back to bed. At the clinic we recommended lots of rest," Meg offered innocently.

"Nonsense." John yawned again. He glared at her, those green eyes fierce and compelling. She felt like he was reaching out into her very being. Oh yes, John Smith had to be what she'd been searching for and she wasn't about to lose him. "I've been here too long already." He stood, but grabbed the chair for support. He looked at her in astonishment.

"You've drugged me. Again."

Meg nodded. "The book insisted you needed rest. And you did say you wanted to leave—I didn't think you'd listen to reason."

"Damn you for interfering, meddling..." His voice slurred and he swayed.

Meg was at his side, tucking herself rather nicely under his arm and tingling a little at the feel of his body pressed against hers. She tried to steer him back toward the storage room.

He didn't budge.

My, he was strong. Meg couldn't wait until she was in his arms when he was healthy. She knew they would be fantastic together. Would their first time be fast and explosive or all night long? She shivered in anticipation.

She wished she could tell him everything she was feeling, but one look at his hard face told her this wasn't the time.

Still refusing to move, he glared at her. "How did you do it? You ate the soup as well."

Meg sighed. "The tea." She nodded at her untouched cup of tea.

Smith shook his head, and some of the tension in his body eased as he let her walk him back toward the storeroom. "I've always hated tea." Once there, he shook her off and lay back on the bed himself.

Resisting the urge to curl up beside him, Meg wondered how long it would take him to fall in love with her.

"You," he accused with a scowl, "are going to be nothing but trouble."

forgotten the urge to curl up inside him. Meg wondered how Angel would take him falling in love with her.

"You," he roared with a scowl, "are going to be more
lasting trouble."

3

HE WOKE AGAIN.

He stirred cautiously, checking out his various body
parts again. Everything moved better, didn't hurt as
much. His ribs hurt only when he breathed, and he was
aware of the knife wound only when he wasn't thinking
about his ribs. The forced rest had done him good, but he
wasn't about to tell his crazy captor that.

He wondered what she was cooking up now. This time
he was getting out of here without eating or drinking anything. His watch told him it was 9:30 on Tuesday. Escape
was in order.

Standing also felt okay. Walking the few feet to the
door was much easier than yesterday. Turning the knob,
he raised a brow in surprise as the door opened. So, for
some reason, Meg Cooper was no longer keeping him
captive. Did that mean she had reinforcements? Nothing
would surprise him about Meg Cooper.

Only a certifiable kook would work in a Looney Tunes
place like this. He surveyed the store as he passed
through it—the crystals and angels, all ridiculous nonsense. Potions and lotions filled the shelves and glass
cases. Meg Cooper was flighty, irresponsible, trouble, and
most important of all, she was history.

Despite his injuries, he moved through the shop
quickly and was at the door when he remembered he
didn't know how to contact Abigail Milton. As a result of
his actions, she might very well be in danger. Meg would
have to tell him where he could find Abigail.

And tell him what she'd done with his gun. Where
would the foolish woman have hidden it?

The kitchen. He knew she'd keep it in the kitchen, probably in a jar of flour like the heroine had done in *Witness*. Damn, now he was thinking like her; he needed to get out of here, fast. Meg Cooper was dangerous to him. The bad guys he could handle. The case he could eventually crack. A woman like her was a different matter.

Walking very quietly, he made his way toward the enticing smells emanating from the kitchen. Baking. He smelled cinnamon and his stomach growled. Too bad, but he wasn't eating or drinking anything Megan Cooper might offer him. He'd find fast food or something later. He rather doubted that pretty Sedona had a McDonald's anywhere on its main street—nothing so commercial and profitable for this place—but he'd eat some herbs and dried grass and whatever else they had to offer. As long as Meg's pretty hands hadn't touched them.

At the kitchen door he stopped again in surprise. Meg was pouring coffee for one of the two women sitting at the kitchen table, both a few years older than Meg. Her partners in crime? As if sensing his presence, she looked up and smiled. "How nice of you to join us." She waved him in and he found himself reluctantly entering. Now what was Meg up to?

A lively redheaded woman turned a perceptive gaze upon him, studying him from head to foot. "Is that *him?*" she asked, as if he wasn't standing in front of her.

"Yes." Meg smiled at him as if she'd won the lottery, her brown eyes turning all gold and soft in the morning sun.

The red-haired one shook her finger at him. "Well, then, good luck, young man. At least you've got good taste. But I hope you learned your lesson. Imagine treating a fine girl like Meg like that."

"Would you like a muffin?" Meg teased him with a plate of warm, home-cooked muffins. He found himself reaching for one before he remembered his vow. Unfortunately, his stomach wasn't cooperating; it grumbled loudly.

"Michelle made them." Meg pointed toward an ath-letic-looking woman in her late thirties dressed in practical safari wear. "She's famous for them."

Deciding to take the risk, he took a muffin and ate it in three swallows, then found all three women staring at him. He felt like a little boy caught stealing cookies in his mother's kitchen. "It's good," he assured Michelle, who only scowled at him. What was wrong with the women in this town, anyway?

The red-haired one patted her curls and smiled flirtatiously at him. He kept a neutral expression as he looked to Meg for help. What story had she told these women about him? If he was lucky, he'd be some distant relative of hers passing through town.

He should have known he wouldn't be lucky.

"So you're Meg's fiancé," Michelle said accusingly, her voice hard.

"*Ex*-fiancé," Meg corrected. "He left me standing at the altar."

"And now you're back to try to win Meg again, to make amends—having realized the error of your ways. This is so romantic," the red-haired one gushed.

"She should shoot him," Michelle declared.

Reflexively, he touched his wounded shoulder, but the two women didn't notice. Meg did, her eyes narrowing slightly, and then she smiled.

He was her ex-fiancé? He had left her at the altar? The woman was one-hundred-percent certifiably nuts. The faster he got out of the store, away from Meg, the better. As soon as she told him where he could find Abigail Milton.

He needed Abigial to explain her suspicions. Since he'd read her confusing letter he'd managed to piece together a lot of the puzzle, but he didn't know who Abigial thought was behind the criminal activity in Sedona. Once he discovered what Abby knew, he'd be able to uncover what Kelly's involvement had been—and decide what to do about it. For the first time in his life, he was actually debating whether or not he would reveal what he uncovered about a criminal activity—the forgery ring in pretty, mystic Sedona.

"Where are my manners?" Meg suddenly said. "Darling, I'd like you to meet two of my new friends, Michelle Stoneaway and Rachel Lunden. They've made me feel so welcome here in Sedona. Naturally, I couldn't help but tell them all about you, about us."

Naturally. He stepped forward to shake hands with Rachel, who fluttered her eyelashes at him. Michelle practically broke his hand. "Meg never told us your name."

Meg turned a curious face toward him, waiting. "Smith," he said, and she made a little moue of disappointment. "Adam Smith." He ate another muffin as the women waited for him to say something else. He wasn't going to help Meg with her crazy story.

"Imagine arriving out of the blue like this, determined to win back Meg's hand." Rachel fluttered. "This is so romantic."

"He hasn't won me back," Meg countered. "Adam has merely realized the error of his ways. He's come crawling back to make amends."

Adam tried to maintain a bland expression as he reached for another muffin. Michelle glared at him and then turned to Meg.

"Men! What else can you expect? Take my advice, girl, turn him down. He's an attractive specimen, I admit, but the best thing he ever did for you was not marry you. Soon you'd find yourself tied down with children while he's gallivanting around." Michelle nodded at her own words. "Marriage is only a trap for women. That's why I've remained single and intend to remain so."

"Not if Jason has anything to say about it," Rachel teased her friend.

"Waiting for any man to arrive and make your life better is just a silly dream."

"Michelle, you're being too harsh. And you have to admit Adam has a certain appeal," Meg insisted.

"I'm not blind, girl. I'll admit he has great shoulders and other...attributes, but don't be fooled by his masculine appeal. Take him to bed if you like, but don't marry him!"

Before Adam could get out any kind of response to Michelle's blatant sexism, Rachel clapped her hands together in excitement. "This is going to be so interesting. I thought you were going to marry Reid Logan."

Meg choked on her cup of coffee. "Reid and I haven't even gone on a date!" she protested.

"Oh, dating is overrated," Rachel insisted. "I've seen the way he looks at you, and how you've looked at him. Why, I'd assumed that you were lovers already. Oh my—" she slapped her hands over her mouth "—I shouldn't have said that in front of *him*."

"That's quite all right, Rachel. Adam gave up his right to be jealous a year and a half ago. But you're wrong about Reid and me."

Michelle stood and glared at Adam one last time. He was beginning to think it was the only facial expression she was capable of. Then she turned to her friend. "Rachel, I think we've disturbed these two long enough. We should leave them alone to discuss their situation. Remember, Meg, you're better off alone. You!" was all she said to Adam, but it spoke volumes. He was overwhelmed by the urge to assure Rachel that Meg was safe from him, but restrained himself.

Only now he was even more caught up in the crazy life of Megan Cooper. He'd known she was trouble and should have just made for the front door when he'd had the chance. Someday he'd listen to his head when it came to women like Meg.

Just as soon as she told him where he could find Abby—and told him anything she might know about Kelly—he was going to get away from her.

Meg only smiled at the two women and walked them to the door. Adam thought about making his telephone call to his boss from her kitchen phone, but decided he'd rather get as far away from Meg Cooper as possible. But first he needed his gun.

"Smith? Adam Smith was the best name you could make up?" Meg demanded as she walked across the kitchen, picking up the mugs and loading the dishwasher. Adam couldn't help but admire her backside in the tight jeans, or when she turned around, her breasts clad by the black T-shirt. Meg had a lot of nice curves for a man to discover. But he wasn't going to do any discovering. Let Reid Logan do that.

"Who's Reid?" he found himself asking.

"A local rancher. His sister Gloria comes into the shop a lot. Adam Smith? You sure don't have a lot of imagination, do you? I always thought whoever I ended up with would."

Ignoring her last words, he merely said, "Adam Smith is my name."

"Then why did you use John Smith last night?"

"Revenge. I knew the obvious alias would annoy you."

"Oh." Meg frowned at him in confusion. "But I haven't done anything to you. I saved your life." Her brown eyes flashed at him as she raised her chin.

He couldn't believe her. "You drugged me twice."

"It was for your own good."

"Now you sound like my mother."

"Ouch. There's no need to be mean." Meg turned away from him and busied herself at the sink for a minute. Adam didn't say anything, knowing she wouldn't be able to remain silent for long.

"So what do we do now?" Meg inquired.

"*We're* not doing anything. I'm going to get my gun and then leave. The farther away from you I am, the better I'll be." He'd never spoken truer words. Maybe he should head back to New York and rethink his case from there. His escape from this crazy situation, however, wouldn't help Kelly.

"Now you're being unfair." Meg crossed her arms and leaned against the kitchen counter. "If you're going to be rude and arrogant, I'm not going to tell you where I hid your gun."

Adam smiled with real pleasure for the first time in days. "You don't need to tell me." He looked around the kitchen, and then moved Meg aside to uncover the canisters she'd been screening with her body. He reached for the flour jar and heard Meg gasp. Digging through its contents, he felt the heavy metal of his revolver.

"How did you know it was in the flour jar?"

"I watch movies, too. *Witness* with Harrison Ford and Kelly McGinness."

"Oh." Surprisingly, Meg sounded happy. "You see, we are meant to be together. We have so much in common," she added enthusiastically.

He had to watch his step around her. She would be more trouble for him than the case, Kelly and the men who had ambushed him combined. "Correction. We have nothing in common." He checked the compartments, glad that Meg had had the good sense to wrap the gun in a plastic bag before burying it in the flour. He turned to her with satisfaction. "And now that I have my gun, I'm out of here."

Meg looked shocked. "You can't just leave."

"Watch me."

"But—but," Meg spluttered, "what about your cover? You are planning to stay in Sedona until Abby returns. I've given you a reason to stay."

Meg had given him a cover story. Plus, he needed to talk to Abby. Because of how…itchy Meg made him feel, he'd forgotten about Abby. "When will she be back?"

"Who knows?" Meg waved airily, not meeting his eyes. "Abby comes and goes as the spirits move her."

"Another one of those." He turned on her. "Why did you make up that crazy story about me being your ex-fiancé?"

Meg didn't look at him, but played with a strand of her soft, shiny hair. "It was the first thing I could think of."

"A fiancé who stood you up at the altar? One who's come crawling back?"

Meg sighed enthusiastically. "I'll admit the last part was wishful thinking, but the best lies are ones based in fact." She raised her gaze to his and he saw the sadness on her face. "A number of residents know my pathetic story. That my fiancé backed out of the wedding just as I was about to walk down the aisle. As I never mentioned my former fiancé's name or said much about him, no matter who you are, you could be him."

Adam felt another small part of reality leave him as he sank deeper and deeper into Meg's crazy world. Her former fiancé should be thankful for his lucky escape. The man had probably woken up in the morning and finally realized what he was getting into. Even so, Adam couldn't help but experience a little twinge of sympathy for Meg. "He left you at the altar?"

"Not quite so dramatic. I exaggerate a little when I tell the story. People rather enjoy my tale of being an abandoned bride who's looking for adventure." She smiled oddly when she said the word *adventure*. "The truth is that Max told me before the ceremony. He married one of the bridesmaids instead."

"The bastard." Adam couldn't help it, he felt bad for her. His divorce had been an unpleasant experience—one he planned never to repeat—but by the time his wife and he agreed to separate, their love had been dead for a long time. He didn't know if he could have faced having the person he loved, the woman he intended to marry, tell him only hours before the wedding that she was in love with someone else.

Meg shrugged. "My thoughts exactly. That's when I left New York. I realized I'd been planning to marry Max for all the wrong reasons. So I went searching for adventure."

All his sympathy died. Now she sounded like his sister, Kelly. Or his ex-wife, Allison. Why was he always attracted to women like that? "Adventure? There's no such thing."

"Yes, there is!" Meg smiled brightly at him. "After fourteen months I was beginning to doubt it myself, which is why I had just decided to go back home, when you rushed in through my door. You're my adventure, Adam Smith…or whatever your name is."

When Meg stepped toward him, Adam moved back. He'd been down this road before and knew it only led to trouble. He had to remember Allison.

Meg stepped closer, still smiling, still smelling like roses, and Adam grew angry. The woman was nothing but a complete little idiot. "I am no one's adventure. Your fiancé probably realized what a mistake he was making and corrected it in time."

Meg sucked in her breath in hurt, but she took another step forward. "Max and I weren't in love. Not really, deeply in love like he was with Emma. Eight years apart didn't change how they felt about each other. It doesn't when you're really in love with someone." She came even closer and then cocked her head to one side. "Have you ever been in love like that?"

"Once. Or rather I thought I was." Why was he telling Meg this? He never talked about his marriage. "Turned out Allison was exactly like the rest of my family. She always needed rescuing. After a while I got tired of it."

"And that was the end of your marriage?"

"Yes."

"How long did it last?"

"Four years."

"That's not so bad. You gave it a really good effort. I like that in a man." She smiled at him and raised her hand as if she was about to touch him, but then stopped. "So you think I'm like Allison."

"Yes." Why had he wanted her to touch him?

"Was she pretty?"

"Yes."

"Do you think I'm pretty?"

"Yes, but that has nothing to do with it. Not every pretty woman reminds me of Allison." He felt his blood pressure rising and knew he had to get away from Meg Cooper as quickly as he possibly could. Now he wanted to touch her. He wanted to see if the color would rise in her cheeks when he stroked her impossibly soft skin.

"Then it's my mind and personality?" Meg was practically on top of him. He felt a bead of sweat trickle down his back.

"Exactly. Allison was flighty, irresponsible, careless, impetuous, unreliable, emotional—"

"Stop." Meg held up her hand to halt the flow of adjectives. "No one has ever described me like that. Usually they think I'm very restrained. A bit of a daydreamer, but also very practical. I like it." She smiled, her brown eyes sparkling with those gold flecks. "Are you involved with someone else?"

"No." Adam tried to get a grip on when he'd lost track of this conversation, but couldn't.

"Excellent. I'm not either, so we have a chance."

Adam was afraid he'd stepped into quicksand, but he tried anyway. "Lady, you're not listening to me. We are not spending any more time together. I am leaving. Now. I'll find Abby by myself." He took Meg by the shoulders and moved her away from him. Then he crossed the kitchen, heading toward the back door and freedom.

Meg called after him. "But your cover as my former fiancé is a good one. Michelle and Rachel are busy spreading the gossip about you even as we've been standing here. Everyone in town will know about you. No one will be suspicious. So you can do whatever it is you came here to do."

Meg's words stopped him at the door. She was right.

"Why are you here?" Meg asked, when he didn't respond to her crazy suggestion.

"None of your business." The little that Adam had put together he wasn't going to tell her. His sister was depending upon him. But he was having to reconsider

Meg's advice. The cover she'd created for him was a good one. The town would be so busy gossiping over the circumstances of his arrival, of him having left Meg at the altar and trying to win her back, that they wouldn't be suspicious. In fact, he could ask a lot of questions under the guise of wanting to know what drew Meg to Sedona.

"Okay," he said. "You have a point. I'll be your ex-fiancé." He felt like he'd just uttered his own death sentence. "Where did we almost marry?"

"The Hamptons, Long Island." Meg watched his reaction anxiously.

Oh great, he was involved with a rich, flighty woman. Maybe even an heiress. A woman who didn't know the value of hard work or the zeroes on her credit card statement. No wonder she had ended up in mystical, kooky Sedona.

He shook his head, knowing he was getting himself in deep. "And I didn't marry you because…?"

"You got cold feet. You told me before the ceremony."

"And now I'm back to try to win you again?"

"Yes," Meg agreed happily.

Humph. Adam knew he was getting himself into danger, but he had to remember Kelly. To find the man who had hurt her, he'd be willing to suffer anything. Even Megan Cooper.

"Of course, I'll be resistant. After all, you did betray me once. But I'm also the forgiving sort, so you should be able to make progress." Meg looked up at him hopefully, as if she wanted him to kiss her.

Considering the ridiculous situation he'd somehow gotten himself into, he knew he'd have to watch himself. A woman like Meg was only trouble. No matter how appealing she looked. Or how much he was thinking that kissing her seemed the appropriate thing to do under the circumstances. After all, they had been engaged…sort of. Now he was already losing himself in her crazy way of thinking. He took a step toward her.

The front door of the shop tinkled. "Hello, Meg?" a

man's voice shouted. The door closed and heavy boots sounded across the wood floor of the store.

"In the kitchen, Greg," Meg answered, looking disappointed. So it wasn't the famous Reid Logan. For some reason Adam found himself curious to meet her suitor.

A blond-haired man in his late twenties walked in. Dressed in chinos and a faded denim shirt, with his longish hair and perfect smile Greg looked like he had stepped out of a Ralph Lauren ad. All that was missing was his Jeep. He crossed the kitchen and kissed Meg on the cheek, positioning himself close to her territorially. Then he surveyed Adam with suspicion. "I met Rachel after I dropped off my last clients from their four-wheeling trip. She said the guy who dumped you was back, looking to do, like, the big reunion thing."

Meg's face lit up as she began to weave her elaborate story. "Yes. Greg Trenton, meet Adam Smith." She waited for the men to shake hands, but when neither made a move, she shrugged her shoulders slightly and turned to Adam. "Greg runs a four-wheel-drive outings company for tourists. Adam is my former fiancé."

Frowning, Greg nodded at Adam, putting an arm around her shoulders. "Meg doesn't want you back, man."

So Meg had more than one suitor. Adam picked up another muffin, wondering how she would react to Greg's caveman tactics.

"Greg! That's not your place to say." Meg shook off Greg's arm and moved next to Adam. He smiled at her and then sat down at a kitchen stool, finishing the muffin as if nothing untoward was happening. He wasn't about to get jealous over a pretty boy like Greg. Meg placed a hand on his shoulder proprietorially, speaking to Greg. "Adam's come to Sedona to apologize for the way he canceled our wedding, and I've accepted his apology. What the future holds is in the future. Or maybe the vortexes."

Vortexes. Adam's situation was only getting worse and

worse. He needed to be careful he didn't get sucked into a vortex. He also hated every pretty inch of Greg.

Greg opened his mouth and then closed it as though realizing whatever he said would be a mistake. But then he opened it again, unable to resist speaking his mind. The boy was very young. It had been years since Adam had been compelled to say what he was thinking.

"But, Meg, he left you at the altar."

"Yes," Meg said. "It was a very difficult day. But if I can forgive Adam, then I think you have to, too."

"But you can't trust him. He might hurt you again."

"That's a chance I'm willing to take." Meg's words were soft but firm. Adam rather liked the way they sounded. *Don't fall for her charms*, he reminded himself.

Adam smiled at Greg. "Meg is a woman worth fighting for."

"Yes." Greg glared at him.

So Greg did want Meg. How many men did she have trailing after her? First the famous Reid Logan, then Greg Trenton. Her allure was potent, but Adam didn't want to get caught up in her trap. He knew better.

Greg frowned at Meg. "Be careful," he insisted. "I can tell this guy isn't trustworthy. Why has he come back now? Have you asked him that? He might have some kind of ulterior motive."

Meg put her hands on her hips and shook her head at Greg. "If you're going to be so rude, I'm going to have to ask you to leave. Ulterior motive, indeed! If he'd wanted my money, he could have gotten that the first time around."

Greg crossed his arms. "I don't want to interfere, but you know that we all care about you. I don't want to see you hurt again. When you first came here, Michelle said, like, she could see that there was a spark missing in you. It's only been recently that you began to give off, like, heat and light again. I've been wanting to ask you out, but I didn't want to rush you." He shook his head, regret on his face. "Now it looks like I'm too late. You." He pointed his finger at Adam. "I'll be watching you."

Meg took Greg's arm and began to steer him away from the kitchen, talking quietly. Adam could hear Greg speaking animatedly once they got to the front door, then Meg's calm tones. Adam sat in the kitchen and considered his situation: bad and getting worse.

"Damn," she said when she came back into the kitchen.

"He's a persistent boy," Adam replied, still drinking his coffee.

Meg glared at him. "A fat lot of help you were. You could have acted a little more romantic around me. Luckily, Greg was too jealous to notice your clear lack of interest."

"I'm not good at playing games. All I want is for you to tell me how to get in touch with Abigail Milton and then I'll get out of here."

"But who are you?" Meg demanded once again. She was persistent. "Are you a private investigator? A corporate spy? A mercenary?"

"Nothing like that." He liked the way she tapped her foot impatiently and crossed her arms in frustration. No masking of emotions or wants. She was the most alive woman he'd ever met.

"Well…?"

"I'm a journalist. I write about business. Profiles on companies, analyzing the stock market, stuff like that."

Meg made a noise that sounded like a harrumph. "If you're not going to tell me, just say so. There's no need to lie." Incredibly, she actually looked upset by his revelation, but then her expressive face cleared. "So what do we do first?"

"*We* aren't doing anything. I work alone."

"Not this time. You need me to help you around this town. I could point you in the right direction a lot faster if you told me what and who you were looking for." When Adam remained silent, Meg only shook her head and tried a different approach. "How did Abby get in touch with you?"

He decided it couldn't hurt to tell her a few of the details. Ever since Abby had contacted him, events had happened so quickly he hadn't had time to stop and analyze the situation. He'd been reacting instead of planning. Going over his case with Meg would help clarify it in his own mind. "Abigail Milton mailed me a letter. Unfortunately, she didn't put enough postage on it so it took a long time to reach me in New York. So I guess I showed up late."

"But what was in the letter?"

Adam considered how much to tell Meg. Not a lot. She'd undoubtedly go blabbing all over town. "Abby suspected high-level computer forgeries."

"What does that mean?"

"Somehow Abby learned that someone she knew was creating computer-generated identities."

Meg creased her brows, analyzing his words. "Abby was always playing around on her computers, claiming she could create a better program than the kids in Silicon Valley, but I still have no idea what you're talking about. What is a computer-generated identity?"

"Basically it's a completely new identity that is almost impossible to prove false. People have been expertly forging passports and other paper identities for years, but if for some reason you wanted to create a completely new life for yourself, a computer forgery is even better."

"Why?"

"Because you would have a past, not just papers," Adam explained. "If you're a criminal or a terrorist and want identification to get into a country, then paperwork is fine, but what if your ambition is for more? If you wanted to work for the government or a high-tech industry and even most of the top corporations, a good security check will reveal that John Doe only came into existence recently. There would be no records on this person. No bank accounts or school reports or medical exams. That's what investigators look for—something beyond your birth certificate, passport and other papers."

Meg nodded in understanding, "So a computer-generated false identity gives you history. In the old days a Russian spy undercover in the U.S.—a mole—had to live for years under a false identity, in order to establish the reality of that identity. Like Kevin Costner in *No Way Out*."

He had to admit she was fast. "What Abby found was a computer program that literally goes into all kinds of existing data banks and adds John Doe. Suddenly there are school attendance records, a credit history, parking tickets, everything that's stored on computers. One day, John Doe doesn't exist anywhere; the next, he has a history that covers everything stored in main frames."

"That's incredible."

"Exactly. If what Abby claims is true, then our government could be hiring fake people—spies—and fully believe that the security check on them is one-hundred-percent accurate. I checked out some of her facts—some of the names—and she might have something." Adam had been scared by what he'd uncovered. If what Abby claimed was true, and his initial investigation showed that it could be, then security in any country could be breached.

Plus there was his personal matter of Kelly. He had no idea how deep his sister was involved in the computer forgeries, but she was connected somehow. Otherwise they wouldn't have tried to kill her. It was why Adam was working alone. His first priority always was to protect Kelly. If she was up to her pretty little neck in illegal goings-on, he'd rescue her, just like he always did.

"And when you began checking out what Abby claimed, the bad guys found out and got nervous?" Meg continued, putting the few facts together.

"It looks like it. I was ambushed shortly after arriving in Phoenix. But they didn't get anything out of me."

"What happened to the letter that Abby sent you?"

Embarrassed, he mumbled the answer.

"What?" Meg asked.

Knowing she would persist until he admitted the truth, he took a deep breath and blurted it out. "I ate it."

Meg's lips twitched, but she only said, "So, the bad guys don't know who your source was or where you were heading?"

"No. That's why I wanted to get here to see Abby right away. I figured she could show me what led her to think someone in Sedona was involved, and then we could go to the police together." Maybe. Depending on Kelly's role.

"But Abby is gone. Every once in a while she says she's had enough of being nice to tourists and playing with her computer and wants to commune with nature. She heads off on a retreat, to be completely alone. I never know how long she'll be gone." Meg remained silent as she considered what he'd told her.

Adam took another sip of coffee. It went down the wrong way when he suddenly remembered something. "Damn." He'd been in such a hurry to destroy the letter. He couldn't believe that despite his amateur spy theatrics he'd made such a mistake.

"What?" Meg demanded.

Adam could hardly believe his own stupidity. "The envelope. I didn't destroy the envelope. It had The Gateway's return address on it. They know I was heading here."

Which meant he couldn't leave. Meg was in danger whether he stayed with her or not, but if he was with her at least he could try to protect her.

She understood immediately. Rather than looking frightened, she gazed at him with pleasure. "So you can't leave me. You'll have to stay to make sure whoever is after you doesn't come after me. In exchange, I'll help you."

"This isn't a game." He was furious with her. She needed to be frightened, to be cautious. "It's a dangerous situation. You can't protect yourself if you don't believe it."

"I'm not a fool. Many people actually believe I'm a very practical, logical person." Adam made a derisive noise, but she ignored him. "I don't want to lose you, either. I've waited my whole life for you. That's why I look pleased."

The woman had only known him for a few hours and she was determined to cast him in the role of romantic hero. She was even more of a fool than he'd feared. Adam considered the situation and Meg. This was supposed to be a very minor investigation, but he felt himself sinking deeper and deeper into a quicksand pit of questions. He needed to regain some control over the situation or he would be lost.

Meg continued to look at him with satisfaction. Well, he could do something about scaring her. He stood and walked over to her and took hold of her by the shoulders, aware of how much bigger and stronger he was. Meg only smiled, oblivious to her situation. "You have no idea what kind of a man I am. Or even if Adam Smith is my real name."

"You're my adventure," she answered.

Ridiculous woman. He tightened his grasp on her shoulders and heard her suck in her breath. He pulled her closer to him, so that they were barely touching. She didn't resist; instead she looped her arms around his neck.

"Are you trying to frighten me?" she asked softly, her breath hot against his cheek. He smelled her perfume again.

Ignoring his sudden desire to run his hand along the soft skin of her cheek, he pulled her hard against him. He felt all of her soft curves. "Oh!" Meg gasped, but didn't say anything more, merely continued to look at him, her expressive brown eyes letting him see into her soul.

With one hand he cupped a breast, waiting for her to push away. Instead her eyes widened and her mouth opened with a sigh. That's when he lost it. He covered her parted lips with his. Kissed her hard and deep and lost himself in her.

She was so sweet. He angled his mouth to take the kiss further. Her passionate response swept him away. She filled all of his senses—she was all he could think of, all he could imagine. He took her bottom lip into his mouth and she moaned and he pulled her even closer. He wanted to be inside her, so he thrust his tongue between her lips, tasting and exploring. Her tongue mated with his, showing her to be just as needy, just as wanting.

His hands explored her body, the sweet fullness of her breasts, the lush curve of her hips. Her body fit him so perfectly, he could easily imagine them together naked. He wanted to touch and kiss every single inch of her.

He wanted to make love to her.

He wanted to make love to Meg more than he'd wanted to make love to any woman in a long time, and considered sweeping her into his arms and carrying her back to the roll-away bed in the storeroom. They would be so good together; he could feel it. She'd be so hot and sweet, giving him everything, trusting him completely.

Instead, he pushed her away from him, noting her flushed face, her kissed lips. His own breathing was ragged, his body aching for release.

Meg smiled at him, gasping for breath. He felt like he'd run a marathon.

"That's twice," she said. "If you kiss me once more, we'll be lovers."

4

"*NO.*" The word escaped his lips as a sound of horror, but Meg didn't seem to notice. "No," he said more firmly and calmly. "We are not going to be lovers. And *I've* only kissed you once," he added on rather desperately. "What kind of stupid rule is three kisses, anyway?" Megan Elizabeth Cooper was not his destiny. She was his ailment and he was going to cure himself of her.

He knew kissing her had been a mistake.

Meg's golden brown hair framed her face as she shook her head, touching her kiss-swollen lips. She sighed, looking bemused, then turned those killer brown eyes on him, and he felt himself losing his footing. She weakened him more than any of his injuries. "True, I did kiss you the first time, but you felt it, too. It wasn't like kissing anyone else. We have that special chemistry…that connection between us. You can make my palms sweat."

Adam made his voice cold and calm, no matter how his insides were quaking. He refused to wipe the sweat off his palms onto the thighs of his jeans. What she was saying was ridiculous. Her kiss had not affected him more than any other woman's kiss. At least he insisted to himself it hadn't. "We're attracted to each other. That's it. Nothing more. You're being ridiculous just like my ex-wife. Are all women like this?" He shook his head. "You still don't know who I am or if you can trust my story, but you want to go to bed with me." He liked the cool logic of his argument. He wished he believed it.

"Crazy, isn't it?" Meg agreed. "And it's so unlike me. That's how I know you're the man for me. I felt it the first time I saw you…a little click, like a missing piece fell into place." She looked encouragingly at him, as if she wanted him to confess a similar response.

Adam shook his head, but Meg wasn't dissuaded. Kissing her to scare her had been a bad plan, one he wasn't about to repeat. He needed to remember why he was here. Kelly. And he couldn't forget about Allison. His ex-wife had thrilled and attracted him, just like Meg, but then she had turned into another obligation. Another person he had to take care of. Just like Kelly and the rest of his family. Now he had his independence and he planned on keeping it. He liked being a loner. He wasn't giving up his freedom for any woman, no matter how alluring she might be. No matter how much kissing her had been more of a mind-blowing experience than he could ever recall.

He'd learned his lesson from Allison and planned his life accordingly. When necessary he would come to the aid of his family. Even Allison. Unfortunately, their divorce hadn't lessened her reliance on him. But he didn't have to be involved in their messy, draining lives on a day-to-day basis. He liked being alone. Sometimes he wished for more, but it didn't seem to be in the fates for him. The kind of woman he always fell for was a needy kook. Meg. He couldn't change his nature, it seemed, but that didn't mean he couldn't learn from his mistakes. He was going to remember every lesson Allison and his family had taught him, and stay as far away from Meg as possible.

Because deep inside he knew that Megan Cooper would be even worse than Allison for his control and his peace of mind. If she caught hold of his heart, she'd be able to keep it.

But he was curious about her—she was such an odd contradiction, one minute capable of saving his life, understanding the intricacies of computer forgery, and then saying silly things like that three-kisses-and-we'll-be-lovers statement. He wasn't going to kiss her again, but he couldn't help asking, "Did you have the same feelings for your ex-fiancé, what's-his-name?"

She was looking at him curiously, and silently he cursed himself for showing any interest. He had to remember not to offer her any encouragement. He remained quiet as Meg frowned, wrinkling her brow as she thought about her ex-fiancé.

"His name is Max and, no, I never did have these immediate...overwhelming feelings for him. Which is probably why it never worked out for us. Neither of us was overcome by passion. Our relationship seemed so practical, it made so much sense that everyone thought we'd be very happy together, including us for a while, but... He married someone else. A woman he felt that overwhelming, complete passion for." Suddenly Meg's face cleared and she smiled at him. "I'm glad you helped me see that." She looked him over and then cocked her head. "Did your ex-wife really hurt you so much that you're not even willing to give us a chance?"

"There is no us," he muttered between clenched teeth. The woman was even sillier and more ridiculous than he'd given her demerit points for being.

"Oh." She moved away from him and looked around her kitchen, as if searching for an answer. She folded some tea towels and then looked out the window at the red rocks. He waited in silence, fully expecting her to continue with her crazy theory. Finally she turned. "You're wrong about us, but you probably need some time. And since you're not willing to talk about who you think you're after, how about going shopping?

"Shopping?" Another silly female hobby—he should have known.

"Yes. You need clothes so you can move around town. While we're at it, you can check out the natives, investigate whatever it is that you're not telling me. We women call it shopping."

She was right. He was a big enough man to be able to

admit when the other person had a point.

He needed to go shopping.

"FREDDIE, I'D LIKE YOU to meet Adam Smith, my former fiancé." Meg introduced him to the tall, elegant man. Dressed in gray linen pants and a white cotton shirt, with a discreet silver bracelet, Freddie put down his jeweler's loupe and rose to shake Adam's hand. His grip was strong but not overwhelming like Michelle's.

"The man who left you at the altar?" Freddie raised an eyebrow and surveyed Adam from head to toe.

"Meg has exaggerated slightly," Adam clarified for the dozenth time that afternoon. He had enough clothing to keep him going for weeks, but the shopping excuse was an excellent way to make the acquaintance of much of the town. Whoever he was searching for had to work in a business that brought him or her—Adam was an equal-opportunity investigator—into contact with the public as a cover. The buyer of the new identity had to spend a lot of time with the programmer so that they could create the identity the buyer wanted. In other words, a "tourist" needed to be able to spend a lot of time with one of the residents of Sedona. Of course, any business, from that of four-wheel excursions to a jeweler to a hotel, could provide the excuse. The programmer and the buyer could consort together in full public view without anyone thinking anything of it. A clever and well-thought out plan. The person he was after was very smart and ruthless, he reminded himself, picturing Kelly's bruised and battered body.

Picturesque Sedona in the midst of red rock country attracted tourists and business people alike, Adam had read in the airplane magazine during his flight in. The tourists came to experience the connection to the Old West, to enjoy the beauty of the vistas. To commune with the mysticism that was Sedona, as he had heard over and over again. It also seemed like the last place in the world to run across men and women who needed new identities: drug runners, spies and other scum of the earth.

Instead, all the locals raved over the beauty and magic of the place. And then there were the vortexes. Meg had told him that the psychic Page Bryant in the 1980s had divined four metaphysical vortexes around Sedona. As a result, the New Agers had arrived in droves. Which meant no one seemed odd in Sedona. Adam bet four guys dressed in their best Mafioso pinstripes, shiny ties and violin cases could walk down the main street and no one would blink an eye.

As if to prove how crazy everyone was, Meg had told him about the Harmonic Convergence. In 1987, over five thousand people had come to Bell Rock, expecting to be transported to the galaxy of Andromeda. Adam had only snorted in response, but Meg had continued unabashed. "Sedona does have an unusual feel. I wouldn't have believed it myself if I hadn't experienced it the second I came to town. I had no intention of staying here, but shortly after coming to look at the beautiful scenery, to watch the rocks change color from violet to red with the changing light, I knew I couldn't leave immediately. That this was the place I was going to have my adventure. Although I was beginning to fear I was wrong until you arrived at Abby's shop on Saturday night. Do you realize we've barely known each other for four days, if you include the time you were unconscious, and I feel like I've known you forever and my life has completely changed?"

"You're nuts," Adam couldn't help saying, but his tone was more amused than harsh, and Meg continued on as if she hadn't heard his words. He was sorry to hurt her, but she had to stop these ridiculous fantasies of hers. He and she were not going to end up together. While he might like to take her to bed and give her a mystical experience, he wasn't going to touch even one inch of her pretty skin. If he wasn't careful, Meg could turn into an addiction, and he needed to just say no.

The business people also fell into the mystical category, Adam learned. Aging hippies or daydreamers, these people combined their belief in the forces of the universe with commerce: stores selling everything from mysticism to Levi's jeans to gourmet sandwiches and cakes. Plus, there were lots of artists. In the small town there were over three hundred professional artists as well as about fifty galleries. Moreover, Meg revealed, most of the art was positive. No matter what the artist drew or sculpted or created in any form or fashion, it was fundamentally positive. "It's because of the vortexes—they exude positive energy. Then again, it could be the sheer beauty of Sedona and the countryside that makes people look for the best."

"Is that what you do?"

"Yes," she responded, considering her words. "I wasn't always like that, I used to be so career driven, but I've changed. No matter what happens between us, I'm a different person now. I have Sedona and my friends here to thank for that."

Naturally, Freddie fit into Sedona, with his jewelry designing and his dapper appearance. Adam continued with his explanation as to why he had arrived in town. "Meg and I agreed before the wedding that we wouldn't suit."

"But now you've discovered the error of your ways and are here to win her back," Freddie said archly. To Adam's irritation, the man took Meg's hand and kissed it. Freddie was far too elegant and handsome for Adam's liking. Another damn admirer of Meg.

"He should!" Meg added vehemently. "He broke my heart. The only problem now is that my heart has healed. I don't know if I want Adam again. He's going to have to work hard to win me back."

Freddie looked at Adam with determination. "Well, that is good news. It gives the rest of us men hope."

Adam stepped closer to Meg and put his arm around her. She leaned into him a little, but didn't look at him. This afternoon, playing the role of her ex-fiancé had given him lots of chances to touch her. He told himself that it helped establish his cover, and refused to admit how much he liked it. Well, he could admit it, but only to himself. Besides, his attraction to her was only sexual.

"Freddie, you are an awful flirt!" Meg's voice was coy and teasing, and Adam didn't like it. "What about that ring you were making for me?"

For a moment, Freddie studied the two of them together and then shrugged his shoulders. "From what little you said about your ex-fiancé, I never imagined the two of you would look so natural together. Maybe Adam will give Reid more of a run for his money than I expected. Now, never mind my blathering—the ring is finished. It's in the back room. Let me go get it." He puffed up his chest. "I think you'll be very pleased."

As Freddie disappeared through the curtains into the back, Adam noted sourly, "Another of your many lovelorn male friends."

Meg stepped out of his arms toward one of the counters, studying the earrings in the locked case, not looking at him. "Freddie? Don't mind him. Abby said there was someone he'd been serious about, but she left. Now he flirts with all the women."

"How about the men?"

Meg grinned at him. "*Tsk, tsk,* now you are sounding jealous. Freddie is quite the ladies' man, but I think he's taken with Gloria Logan. I don't know." Meg's mouth twisted and her pretty brown eyes filled with concern. "Freddie has good taste, but there's something about Gloria... Maybe I'm just jealous. She is gorgeous."

Adam smiled. "Really? Maybe I should meet her."

Meg punched him hard on his healthy shoulder. "You're here to court me, not Gloria Logan."

"What about Reid? When am I going to meet him?"

"You can meet him Thursday night. I've been invited for dinner at the ranch."

"The famous ranch and the famous cowboy. Should be fun. You and Reid. Me and the beautiful Gloria."

Meg smiled back, barring her teeth. "She's incredibly

beautiful. Angelic, in fact. I've seen men walk into walls when she glides by."

"Not sure I'm into the angelic type."

"Of course not. They're boring. You much prefer a woman who can think and take care of herself. A woman who's not afraid to tell you what she's feeling."

"Someone like you?"

"Exactly." Meg smiled at him with real pleasure, her brown eyes shining, and Adam felt a little click. *Oh no*, he told his libido. Not his heart—his libido. He wasn't falling into this trap again. He just enjoyed talking to Meg; she had a quick wit and a goodness that he found appealing. Nothing more. Absolutely nothing.

But after most of the day with Meg, he was becoming curious about her. He knew he was falling into a trap, but suddenly he didn't want to extricate himself too quickly. Instead, he wanted to get to know Megan Cooper. "When he—your ex-fiancé—left you at the altar—"

"He didn't exactly leave me at the altar. He told me the morning of—"

"When he told you, were you devastated?" Adam wondered why he wanted to know. He couldn't feel sorry for her, or wonder what kind of man would have left her at the altar. Wonder if the man had realized he'd made a mistake.

"Yes." Meg stared at the jewelry counter and then finally at Adam. "I was planning to spend my life with Max. I thought he would make a good husband, and that I would make a good wife to him. When he told me he was in love with someone else, that he was going to marry Emma, of course I was hurt. Badly. I'd suspected that Max and Emma had a past, but I still thought he was going to marry me. Or I did until almost the morning of the wedding.

"That's why I left. I caught the first plane out of Manhattan and have spent over a year trying to figure out what I want." She smiled crookedly at her impulsiveness. "I'd always planned out my life so carefully, always had very specific goals, but at the same time I always kept expecting…something…to happen. Something profound that would change my life and me. I finally realized I had to go searching for what I wanted."

"Which is why you ended up in Sedona?"

"Yes. Sedona just felt…right. Like I was meant to be here."

"And the adventure?"

"Until you walked through my door, I wasn't sure if I'd ever find it." Her compelling brown eyes met his and he felt a tug on his heart. *No*, he told himself. Adam had just opened his mouth to deny that he was her adventure when Freddie walked back in carrying a ring.

Adam recognized the design immediately. It was an exact replica of the ring that had been found on Kelly's body.

HE WOULD NEVER FORGET how bruised and how small Kelly had looked in the hospital bed. When she'd opened her eyes and smiled weakly at him, he'd felt tears running down his cheeks, over his smile. He hadn't cried since he was five years old and his father had taught him it wasn't manly. Kelly had lapsed back into unconsciousness, and Adam and their mother had continued to spend days at the hospital, wishing and waiting for Kelly to wake up. To recover from the coma.

To live.

It had been touch and go. His mother was the one who had been convinced that Kelly would live, that she would recover. When Adam had begun to doubt, it had been his mother's faith that had kept him returning to the hospital time and time again. Holding Kelly's hand, talking to her, begging her to open her eyes.

It had been his turn with her when Kelly had finally rejoined the world. She'd then spent weeks recovering, gradually regaining her strength and part of her memory, but to Adam's frustration, she wouldn't talk about what had happened to her. Somehow she had made it to the hospital in Queens and collapsed in the emergency room. The only piece of identification Kelly had had on her was her library card, which had led the authorities to their mother.

Adam thought it appropriate that it was Kelly's library card that had brought her back to her family. As kids, he and Kelly had had little in common except for their love of books. Kelly always enjoyed fairy tales and stories of adventure, and had quickly become an afficionado of fantasy and science fiction—worlds where beautiful princesss and noble knights ruled, where right won over might. Adam had been much more interested in how things worked. He enjoyed the real world: history, economics, politics. Their childhood choices had shaped their adult lives.

The doctors guessed that Kelly had been in some kind of accident and the trauma included temporary amnesia. They believed her memory loss would be short-term. But even after some of her memory did return, Kelly wouldn't reveal what had happened to her.

Adam, however, believed that someone had tried to kill her.

After Kelly recovered and was able to come home to their mother's house, she was a different person. She spoke very little, only in response to direct questions and then only in monosyllables. Even more than her life-threatening injuries, it was the stealing of his sister's vitality that sent Adam out on his quest for vengeance. Before her accident, Kelly had sparkled. She'd entered a room and people had responded to her. And she'd talked, incessantly, about everything. About her day, her thoughts, her dreams. Adam usually shut out his sister's silly, inconsequential chatter, but now he'd give anything to have the old Kelly back.

But Kelly hadn't come back. She'd returned to consciousness, but then retreated into herself. He could hardly believe it was six months since their mother had taken Kelly home. At first Adam had continued to demand she tell him what had happened to her, who had hurt her, but Kelly had only retreated even more into her shell.

He'd realized he was only making Kelly worse, and had stopped his harassment. Instead, to give his mother a break from the twenty-four-hour nursing routine, he spent two afternoons a week at the old house with his sister. But the sibling he knew and loved wasn't the one who lived in his mother's house. For the first time in his life, he and Kelly didn't talk. He'd tried, but she never responded beyond short answers. Just as disconcerting was the fact that she clearly preferred having someone in the house with her; she was scared to be alone. His anger at whoever had done this to Kelly grew daily, as did his frustration at not being able to do anything for her. He needed to help her, but he had no idea how to begin.

On his last visit, he'd brought a large pile of mail that had gathered for him at the newspaper. Adam was a good investigative reporter and good at going undercover to get to the heart of a story—his military training helped him with that—but his specialty was business reporting. With the amount of influence that large corporations and stock markets held over the lives of ordinary people, his editor had given him free rein to tackle financial stories other reporters ignored. And with luck, and a great deal of skill, Adam had uncovered several stock scams, a couple of embezzlers and a number of products that were hazardous. Every story that revealed another crooked businessman or inept government bureaucracy brought him more and more mail.

He'd sorted the letters into piles: those that seemed important, those he would write to as soon as he had some free time and, finally, the crackpots. Kelly had been idly sorting through this last pile when he'd sensed something was wrong. She had grown extraordinarily still, staring fixedly at one letter. Then, noticing Adam's attention, she had reached for the next piece of correspondence, but he had managed to catch a glimpse of mysterious letter's stationery. He'd wanted to demand what it meant to her, but didn't dare. He didn't want to push Kelly back into her shell.

Instead, he'd hardly been able to wait for his mother to return home, to eat the overcooked pot roast, for his mother and him to make strained small talk that Kelly ignored, until he could at last escape to his car with the correspondence in his briefcase. That's how Abigail Milton's letter had come to his attention.

Abigail Milton of Sedona, Arizona.

The last communication from Kelly until she'd shown up at the hospital four months later had been a postcard she had mailed to their mother from the Grand Canyon. His reporter's instincts humming, Adam had spent the next day investigating Abby's letter.

First, he'd had to translate Abby's free-flowing statements to what she actually suspected. It turned out that she had read his column for years, believing he was a supporter of the underdog. She even acknowledged that occasionally he showed that big business had a conscience, that he could listen to both sides of the argument, and that was why she was sending him her suspicions. She didn't trust the security of computers, Abigail had continued, which was why she was writing him by mail. It was still difficult to tamper with the U.S. Postal Service, she asserted.

The letter was dated three months previously. When Adam checked the envelope, he discovered Abby had forgotten to include the correct amount of postage and the missive had taken a long and leisurely route to him. It might be illegal to tamper with the mail, as Abby had claimed, but a stamp helped, he'd muttered to himself.

Too caught up by the excitement of a clue that could lead to what had happened to his sister, he hadn't paid attention to Abigail's warning against using computers. No, he'd used his home computer to connect to his paper's main frame and check the two names and dates Abby had sent him: Justin Stone, October 10, and Philip

Black, November 15. To his shock and growing excitement, Adam discovered that what Abby claimed was true. While both men existed according to birth certificates, school records and social security numbers, Abby had challenged him to go further and he had. The men had credit cards—platinum, with long billing records—reports on medical tests and lots of other documentation. Adam decided he needed to check minor details and found neither man had ever donated blood, held a library card or, most importantly, been sent an envelope from Ed McMahon declaring they could already be a winner in the Publishers Clearinghouse Sweepstakes.

The direct-mail connection was Adam's best test as to the real identity of a person. If Jason Stone or Philip Black had existed before the dates Abby supplied, then Publishers Clearinghouse would have found them—from credit card mailing lists or magazine subscriptions—and they would be in the sweepstakes system.

Since they weren't, they were fakes. Elaborate computer forgeries. Fake American identities including citizenship.

Extremely valuable.

That was the scam some very clever person was running out of Sedona, Arizona. What Abigail Milton somehow stumbled across while playing on her computer. Moreover, Adam was convinced that her having sent her suspicions to him wasn't a coincidence. She'd known he'd be interested because of Kelly. Only Abigail was off on a retreat, and Adam had been chasing dead ends ever since he'd caught the first flight out of La-Guardia to Phoenix, Arizona.

Stupidly, he'd ignored Abby's cautions. Whoever had been clever enough to create a program that could make these false identities had set a number of flags into the program as well. While Adam hurriedly checked one database after another, he must have tripped an early warning signal the criminal had encoded to alert him if someone got too curious about the new identities. Clearly,

Adam had been traced. Discovering what airline flight he would be taking into Phoenix, Arizona, had been easy for the computer genius.

As a result he'd promptly been ambushed.

And then he'd met Meg, which for him was even more dangerous.

He brought himself back to the present, to his first clue. He remembered the ring on Kelly's finger as he'd held her hand through the long nights. The same design that Freddie had made for Meg.

"Oh, it's beautiful," Meg exclaimed, putting the ring on her finger. Composed of silver with turquoise and garnet, the ring gave grace to her elegant hand. "It's exactly the colors of the rocks here in Sedona. I love it, Freddie." She hugged him, and Adam had to restrain himself from pulling her out of the man's arms. He didn't know if Freddie was the one who had hurt his sister, but there was clearly a connection. Meg opened her wallet, handed Freddie her credit card, and he rang through the transaction as Adam tried to figure out exactly what this clue meant.

He wished he could throw Freddie against the wall and choke the truth out of him. Instead he followed Meg out of the store, plotting his course of action.

And analyzing the course of events he had set into action by using his real name. The townspeople knew him as Meg's ex-fiancé, Adam Smith. The forgers knew him as the journalist Adam Smith. Without really considering the consequences, but wanting to flush out his quarry, he had announced his existence. Now all he had to do was wait for them to come after him—again. Only this time he would be ready.

And he was looking forward to breaking every one of Freddie's fingers.

5

BREAKING EVERY ONE of Freddie's fingers might be too good for him, Adam decided, as Freddie droned on and on about stocks at the investors' club meeting, a regular event on Wednesday evenings at The Gateway. With surprising ease, Meg had cleared out a corner of the shop—the display units were on rollers—and put out a dozen chairs and a table for coffee and food.

"Everyone brings something," she had said, a smile playing along her lips, "so you won't have to trust my cooking. Although I've really become quite a culinary expert since moving to Sedona. You don't know what you're missing." Adam had refused to eat anything that Meg had cooked since he'd regained consciousness. He planned to keep it that way.

Last night, after a full day of meeting Sedona's businesspeople, he had claimed fatigue and disappeared into the bedroom Meg had fixed up for him. He'd wanted a chance to think without the distraction of her presence. Or thinking about *three kisses*. Today, he'd tackled Abby's computer, but she had set up a good password system and he'd been left frustrated. He'd been forced to abandon the process, wishing that he'd taken one of the computer security cracking courses the army and his newspaper had offered. Instead, he'd walked around town again and then helped Meg in the shop in the afternoon. Local residents had developed a sudden need for items from The Gateway, obviously wanting the chance to observe Adam Smith, the scoundrel who'd abandoned Meg at the altar. Surprisingly, he'd had fun. Meg was easy to work with and possessed a quick wit. They'd turned the spinning of their misbegotten romance into quite a tale, each trying to out do the other.

"Cookie?" Rachel asked, dressed for the meeting in a pink flowing skirt and matching blouse. She fluttered among the guests, offering refreshments and gossiping with a skill and ferocity that Adam had to admire. He would have to cultivate her acquaintance better, for she could fill him in on a lot of what was going on in pretty, peaceful Sedona. She was the one, after all, who had referred to Meg and Reid as lovers. Adam speculated that if he hadn't broken into The Gateway and set Meg's heart all aflutter, Reid and Meg might actually be lovers by now.

He banished the irritation he felt at the idea of Meg in another man's bed and took several more of the amazing chocolate-cookie wonders. Rachel might be handing them out, but his stomach recognized Michelle's handiwork. He winked at Michelle, but she ignored him. A dark-haired man in his early thirties standing next to her, dressed in black jeans and a black vest decorated with Indian petroglyph figures, eyed Adam suspiciously when he did so.

Freddie finally sat down to sporadic applause from the fifteen members of the Sedona Wednesday Night Investment Club— apparently a splinter group from the Sedona Tuesday Evening Investment Club—and Adam quickly made his way over to Michelle.

As he approached, the younger man leaned close to Michelle. "Some more coffee?" he asked her. "I blended a dark roast especially for you."

Michelle took the coffee without smiling at the man. Her eyebrows rose in surprise when she saw Adam. "Mr. Smith, I didn't think our little investment club would hold any interest for a financial reporter like yourself."

Adam flashed his best smile, but knew he hadn't weakened Michelle's defenses. "How could I do anything except enjoy myself in a room filled with so many charming ladies?" He turned to the man, who was now scowling at him, and extended his hand. "How do you do?" he said, and tried not to wince as the man crushed his fingers in response. He'd shaken hands with a lot of teamsters, yet it was the residents of quiet, pretty little Sedona who were threatening to destroy his grip. "I'm Adam Smith."

The other man immediately relaxed his death grip. "Jason Stavropoulos. So, you're Meg's ex-fiancé," he said, obivously no longer viewing Adam as a threat. "You're all the town has been talking about since Monday."

Which was exactly how Adam had planned it. He wanted the whole damn state of Arizona to know he was alive and investigating. What he didn't want was for the criminals to know he was waiting for Abby, but for them to worry about what he knew. If the bad guys were worried, they might panic and do something stupid—and lead him right to them.

"You were the main topic of conversation at my restaurant from breakfast through after-dinner drinks."

"I suppose my past relationship with Meg could be seen as interesting." He took a sip of the excellent coffee as he continued to study the unusual pair. Jason had the striking olive features of his Greek heritage. Slim but strongly built, he was almost as tall as Adam's own six-two. Would he be the kind of man Kelly would be attracted to? Adam acknowledged that Jason could very well have drawn his sister's interest, but at the present, he was making eyes at Michelle. But that didn't mean anything. Jason's attraction to Michelle could be a cover.

Adam knew that finding the man who had been Kelly's lover would lead him straight to whoever had threatened her life—and to the forgers. Unfortunately, with so many flakes in Sedona, the list of suitable men was long.

A flake was just the kind of man his sister had a penchant for falling in love with. After the accident, Kelly might not have remembered what had happened to her, but he knew that she'd begun to regain her memory after a couple of weeks. But she'd refused to say anything about where she'd been, who she'd been with or how she'd been hurt.

As a result, Adam knew without a doubt that Kelly was in love with the wrong kind of man. It was her pattern. When she'd reacted strongly to Abby's letter, he knew he'd finally found a lead. And when he'd read what Abby suspected, he'd been very afraid that Kelly was involved. Abigail Milton claimed she had written to him because she had read his column, but no matter how big a fan she was, there were hundreds of good journalists in the country. No, Abigail had picked him because of his connection to Kelly.

When Meg wasn't with him, he'd shown Kelly's picture around Sedona, and a couple of people had recognized her as a girl they'd seen once or twice in town several months ago. No one could remember where she'd lived, however. The coffee shop woman had remembered that Kelly liked spending time at The Gateway, so Adam knew he was on the right path.

Once again he considered Jason, wondering if he was the man for whom Kelly was willing to sacrifice her life.

"You must bring Meg to my restaurant for dinner. I could make a reservation for tomorrow," Jason offered, sounding friendly, as if he'd remembered that Adam was in romantic pursuit of Meg.

Adam was about to ask Jason about his restaurant when he smelled roses. Meg slipped her arm through his. She whispered into his ear as if they were sharing lovers' secrets, and for a second, all he was aware of was her soft breath against his skin. Her scent enticed him, causing a curious fluttering in his stomach. "Watch it, Jason is jealous of anyone who spends too much time with Michelle," she breathed against his ear.

He turned his head to say he was aware of Jason's jealousy, then realized his lips were only a fraction of an inch away from her mouth. She leaned against him gently, solicitous of his injuries. He only had to move forward a touch and he would taste her. And convince everyone in the room that he really was Meg's ex-lover, determined to win her back.

Adam moved forward, but Meg stepped back to let another member into their little circle. "Freddie, that was a wonderful talk," she exclaimed as the man weaseled his way next to her. When she smiled warmly at Freddie, Adam put his arm around her waist, pulling her close to him.

Meg wiggled a little in protest, but he didn't loosen his hold. He rather liked the way she wiggled against him. He refused to consider how annoyed he felt at not being able to kiss her.

Continuing to ignore him, Meg turned her attention to Freddie. "Tomorrow night we're having dinner with the Logans. At the ranch."

"Oh, my," Freddie said in amused tones. "Adam and Reid together. *That* should be interesting. I can't wait." When Meg looked puzzled, he added, "I'll be there, too. The beautiful Gloria asked me personally."

Adam glowered at the jeweler and then looked at Jason, who nodded in sympathy.

But Freddie wasn't about to be stopped so easily. He fixed his attention on Adam. "What did you think of my little talk? I'll value your expert opinion. I believe Meg said you were a business writer. Would I have heard of your paper?"

Adam decided to ignore the veiled slur regarding his credentials. He was a good writer, damn good. Plus he'd been successful very quickly, winning a couple of awards while working for a Philadelphia paper before moving on to writing his own column for one of the world's most prestigious ones. As a result, he didn't need to play one-upmanship games. "I found your topic interesting, but bioengineering stocks are a bigger gamble than the lottery."

"Only if you don't know what you're doing."

"Many investors who thought they understood bioengineering have regretted their foolishness." Freddie ruffled his plumage and Adam decided to give him a little room to maneuver in hopes that he'd trip himself up. Adam needed to find out more about this man; he couldn't base all of his suspicions on the ring or on the proprietal way Freddie looked at Meg. Indeed, if Freddie was innocent, he and Meg would make the perfect couple. Two fruitcakes.

Over Adam's dead body.

"The stock you recommended, however, is one of the best," Adam admitted.

Freddie preened. He brushed back his silvery locks and puffed up his chest. "Thank you. I am known as something of an authority in our little community."

"How do you know so much about Lab Janzen? The small company is obscure—I believe it only listed on the exchange two months ago."

Freddie's lips curled in a condescending smile. "In my other life I was a scientist. Like many people here in Sedona, I was quite an authority before I decided to abandon the rat race for a truer way to live. I still keep up-to-date with the scientific journals, however." He smirked. Adam was sure that if the man had a mustache he would have twirled it. Freddie continued, determined to one-up Adam. "Where did you say I can find your column?"

"I didn't, but you may have read the paper. The *New York Times*."

Freddie spluttered over his drink. Jason smiled. Even Michelle's lips twitched in what Adam believed might be a small sign of pleasure. He felt Meg grow curiously still next to him. She looked at his expression of pleased satisfaction and then muttered something about being in the wrong company and excused herself.

He was puzzled by her reaction, but at the moment he needed to question Jason. "Magnificent woman, isn't she?" Jason asked as Adam watched Meg escape to the kitchen. What in the blazes was wrong with her? It was as if she found the truth about him to be disconcerting. "Yes," he agreed absently, and then realized that Jason was watching Michelle leave them and join Rachel at the food table.

Adam nodded in her direction. "She doesn't give you much encouragement."

Jason shrugged, turning his attention to Adam, but periodically darting a glance at Michelle. "Not in public. But then nothing worth winning is easy."

"Sometimes the price of love can be too high," Adam said, and then wished he'd kept his mouth shut. He was supposed to be investigating, not offering advice to the lovelorn. Clearly, kookiness was catching. "What brought you to Sedona?"

"Michelle." Jason's face glowed as he talked about his lady love. "I had a restaurant in California but wasn't very happy. So my girlfriend at the time and I took a driving vacation through Arizona. As soon as we entered the town limits I knew I wanted to sell my California restaurant and open one here. Then I met Michelle. Right away—it was like the earth shifted on its axis and for the first time I could see really clearly—I knew I wanted to spend the rest of my life with her. Now all I have to do is convince her."

Surprised at how easily Jason talked about his feelings—but then he was a former Californian—Adam asked, "Why is Michelle so resistant?"

"She thinks I'm too young for her. That I'll break her heart." Jason's gaze strayed after Michelle, who was talking to Freddie.

Adam studied the younger man. "None of the obstacles worry you?" He meant the decade separating their ages, their clearly different temperaments and outlook on life.

Jason returned his attention to Adam. "None of that matters. Not when it's true love." Then he flushed under his olive complexion and shrugged. "You'll have to forgive my extravagance. It's my Greek heritage. We believe that when you've met the woman of your dreams, you can't let any obstacle stop you."

Jason excused himself to follow Michelle, and Adam

found himself silently wishing the young man good luck. Adam would have to be careful not to stay in Sedona too long or he'd turn into a touchy-feely emotional wreck himself.

In his investigations so far, he'd learned that Rachel and Michelle operated a small hotel that included a sophisticated conference center. The entrepreneurial pair attracted a lot of business groups conducting corporate retreats, both from northeastern companies looking to escape the weather and California entertainment executives wanting to commune with the vortexes.

Pretty-boy Greg Trenton, the owner of the local four-wheel drive excursion company, wasn't a member of the investment group, but his tall, slim office manager, Dana Griffins, was. Adam made his way over to her. Thick glasses, a makeup-free face and pale skin made her an unusual Sedona resident, especially working for such an outdoorsy company as Get Going! Dana was meant for the indoors, or elegant British gardens sipping iced tea under a parasol. Adam wondered if she was pining unnoticed for the gorgeous Greg.

Dana blushed furiously at Adam's mild flirtation. She readily admitted she was a computer nerd, an escapee from a liberal arts college and literary family. "My parents think I dropped out to write a novel. They'd freak if they found out I was writing computer software."

He liked the way her face became animated as she talked about computers. "Why Sedona and not Silicon Valley?"

She returned his smile and blew her hair out of her eyes. "My programs will get me where I want to be. I don't need to become corporate in order to accomplish my goals—at least my parents' and my philosophies have that much in common."

"And once you sell your software?"

"I'll be rich and live wherever I want." She looked at him determinedly.

"Wherever Greg is?"

"Yes." Her self-confidence collapsed, her shoulders sagging. "As soon as he notices me. Will you be taking Meg back to New York?" Dana asked hopefully, clearly aware of Greg's interest in her.

"We haven't set any definite plans," Adam hedged. Dana spoke obscurely about her software programs, and despite Adam's regular perusal of the computer magazines, she lost him quickly. Still, he waited for her to mention something about computer-generated identities, but once she'd stopped talking about RAM and artificial intelligence, she returned to her favorite subject: Greg.

"This has been fun," she said suddenly. "Most people's eyes glaze over as soon as I start talking. You held out for a long time before I lost you. Maybe we could talk again some time." She blushed again.

"Maybe we could do it over dinner. Somewhere Greg would be sure to see us."

Dana nodded, and then, as if not able to say any more, she walked away from him. She really was very shy, Adam realized. She could talk about computers and Greg with ease, but after that she froze. Unfortunately, he doubted that Greg would ever notice her. Then again, in Sedona, one just never knew.

"Hi! We're Nancy and Brian Masters," a man's voice boomed as a tanned and fit couple in their early fifties took over Dana's spot. Brian was a retired real estate agent, Nancy a former teacher. A long-time-married couple, they explained how they spent the winter months in Sedona and traveled the rest of the year. Brian had gotten out of the real estate market before the bust, he admitted, but Nancy was the one who increased their retirement fund through investments.

"She's a genius," Brian exclaimed as he kissed his wife's cheek. "To think she spent all those years in the classroom—"

"When I should have been on Wall Street. Brian thinks I would have been—"

"A huge success. You're brilliant."

Nancy patted his arm and smiled at him fondly. "I liked teaching. And kids."

"We're thinking of adopting. An older child. So we'll do less traveling, and Nancy can spend more time on the computer. Internet and the stock market. You can't go wrong." Brian grinned from ear to ear and squeezed his wife around the waist. "You're Meg's guy, aren't you? The one who left her standing—"

"Standing on her own two feet. So many of us girls make the mistake of marrying far too young." Nancy poked her husband in the ribs.

Brian grinned at his wife. "You were just a baby when I married you, practically stole you out of the cradle." He turned his round, fresh-scrubbed face to Adam. "We eloped when she was seventeen and I was nineteen. Been the best thirty years—"

"Neither of us could have imagined it would turn out so well. But eloping isn't for everyone." Nancy stressed the last word, trying to stop her husband from putting his foot any further into his mouth. "Why, from what Meg has told us, your wedding was a big society do."

Two sets of curious eyes turned on him, and Adam didn't know what to say. Meg's marriage had been a big society affair? He'd concluded that she came from a well-to-do family who had spoiled her silly so that she thought she could get whatever she wanted, including him, but he hadn't actually thought about her wedding day. She must have been humiliated—no matter what she claimed. Suddenly he was coldly angry with the man who had let Meg down, who had hurt her so badly that she had fled her life looking for a new one.

He murmured some inanity about the wedding and then asked the Masterses about their grown children. Adam let them finish each other's sentences for some time, but he didn't learn anything interesting from Brian or Nancy. Except, of course, that Nancy knew computers, as did Dana Griffins. Whoever Adam was looking for had to be an expert.

Of the other regulars—Anna Brown, a gift shop owner; Steve Gruber, a writer of detective novels; Reginald Truman and Ben Holden, drivers in Greg's company—Adam didn't find anyone even slightly suspicious. They were all potential suspects, but none of them had set off internal alarms.

Adam was the last person on earth who would believe in any kind of extrasensory hocus-pocus. But he did trust his instincts. On more than one occasion, his gut reaction to someone had proven correct.

He should know soon enough if he'd attracted the attention of his enemies. Everyone in Sedona knew he was here. Everyone except Abigail Milton, unfortunately.

Meg came out of the kitchen and glared at him. He was by her side in a few quick steps. "Is something wrong?"

"You!" she whispered angrily.

"What about me?"

"You're a writer. A *business* writer!"

"I told you I was." He was honestly bewildered. This woman was even more of a kook than he'd imagined. What was wrong with being a business writer? He was a very successful one who worked for the *New York Times*. He'd written rags-to-riches stories, uncovered crooked CEOs, always been ready to tackle any kind of assignment. But he couldn't begin to tackle Meg's logic.

She turned on him, hands on her hips, leaning in close so that no one could overhear. "You don't understand. I've spent my whole life surrounded by writers. And Max, my ex-fiancé, was a businessman."

Before Adam could try to make any sense of Meg's convoluted logic, a gentle hand touched his shoulder. He turned around to behold a blond goddess.

"Oh, I'm sorry. I'm interrupting." She had the honeyed voice of an angel, wide blue eyes, big blond curls and perfect teeth. He'd never known a woman's teeth could be so alluring.

Adam smiled his most dashing smile at the ethereal beauty. He had the overwhelming urge to protect her from the big, bad world. "I don't believe I've had the pleasure. I'm Adam Smith."

"The writer?" Her pretty blue eyes widened in recognition.

At least someone knew and appreciated his work. Next to him, Meg made a curious strangled sound.

The blond angel batted her eyelashes at him. "I've read your column for years and am thrilled to be able to make your acquaintance. Keeping up with business is a hobby of mine. You're very good, Mr. Smith."

"Call me Adam, please."

"Adam. I'm Gloria Logan." She took his hand in hers and gazed up at him with wonder. Adam would bet anything that this was a rational, logical woman. The kind he'd been searching for his entire life.

The kind he'd been trying to avoid his entire life elbowed him in the side. Luckily she missed his injured ribs. "Adam's my fiancé."

"I thought you weren't engaged anymore." Gloria didn't exactly pout—Adam couldn't quite describe what she did with her bee-stung lips except he wished she'd do it again. Moreover, she made it clear that she thought Adam being engaged was a loss to herself.

"Adam is trying to change my mind," Meg said in a strained voice.

Glad that for once Meg was annoyed with him instead of the other way around, he leaned closer to Gloria. "I believe we're coming to dinner tomorrow night."

"I'm so pleased." She smiled and a chorus of cherubs burst into song. "I'm sorry to interrupt. Meg has so many *interesting* hobbies, I'm afraid I could never keep up with her. Why, she's had such a number of adventures after your aborted wedding…" She let her veiled criticism trail off, and when he didn't jump to Meg's defense, Gloria smiled again. "I came to remind you about our invitation. With so much excitement in town, I didn't want you to forget."

"Not a chance of that," Meg noted sourly, and stalked

off. Adam watched her retreat, eyeing the short denim skirt she'd worn all day long. He'd been right; Meg did have great legs.

Gloria touched a pink fingertip to his arm. Turning his full attention to her, he held her much smaller hand in his. "You must excuse Meg," he said. "She becomes jealous easily. That was one of our problems."

"You poor dear. But now you're back to win our Meg all over again."

"I didn't realize you and Meg were such good friends."

"I could certainly never treat a man how Meg treated you."

"But I'm the one who treated Meg so shabbily."

Gloria quickly retreated from her miscue. "But you're a big enough man to admit the error of his ways. To come back asking for forgiveness." She ran a hand up his shirt. "I hope Meg realizes how lucky she is."

He looked up to see the topic of their conversation march out of the room. Glasses clattered dangerously in the kitchen. He smiled at Gloria.

She must have realized she was treading on thin ground. She looked around the nearly empty room. "Goodness! We're the last ones still here. I should go home as well." Gloria paused, then added, "I look forward to dinner tomorrow."

"So do I. Immensely."

And he did. Alarm bells were ringing inside of him and Adam always trusted his instincts when it came to a story. Not when it came to women, but in everything else.

At the door, Gloria briefly touched her lips to his. Adam felt Meg's gaze on him, but when he turned around he only caught a glimpse of her heading up the stairs.

As Gloria was the last person to leave, he locked the shop. Full of questions, he felt restless, so he cleaned up the last of the cups and plates, loading the dishwasher. He tidied and straightened in the kitchen for several minutes, but the only response from Meg was the slamming of the bathroom door. He waited until he heard her bedroom door slam before taking the back stairs to the small room that was his for the duration of his stay.

After several hours during which sleep evaded him, Adam began to contemplate his stay here. The single bed held no appeal for him. As soon as he lay down he'd hear Meg's voice: "Three kisses and we'll be lovers." His flirtation with Gloria this evening had been aimed at making Meg angry. To make her keep her distance from him.

Lost in his reverie of exactly how impassioned Meg could become, Adam heard a thunk in the kitchen. Grabbing a heavy book, the only weapon at hand, he headed out of his room and down the back stairs to the kitchen. His plan, such as it was, had been to announce his presence in town loudly and clearly, to draw out the opposition. But he didn't want Meg hurt.

He heard quiet footsteps in the kitchen. Taking a deep breath, he jumped around the corner, rushed forward and threw a hammerlock around the intruder's neck cutting off his air.

When the man struggled, Adam wrapped an arm round his chest and encountered an armful of soft female breast. He smelled roses and let go of Meg.

Gasping, she stepped away from him. He held his arms out, wide and unthreatening. "I heard a noise. I thought you were an intruder."

"I came down for a drink," Meg explained.

"Here." Adam picked up the glass of warm milk on the counter. "You should have turned on the lights," he said, as he flipped the switch, and then wished he hadn't.

"I didn't want to wake you." Meg, dressed in a clingy negligee, gratefully took the glass he was holding.

He couldn't help but watch the milk touch her lips, the swallow of her throat. Then he let his eyes dip lower, to her negligee-clad figure. Clearly Meg hadn't expected him in the kitchen and hadn't bothered belting her robe. The yellow satin hugged her curves, especially her breasts. When she finally noticed his stare, their tips hardened in reaction. "I didn't…" she began, flustered, and reached for the lapels.

"Don't," he said, his voice rough. "You look good. I like looking at you."

"What about Gloria?" There was a hint of outrage in her voice, and he had to bite back a smile.

"That was just to make you mad."

"It worked." She swallowed convulsively and took one step closer to him, raising her chin, her eyes meeting his, searching for answers. "Is this all you want to do? Look?"

"No. I'm going to touch you." With one hand on her hip he drew her closer to him; he ran the other up and down her side, stroking and exploring. She was lovely. The pull of the satin material aroused her nipples even further and he watched her eyes flame with desire.

She didn't offer any protest or encouragement, but let his hands move over her. Let him discover his needs and wants. When his hands molded her breasts, his thumbs brushing insistently against her swollen nipples, her mouth fell open, but still she said nothing. Waiting for him.

He couldn't fight his desire for her a second longer. He leaned close so that their lips almost touched. "How many times do I have to kiss you before we're lovers?" he asked in a harsh whisper.

"Three."

"How many times have we kissed?"

"You've kissed me once."

"Twice more then."

"Yes."

He touched his lips to hers, and all he could feel was heat and need and flame and smoke and…

"Damn." He took her shoulders and pushed her away from him.

"Fire!"

6

"HOW ABSOLUTELY DREADFUL," Freddie said, holding on to the roll bar as Adam unsuccessfully tried to avoid a large hole in the dirt road. Meg muttered something under her breath about male drivers, but Adam refused to respond. He'd rented a four-wheel-drive Jeep from Greg's operation earlier in the day and he was enjoying the feel of the desert all around him as he drove. Even his ribs felt better. His office had shipped him money and the extra credit cards and identification he kept for unexpected circumstances like this.

"You must have been dreadfully frightened," Freddie continued.

"I was more shocked than anything else. Adam acted so quickly that we were able to grab the fire extinguishers and put out the flames before they spread through the store," Meg answered, her voice quiet at the memory of what could have happened.

"Did the fire chief say how it might have begun? A fire in that shop, with all those books..." Freddie shuddered. "It could have been an inferno. What if neither of you had woken up in time?"

"Bill thinks someone threw a cigarette into some garbage that was too close to the shop, but still...it was scary. Someone from our meeting probably had a cigarette afterward and wasn't careful. Because of the hot night air, it smoldered for hours...."

"It's a good thing both of you were awake so late," Freddie hinted suggestively.

"Yes," Meg responded blandly.

"Meg and I were lucky," Adam agreed. Very lucky. He

doubted the fire had been an accident, but he also doubted that it had been meant to kill them. It had been a warning. His last chance to drop the investigation and leave.

He couldn't just wait for Abby to come back and tell him her suspicions. Adam was glad to be able to get to the Logans' ranch. As much as he didn't like trusting his feelings, he'd felt that familiar prickling at the back of his neck when he'd spoken with Gloria. That reaction needed to be checked out. She had been interested in him more than as the new single man in town—or as a man she could steal away from Meg. Gloria has been as suspicious of him as he was of her.

He was also looking forward to the opportunity to meet Reid Logan.

The last thing the fire had done was scare him off. Now he was angry and even more determined. However, Meg's involvement worried him. He was putting her in danger. She was heedless of it, or rather, uncaring. Today when he'd suggested she might like to return home to her family for a visit, she had thrown a book at him and stormed out of the shop. She was fearless and beautiful and passionate, but she refused to listen to reason. He couldn't deny, though, that if that fire hadn't interrupted their kiss last night, reason wouldn't have saved him. He and Meg would have made love. He wasn't being conceited; she had made it clear that she wanted him. No, he was the one who had to remember restraint. To remember his ex-wife. To remember he wanted to find the man who had hurt Kelly.

And not to kiss Meg Cooper a third time.

The Logans' sprawling ranch house appeared in the fading sunlight. "We've been on the Logan property for the last twenty miles," Freddie said. "Pretty impressive."

"Reid has one of the most spectacular ranches in the state. It's been in the Logan family for over four generations. Gloria runs a very exclusive dude ranch operation catering to only one or two guests at a time," said Meg.

"Impressive," Adam agreed, curious to meet Reid and to continue his acquaintance with the angelic Gloria.

A tall, fair-haired man with the lope of a cowboy met them by the side of the house, where Adam parked the Jeep. "Hello," he drawled, helping Meg out of the vehicle. Keeping a casual arm around her waist, he extended his hand toward Adam. "I'm Reid Logan and real glad you were able to join Meg. Gloria has been looking forward to seeing you again." Reid turned his attention back to Meg, a slow smile spreading to the crinkling corners of his blue eyes. "Meg, you look beautiful as always."

"Thank you, Reid." She stepped away from him a little, so that his hand fell from her waist, but she continued to smile with delight at the tall cowboy. Adam resisted the urge to pull her to his side.

"Freddie." Reid acknowledged the last guest, but then stepped closer to Meg, who practically fluttered her eyelashes at him, Adam noted with disgust. He moved to take her arm but Reid was already leading her toward the well-lit house.

Adam didn't have much time to admire the ranch house or the buildings in the back that must have been the barns, for the front door was open and the sounds of conversation and laughter drifted out. Gloria met Adam in the pine-walled hallway, her blue eyes sparkling as she touched his arm with her long and slender fingers. Lovely and feminine as she was, he wished it was Meg touching him. "I'm so glad you were able to join us for dinner. I was afraid Meg might decide to keep you all to herself," Gloria said softly, drawing him into the living room. "Have you had any luck with our Meg?"

"Luck?"

"At winning the fair maiden's hand, of course. You had better hurry. I think my brother has decided to become more aggressive in his campaign now that he has competition. My brother can be very persuasive. Plus, he hates to lose."

Reid was pouring Meg a glass of red wine, placing his

hand over hers to steady the glass. Adam stopped Gloria in the doorway of the living room, continuing to hold her hand. "Are you hoping to have Meg as a sister-in-law?"

"She's a sweet girl, but that's not why I wish Reid luck."

"Then why?"

Gloria crinkled her baby blues at him. "Because you'd be lonely, brokenhearted and on the rebound."

"And you'd nurse my broken heart?"

Gloria laughed delightedly, arching her slender neck. "I live for the opportunity to show how...*sympathetic* I can be."

Adam couldn't help joining her in her amusement. "Do you always go after what you want so directly?"

"Usually. I don't like to play games. Why waste time when the man and I could be doing much more *interesting* things together?" Her voice faded into a husky whisper and Adam felt it to his stomach. "But I'm being a bad hostess and monopolizing you. Come meet the others."

The Logan ranch could put the Ponderosa to shame. Everything was large and solid. In this room, a massive brick fireplace was slightly off center. Windows covered one entire wall, offering a view of the patio and swimming pool. The house was built in a large U around the pool. Western-style furniture—large, made of solid wood and leather and fabrics in Santa Fe colors—suited the house.

"Let's go interrupt my brother and your ex-fiancée before they get too cosy." Gloria led Adam to the man commanding the center of the room. Dressed in jeans and a white Western-cut shirt, Reid Logan exuded masculinity and confidence. He was good-looking but not handsome. He had a settled looked about him, as if he was comfortable in his own skin.

Adam judged him to be a few years younger than his own forty-two. Reid and Meg were in conversation with a plump, brown-haired woman when Gloria interrupted. "This is Betty Henderson, a former schoolmate of mine.

When Betty wrote that she would be traveling through Arizona I just had to invite her to visit. Now I'm hoping to convince her to stay with us another week. It can get so dull out here without any female company. No matter how much I try, I just can't interest Reid in my decorating ideas. Betty, I want you to meet the famous Adam Smith, Meg's former fiancé."

Reid offered Betty a drink from the bar and then turned toward Adam and Gloria. "Dear Gloria, as tactful as ever." He belied the edge to his words by putting his arm around her shoulder. "You'll have to excuse my sister, Mr. Smith, but she's very protective of her older brother."

"That's what families are all about. I feel exactly the same way about my sister." He took the beer Reid proffered. "Call me Adam. Your ranch is very impressive." Could Reid be the one who had hurt Kelly? Their gazes locked and challenged, but then Reid glanced toward Meg, who had joined Freddie at the bar. Jealousy. Adam had almost forgotten that Reid was jealous of him because of his supposed relationship with Meg. He smiled at Meg and Freddie. "A wonderful woman. I was a fool to let her get away."

"Why did you?" Reid asked coldly.

Adam felt the familiar prickle of warning on his neck and stiffened. He was only reacting to Reid's jealousy. Maybe.

Or was it Adam's intuition—his damn sixth sense or whatever other foolishness you wanted to name it? Usually Adam called his *unusual* ability luck—or at least that's what he claimed whenever a colleague questioned how he followed a story in a direction no one else had considered. He would never admit the truth.

Sometimes he just got this…feeling. His neck prickled, his palms would sweat and he would just *know* that he'd suddenly stumbled upon the key to unlocking a puzzle. That the quiet accountant who was remaining silent in the crowd of corporate suits facing him had the answers he needed. Or that the executive vice president was lying through his teeth.

While he never talked about his ability, Adam had learned to trust it. And right now all his senses were on alert. Something about Reid Logan was wrong, but that didn't mean he was involved in the forgery ring. Reid might be sending out strong signals because of his feelings for Meg, and as a result, for Adam, Reid's supposed competitor.

The damn woman had too many suitors by far. All this evening needed was for Greg Trenton to be one of the guests.

Adam turned his attention back to Reid's question. "Letting Meg go was a bad mistake. One I plan to rectify. Meg tells me you have one of the biggest ranches in the state."

"Yes. The Liberty L has been part of the family for over a hundred years." Reid's drawl held pride.

"A heritage he plans to leave to his children as soon as he finds the right woman," Gloria added.

Reid frowned at Gloria. "My sister seems to enjoy nothing more than setting grown men against each other. I think it's why she's so good at business."

"Reid, you're being unfair. I'm teasing." Gloria turned her limpid eyes on Adam and he felt their effect down to his toes. Dressed in a white halter dress with tiny pink flowers, she looked sweet and beautiful and very sexy. His palms began to sweat. "Let me freshen up that drink," she said, pointing toward the bar. "Reid wants to say hello to the rest of the guests."

Adam let her lead him to the bar and hand him another beer, one he planned to nurse for the rest of the night. He needed his full wits about him among the wily Logans. Gloria poured herself a glass of champagne. "My favorite," she said with a sigh. "It's not really a party unless there's champagne."

Adam wanted to know a lot more about Gloria and her brother. "Did you grow up on the ranch?"

"Yes. And I was always dreaming of being elsewhere. Especially a big city—New York, Paris, London. I covered the walls in my bedroom with pictures of the Eiffel Tower and the Empire State Building, while other little girls plastered teen idols on the walls. My parents told me I could study abroad, so I begged for a language tutor and spent many of my afternoons conjugating French verbs and learning German pronunciation."

"A determined child. Are you the same way today?"

"Yes, except I knew better what I wanted when I was young. After our parents died, Reid let me go to all the places I'd dreamed about. I studied in London and then in Paris. And the whole time I missed Arizona. I missed the colors and the heat and the spaces, and so I came back home." Gloria shrugged her delicate shoulders and Adam noticed all the soft bare skin.

He waited for his body to react to Gloria. When it didn't, he asked, "What did you study?"

"English history, French literature, Arabic. I flitted from subject to subject, until I finally decided it was time to go home and figure it out for myself. What I wanted."

"And have you?"

"Part of me. I don't think we ever know everything we're capable of. But I do know that this is home. It gives me security and roots and family. And Sedona in all its quirkiness lets me explore. That's why I so adore Meg. She helps me find books to expand my knowledge. This place attracts all of us lost souls."

"Is Meg a lost soul?"

"Definitely. Although now that you're here, she seems much more—I don't know—like I think she should be...." Gloria bit a pale pink lip and looked up at him from under her lashes. She moved closer. "It's difficult to explain. It's a feeling."

There were too many damn feelings in this place—including Adam's own now that Reid was standing too close to Meg and she was laughing at something he'd said. Adam asked, "How did you decide to include a dude ranch on the Liberty L?"

A small frown crossed Gloria's face, but it was quickly gone. "Necessity and boredom. I needed something to do, and my eclectic education had little practical use. While Reid tried to make work for me, he didn't need me for anything. He's a good rancher and manager and he'd hired an excellent staff. Poor little old me was only in the way, so I began to invite my school friends for vacations. I would show them the land and explain the operations, teach them to ride. I know the history of the local area and of our country—one of my majors—and I'm fluent in five languages, with a smattering of more.

"So after one of these vacations, when one of my friends phoned to say that her father and two of his business colleagues wanted to pay me handsomely to take exactly the same vacation, I knew I'd found my business."

"Niche marketing."

"Exactly. I advertise through word of mouth and with an impressive, glossy brochure with lavish photographs. I mail only to people who have requested it."

"And then wait for your customers to call you." He raised his beer in a toast. "Brilliant."

Gloria smiled and the air sparkled. "I've been fortunate that it turned out so well. Running the dude ranch has also left me with a lot of free time. I can continue to study what pleases me. Another interest might pay off just as lucratively one day. I've been lucky," Gloria added modestly, but there was a self-satisfied gleam in her eye.

"You have every right to be proud of what you've accomplished. I'd love a tour of the Liberty L sometime."

"Soon," she promised him, and tucked her arm under his. "But now it's time for dinner."

Meg glared at him as Gloria led him into the dining room, which could comfortably seat twenty. He lingered over Gloria as he pulled out her chair. As there were only six of them—Reid, Gloria, Freddie, Meg, Betty and himself—they took one end of the polished oak table. Reid had seated Meg next to himself.

They were served by Peter, a college student who helped out whenever the Liberty L had guests, Meg informed him. Once their food was in front of them, Gloria leaned toward Meg. "You never told me your ex-fiancé was such a famous journalist."

"Yes, Adam has been nominated for the Pulitzer twice and won countless awards for his business coverage. But I wasn't marrying him for his brilliant writing, so when we didn't..." Here Meg stopped, her eyes filled with tears and she blinked quickly. Adam had seen her perform this act several times and he still marveled over it. "I just didn't want to talk about him. But he is a brilliant writer," she added, and glared at Gloria.

"You would know," Gloria agreed, as she helped herself to more grilled vegetables.

"My personal favorite was his profile of JB Design Inc., Manufacturing," Meg continued. "The company was about to be closed, but the employees bought out its multinational owner and pulled together to keep the business running. Adam has been profiling them every year since his original story in 1989."

Adam shot Meg a quick look; she returned it unperturbed. So she did know his work. The JB Design Inc., Manufacturing takeover hadn't been a complete success, but the employees had saved the business and a lot of jobs. Last year they had even discussed expansion. It's what he wished could have happened to his father's company. Instead it had gone belly-up and his father had died shortly afterward. That's when Adam had asked to be assigned business stories. He was interested in those who got the job done. Who made something new. Who innovated and took risks. Who won.

He uncovered foolishness, mismanagement, inflated egos, and loved exposing it in black and white. He believed in the truth. He tried to occasionally reveal where and how people had gone wrong, hopefully enabling others to learn from their mistakes.

"Adam is more known for his investigative stories, but I think he likes writing about the success stories best." Adam stiffened at Meg's accurate observation. "He doesn't like to admit it, though. It would spoil his tough, cynical-journalist image," she added. She reached for his hand across the table and squeezed it lovingly. No one else saw her pinch him hard.

He leaned closer and whispered, "So that's what you were doing in the library this afternoon?"

"I told you I had some research I needed to do."

Adam turned to Gloria. "Meg exaggerates, but I do find the success stories a good change of pace, and they provide inspiration to the readers. My editor certainly likes the letters those pieces pull in. I'd like to be able to write about you and your exclusive dude ranch. I don't think I've ever heard of another operation like this one."

Reid frowned. "We don't need any more publicity. I don't want a bunch of tourists coming round and gawking at us."

Gloria shook her head at her brother. "Now, Reid, it might be kind of fun. We should think about it."

"Oh, do consider it," Meg urged.

"Could I perhaps have a tour of the house after dinner?" Adam asked Gloria. He wanted to get a sense of the place and an opportunity to talk to Gloria one on one. Meg had promised to keep Reid occupied. He ignored the fact that he no longer liked that idea.

"I'd love nothing more than to show you my home." Gloria smiled beatifically and Adam let her glow wash over him for a few seconds. For the remainder of the meal he said little, watching the interaction between Reid and Meg. Once they'd finished their desserts, Gloria stood. "If the rest of you will excuse us? Freddie, perhaps you could help Betty choose a Santa Fe motif for her next afghan— she's a fabulous knitter. You could probably design something spectacular for her."

Freddie, who had risen to join them on the tour, sat back down. He wiped the kicked look off his face and then turned to Betty. As much as he disliked the man, even Adam wouldn't have wished picking knitting patterns on Freddie.

Gloria toured Adam through the sprawling house, showing him the four guest bedrooms they used for paying guests, the library, the TV room, the playroom with its pool table, and the kitchen where Peter was cleaning up from dinner. "As soon as you've loaded the dishwasher you can go home. I'll empty the machine in the morning," Gloria told him, and the young man shot her a grateful look.

"Thanks, Gloria. I have a paper I wanted to finish writing tonight." He clattered the dishes together even faster, and Gloria winced slightly but didn't say anything.

She took Adam down a hallway from the kitchen and pointed toward the west wing. "Reid has his bedroom and office there, but he likes his privacy, so I'm afraid it's off-limits. Plus I don't think Reid would take very kindly to you being in his space." She stopped in front of another door. "Here are my rooms."

Adam suddenly felt awkward in Gloria's white bedroom. She had a lot of lace covering the four-poster bed, an ivory stripped couch and a glass table under the window. She pointed to a door. "I keep my books, research papers and computer in there."

"May I?"

"Sure." Gloria opened the door to a small room that was in sharp contrast to the feminine trappings of her bedroom. "These two rooms were meant as a minisuite for guests, but Reid suggested I use them for my personal area."

The workroom had lots of windows, but it was the floor-to-ceiling bookshelves crammed with reading material that caught Adam's attention. He read some of the titles. Gloria had everything from Spanish dictionaries, to books on astronomy and physics, to piles of fiction paperbacks. He picked up one randomly and saw a bare-chested pirate holding an armful of lush female. He looked up at her in surprise.

"I read everything, and there's nothing better than a good love story with a happy ending."

Adam put the book back down, noticing the photographs on her desk. In one, a slightly younger Gloria grinned broadly back at the camera, her arms wrapped around the waists of a young man and woman who had to be brother and sister.

"That's Susannah, a friend from my school days in Paris, and her brother. Her father was our first paying customer." Gloria took the photo out of his hands and stepped closer to him. "What do you think?"

"Your home is beautiful."

She closed in, her golden curls almost tickling his nose. Adam had to stop himself from stepping back. He was only inches away from a lot of bare female shoulders and back, her neck had a lovely arch, her breasts and hips curved nicely, yet he didn't itch to touch her like he did Meg. If Meg were standing so close to him and looking at him so invitingly, he'd haul her into his arms and lose himself on the four-poster bed with her.

Gloria shook her head and her smile turned to one of regret. "You can't blame a girl for trying. You've got it really bad for her."

Adam didn't answer, but he feared the answer was yes.

Gloria trailed a finger down his shirtfront, stopping at his belt buckle. Absolutely nothing reacted, and Gloria sighed and stepped away from him. "Let's go back to the living room for coffee."

Adam wished there was something he could say to Gloria, to be able to explain that Meg fell into a pattern of falling for the wrong kind of woman and letting the right kind lead him out of her bedroom. Why was it that his logical brain could never control his illogical heart? He was an idiot, he told himself.

In the living room, as planned, there was no Meg and

Reid. Gloria ignored Adam, poured herself another glass of champagne and went to join Freddie and Betty in front of the fire. Freddie had drafting paper in front of him and sketched busily, never looking up at Adam. Adam scowled and prowled toward the window. Meg had promised to take Reid out of the house and keep him occupied.

Now he wondered exactly how Meg would keep Reid occupied. Was she letting him kiss her, touch her? Had the cowboy taken her to the barn in time-honored Western tradition, planning on making love to her in the hay? Adam peered into the darkness but couldn't see anything.

Telling himself he was acting the part of the jealous lover, just as they'd planned earlier in the afternoon, Adam opened the glass doors and stepped out into the shadows. Quelling the urge to search for Meg, he headed to the west of the house and counted windows until he was in front of Reid's office. The window slid open easily and he climbed inside.

This room was all dark wood and included two sets of antlers on either side of the fireplace. From their age, Adam could tell they were hunting trophies of one of Reid's ancestors. Reid had a very nice collection of western art on the walls and first editions of Zane Grey and Louis Lamour. "Cowboys." Adam snorted and wondered if the Liberty L earned enough to sustain Reid's expensive hobby of collecting rare books.

In the desk Adam found the account ledgers and began to read. The ranch had experienced both windfalls and setbacks. He hadn't expected to find anything different; a lot of profit would have looked far too suspicious. He put the ledger back in the desk drawer, stopped and looked around the room, considering what he should do next. He could turn on Reid's computer and try to break into files, but what exactly did he expect to find here? That was the question Meg had asked him, and he had told her he just wanted to take a look around, to get a sense of Reid.

Of course, that was only half of the truth. He wanted to

sit in Reid's chair, in Reid's office, and discover if he felt anything. To see if his skin prickled or alarm bells went off. He leaned back in the rich leather chair, letting himself be enfolded by the buttery softness. Closing his eyes, he smelled leather, smoke and something that he assumed was horse. He was letting himself drift, imagining Reid working here, when he experienced a sharp jolt through his system. All of his senses screamed that something was terribly wrong. Opening his eyes, he saw Reid and a very pale Meg standing in the doorway.

"I suspected I would find you here," Reid said coolly as he stepped inside, pulling Meg in with him.

Adam stood casually and shrugged, determined to get him and Meg out of this difficult situation and away from the Liberty L as soon as possible. "You'll have to forgive me. My journalist instincts got the better of me. I got a little too curious after the house tour," Adam began, but Reid held up a callused hand.

"No need for explanation. I know all about you." He stepped farther into the room and closed the door behind him. He smiled coldly. "Just the three of us. Now we'll have a real opportunity to talk."

7

REID'S FACE WAS HARD, his eyes narrow, as he pulled Meg along with him. "You shouldn't be in my private office. I don't like anyone being in here, not even my sister."

Trying to look innocent and friendly, Adam took a step toward Reid, his palms open. If the cowboy didn't take his big paw off Meg's arm soon, he would make him. He must have shown something of his thoughts on his face, for Meg frowned at him. He relaxed his expression and tried again. "My reporter's curiosity got the better of me. I've always found that a man's office reveals a lot about himself. As a writer, I haven't come across a successful rancher and I wanted to get a better sense of the man behind this impressive operation."

Reid looked unconvinced. "Then you could have asked me."

"I apologize. Acting on my reporter's instinct is a bad habit of mine."

Reid looked at the desk that held the account ledger that Adam had placed back in the drawer. "Did you find anything of interest?"

Adam felt heat color his cheeks and was glad that he looked embarrassed. "I only took a very quick look."

"Then, if you knew anything about ranching, you'd know that despite the amount of land and livestock we have on it, survival is always our ambition. The Liberty L looks impressive, but we've also experienced a lot of bad fortune with weather and animal disease." Finally Reid let go of Meg, as if ashamed of what he was revealing. "As much as I don't like to admit it, Gloria's tourist business has helped out the finances of the ranch quite a bit."

Meg touched Reid's arm, concern on her lovely face, and then stopped as if she didn't know what to say. She turned to Adam. "Perhaps we should call this a night," she said in cool tones.

Then once again she grasped Reid's hand. "I'm sorry, Reid. I never thought Adam would betray your trust like this. I'm embarrassed." Her cheeks bloomed a pretty pink as she shot another glance at Adam. "Believe me, as his former fiancée, I'm going to give him a piece of my mind tonight. I'll understand if this changes our plans for tomorrow."

Reid looked at their clasped hands. "No, I'd like some time for us to be together. Alone." He glanced at Adam meaningfully. "I'll pick you up at six."

"Good." She smiled at him. "I'm looking forward to our date." She leaned up and brushed her lips against his cheek.

Reid smiled. "I'm looking forward to our date as well." He opened the door, ushering Meg out and leaving Adam to follow them. Adam felt like an idiot for being caught snooping through Reid's office. Nor did he like the look that Meg had shot him or the fact that she had a date with Reid tomorrow night. He seemed to have blown it completely.

Reid kept his hand on the small of Meg's back as the trio made their way to the front hallway. Reid stopped by the big front door. "I'll go tell Freddie you two are ready to leave."

Meg waited until Reid was out of sight and then she punched Adam in the arm.

He cradled his arm—the one that had been nicked by a knife in the ambush—and scowled at her. What did Meg think she was up to? "That hurt!"

Meg's cheeks flushed as she glared at him. "Not as much as you're going to hurt when I get through with you. What kind of investigative reporter are you? You asked me to keep Reid busy so you could look around and get a sense of the ranch. I didn't expect for us to find you in his office, sitting calm as day at his desk with your boots up! Woodward and Bernstein didn't get caught. My God, Mike Wallace is old and he doesn't get caught."

To his dismay, Adam found his body reacting to Meg's anger. All he could think of was how passionate she would be in bed. Why couldn't he be attracted to Gloria? "Keep your voice down—Reid might overhear us."

"It's kind of late to be cautious now," Meg grumbled, but she quieted. She shot him a couple of dirty looks and muttered under her breath. Adam tried to ignore her scent as he considered his next steps. Eventually, Freddie joined them, looking a little puzzled, especially at the cool exchange of good-nights that were made between the two men.

Back in the Jeep on the road to Sedona, Freddie broke the silence. "Well, that was even more interesting than I had expected." He turned to Adam. "What happened between the two of you? Did Reid challenge you to a gunfight at high noon on Main Street?"

Adam kept his eyes on the road and shrugged. He was still cursing himself for letting Reid discover him in the office. "Not quite. But Reid wasn't happy about me being in town to try to win back Meg."

"Oh, right." Freddie didn't sound convinced. "Funny, I thought it was something else."

Adam decided he needed to follow another lead in his investigation or he wouldn't get anywhere. He would gamble on Freddie. "I also thought the ring you made Meg was an original."

Freddie sat up straight, studying Adam through narrowed eyes. "It is one of my original designs. I don't make only one ring—that would be economic suicide. I take it you've seen my design before?"

Taking one hand off the wheel, Adam reached into his pocket, pulled out Kelly's picture and passed it to Freddie. "Do you recognize her? She had the same ring as Meg."

Freddie studied the image and then was quiet for a minute, before he said, "This is Kelly Smith."

He turned to Adam. "Adam Smith. Are you related?"

"I'm her brother."

"Then please tell me if she's all right," he demanded.

"She's doing okay." Adam eyed Freddie suspiciously. "Why?"

Freddie let out a breath. "Let me explain. I made the ring for Kelly several months ago. She came into my shop frequently to check on its progress and we became friends. But I was worried about her. Kelly was scared of the man she was with."

This was the information Adam needed. Plus, it showed that his instincts were right. Kelly was in trouble because of a man. "She told you this?"

"Not in so many words." Freddie shrugged elegantly. "Women confide in me. I like the female sex and seem to understand their concerns better than most men. Or maybe I'm just willing to talk about feelings. Whatever it is, I'm popular with women."

"That's true," Meg interjected. "Freddie is one of the few straight men who have a lot of women friends."

Freddie looked off into the distance as if searching for the right words. "Kelly and I struck up a conversation the first time she came into my store, and, well, I kind of fell for her. She was looking for a special ring, so I offered to make one. I knew she'd have to come back to the store to check on its progress and to have it sized. Well, she didn't need to return nearly as many times as I asked her to, but I was looking for a way to spend more time with her.

"Kelly liked me, I could tell that. And if there hadn't been some other man in her life, I would have had a chance. But whoever Kelly was involved with frightened her."

"Frightened her? How do you know?"

Freddie considered his words. "Because she wouldn't even tell me who he was. From the beginning I knew she was worried about something, but it took several conversations before she confided in me, and then she told me only the barest details. From what I was able to gather, she was traveling through Sedona, intending to stay only a day or two—she wanted to commune with the vortexes and try to get her psychic karma back in shape—when she met this man. She said that in the beginning everything was wonderful. That the first time she saw him she felt this curious tingle, a sensation like everything was right." Adam shifted uncomfortably. "Kelly got all starry-eyed when she talked about how they fell in love. Love at first sight for both of them, she claimed. He treated her well and she moved in with him almost immediately. I'm not sure what happened next, but I got the feeling that Kelly began to wonder where all his money was coming from. One day she came in very frightened and silent. She wouldn't tell me what was happening—but, well, she sort of said goodbye."

"That was the last time you saw her? How long ago was that?"

"It was six months ago. I saw her twice more, but she remained distant. She certainly didn't share any confidences. The last time, she picked up her ring. Then she disappeared. I asked around town about her, but she hadn't made any other friends here. Abby knew Kelly, but she, too, didn't know much about her. Abby was worried about her as well."

"You sound like you cared for Kelly a lot," Meg noted.

"I did. I think I fell a little in love with her. I offered to help her with whatever kind of trouble she was in, but she wouldn't confide in me. Then she was gone and I haven't forgotten her."

Adam considered Freddie's words. The man had given him the best information he'd gotten about Kelly so far, and it sounded as if Freddie had cared about Kelly a great deal. Freddie had more character than Adam had suspected. More than he would have likely given the man credit for.

First he had to make sure that Freddie's story was accurate. If only Abigail Milton would return! Tomorrow Adam would check into Freddie's background and ask more questions about him around town. Someone else was bound to have made friends with Kelly—Kelly always made friends so easily—and might have a better sense of who the man Kelly had been in love with was.

At least, for the first time, Adam knew he was on the right track.

MEG COULDN'T BELIEVE she had been so wrong about Adam.

The man hadn't been the least bit open with her. Adam had never mentioned a word about his sister, Kelly. Before dinner he'd disappeared into his room to make phone calls. He'd tried to utilize Abby's computer, but she'd included passwords and other security measures so that he hadn't been able to access any information. Only out of sheer frustration he had actually asked for Meg's help so that he could take a quick survey through the ranch house.

She'd never imagined that Adam would be so foolish as to be sitting behind Reid's desk when they walked into his office. Meg had tried her best to delay Reid, but he hadn't been interested in a long walk in the moonlight or flirting on the patio. Instead, Reid had been anxious to find Adam. She had to wonder why. Was it more than jealousy? It must be. Reid hadn't taken the clearly offered opportunity to romance her.

Then again, Reid was a very private man and he must not have liked having a well-known journalist snooping around his house.

Meg sighed. She was getting a headache from all this round-and-round thinking. Certainly putting all these clues together was much more difficult than Jessica Fletcher made it look!

Which led her back to Adam again. Meg had foolishly believed that he'd told her the important details of the case. That he was willing to work with her. But he'd never breathed a word about his sister. Kelly was the real reason he had come to Sedona, the reason he was willing to risk his life. She'd thought he was a dedicated journalist who didn't like someone threatening him. But it turned out he had very personal reasons he'd never shared with her.

They dropped Freddie off at his shop—he had an apartment in back—and then Adam parked in front of The Gateway. Meg unlocked the door and stepped inside. How she loved this store with its shelves of treasures. The books and the dreams. All her silly dreams. She felt like they were being crushed.

"Kelly is your sister and she's the real reason you're investigating these false computer identities."

"Yes," Adam said.

"Were you going to tell me about her?"

"There was no need."

"No need!" She whirled on him, anger threatening to take over, but she pushed it back down. "No need to keep me informed because you don't see us as partners."

"No, I don't."

His words hurt her so much, Meg thought she might cry. Here she was feeling everything a woman could feel for a man, and he wanted nothing to do with her. Oh, he'd told her that, but she hadn't really believed him. Was she making the same mistakes she'd made with Max?

The negative signals had been apparent in her relationship with Max, but she had thought that they would get past them. That once they were married there would be more passion. Was this the same situation in reverse?

She and Adam had lots of passion—she knew that Adam wanted to make love to her—but she'd assumed they had more.

From the first moment she'd seen Adam he had felt so right. She'd been positive that he'd experienced the same overwhelming emotions. She'd realized he was more conservative and less likely to act on emotion and intuition than her, but she'd believed he would try. It turned out he wasn't willing to try at all.

Adam would like the old New York Meg. The woman who was always rational, logical and lived by her well-calculated plans. But she was tired of being that women; it wasn't who she really was deep down. She'd changed—and she'd thought her feelings for Adam were part of those changes. Including becoming a woman who was willing to be more adventurous in love.

The old Meg had been willing to settle for reliable, practical Max.

The new Meg wanted passion and thrills and adventure—everything she could find with Adam. But he didn't seem to think or feel the same way at all.

She had backed herself into a corner she could see no way out of.

"We're not partners," she repeated, surprised at how firm her words sounded when she felt so numb inside.

"Don't get me wrong, you've been of help, but—"

"You prefer to work alone. You don't really believe I can help you."

"No. That's not what I meant. Meg, you're twisting my meaning."

"I don't think so. I think I'm finally hearing you for the first time. I don't know why it took me so long, except that I really didn't want to believe you thought so little of me."

"Meg—"

"No." Meg held up her hand, cutting him off. "I think it's better if we end this conversation here before you say something else I'll regret."

"GOOD MORNING," Adam said almost hesitantly when he walked into the kitchen the next morning. He had spent far too much of last evening thinking about Meg and how hurt she had looked. Which was ridiculous. He was only trying to spare them both pain. The chemistry between them was potent and, well, he had to admit he kind of liked her, but being together would only be disaster.

Other than his ex-wife, he'd stayed away from women like Meg and, as a result, had been bored on every date. He'd tried to establish relationships with several successful, rational women and his interest in his love life had slowly died. No, Meg thrilled and attracted him more than any woman ever had. Therefore, he planned to stay as far away from her as possible. But that didn't mean he couldn't apologize for his rude behavior last night.

But he didn't plan to tell her how he felt about her, how much he wanted her. "I wanted to apologize for my words last night. I'm afraid I said more than I meant."

"So now you think I'm capable of running my own life successfully?" Meg waited a minute and then smiled crookedly. "I didn't think so. I had time last night to think about us…and, well, if you don't want to explore what there could be between us, then I'm certainly not going to force you."

"No more 'three kisses and we'll be lovers'?" he asked.

"Nothing so silly," she agreed, and he was dismayed. "Instead—" she held up a list "—I've been putting together a list of potential suspects. Don't give me that negative look."

"Sorry," he said again, meaning it. "How have you chosen your perpetrators?"

"I went through the store's computer records last night and pulled off the names of anyone who bought more than one computer book. Unfortunately, the list is fairly extensive."

Adam took the list and read the names: Dana Andrews, naturally, Freddie, Michelle, Gloria, Ben Masters and a couple of other people in town he hadn't yet met. "Thanks. This will give me a good place to start. I appreciate your efforts." Meg had provided him with a good beginning. So why was he so disappointed about the three-kisses rule? "I don't suppose the store computer system has access to Abby's personal system?"

"No. Abby always said she wanted her personal computer to be completely separate so no one could hack in.

She didn't really care if some hacker plugged into The Gateway's records, but she was determined to keep her personal records private. Which I understand now after what Abby uncovered, but it doesn't make our life much easier."

"Agreed. Too bad about the computers. I'll check out everyone on the list."

"Will you be out all day?"

"Probably." Adam thought about asking her to join him but didn't.

Meg looked at him with a curious expression on her face. "Good luck."

Adam could have used a lot more than luck, he decided, when he came back to The Gateway later. His day had been fruitless. He'd contacted his office and asked one of the junior reporters to investigate the background of everyone on Meg's list. He'd drunk too many cups of coffee with Ben and Nancy Masters and learned nothing new except that the pair could keep finishing each others thoughts forever—or at least what seemed like forever to him, trapped with the happy couple. Steve Gruber, the adventure writer, had been cordial to Adam but suspicious as to why he was asking so many questions. Adam arrived back at The Gateway just in time to catch Meg spraying a spritz of her rose perfume on her wrists.

"How do I look?"

"Delicious." She wore a short brown suede skirt with a fringe along the hem and a bright yellow silk blouse tied around her bare midriff. "Won't you be cold in that?"

"I have a jacket." She grabbed a denim jacket and her purse. "I think I hear Reid out front."

Adam looked out the front door and saw Reid pull up in his Jeep. "You're still going out with him?"

"Of course. I said I was last night. Besides, I figure I'd better appease him a little about your foolish actions last evening. Plus, I like him." She checked her lipstick in the hallway mirror; her lips were kissably perfect. She rifled through her purse, not looking at him. "You can always drive out to the ranch and keep the beautiful Gloria company. No need to wait up for me."

Meg fluffed her hair one last time and then, continuing to ignore him, rushed out the front door of the store. "Oh, you'd better lock the door," she shouted. "You never know what kind of ruthless criminals are lurking about."

With that, Meg was gone, leaving Adam feeling distinctly peculiar.

8

"ADAM, THIS IS A very pleasant surprise." Gloria glowed at him from the doorway of the Liberty L. She opened the door wider, motioning to him. "Please come in, although I must admit I wasn't expecting to see you again so soon."

He stepped in, still wondering exactly what he was doing. "You must have thought me a very rude guest last night."

Gloria pouted her bee-stung lips. "You and Meg did rush out of here. I gathered something had happened between you and my brother, but Reid wouldn't tell me what. I presumed it had something to do with Meg."

"Yes, it was something like that," Adam agreed, wishing he didn't think he was making a fool of himself.

Gloria considered him for a moment and then smiled again. "Come along," she offered, and preceded him along the hallway to the recreation room.

"You look lovely tonight," he told her, and she did. Dressed in snug, faded jeans and a white shirt, her pink toenails tantalized as did her tousled hair. Her face was bare of makeup except for a touch of pink lipstick. She was the ideal combination of innocence and sexiness, and Adam appreciated every lovely line of her.

She took him to the TV room, where an episode of *N.Y.P.D. Blue* was playing on the set. A pile of magazines and a nail polish bottle lay on the small table next to the leather couch. "I'm glad you decided to visit me. Betty left this morning, and it can get pretty lonely out here."

"I wasn't sure if I'd be welcome."

"After rejecting me so cavalierly last night, you should be wondering." She glanced at him from under her lashes, then her lips broke into a broad smile. "I'm not very good at sulking, but why do I have the feeling that the real reason you're here tonight is more because Meg is out on a date with Reid than because of any of my potent female charms? No, no need to answer me. I think we both know the answer. But I'm still glad you came. Perhaps a further acquaintance can help us appreciate each other more."

"That sounds like an excellent plan." Adam returned Gloria's smile, appreciating her openness and wit. Gloria was a very beautiful woman who should be sending his blood pressure sky-high. Instead, nothing. If it was Meg in her short brown skirt with the enticing fringe standing in front of him, looking at him as if she wished he'd kiss her, he'd be doing a lot more than checking his pulse rate.

"Tell me more about your dude ranch," Adam asked instead.

"Would you like a drink or coffee?"

"A drink would be better," he said. Gloria pulled a bottle of Scotch from the drink cart and poured them each a drink. She moved to the couch and patted the cushion next to her. "Sit beside me. I promise not to jump you, and we can at least enjoy the feel of another person's body heat next to us."

Adam sat down, intrigued by her. Not only were the women of Sedona headstrong, but they were also painfully honest. "I'm surprised you're not involved with anyone. A beautiful woman like you has to have had a lot of admirers."

Gloria crinkled her pert nose. "You'd think so, wouldn't you? I think that while I was in Europe I missed much of the mating ritual in Sedona. By the time I decided to make this my home, most of the kids I went to school with had coupled up and settled down."

"But you must have some interesting clients."

Gloria took a sip of her drink. "Call me old-fashioned, but I don't like to mix business with pleasure. Plus, most of my clients are too old." She put her drink down on the table and turned the full effect of her baby blue eyes on him. "So you can't blame a girl for trying when a great looking, successful guy like you comes into town."

"I hope Meg isn't going to give me up so easily," he said with a smile, enjoying his flirtation with Gloria but also realizing his words about Meg were true. He truly was a fool, he thought.

Gloria moved a smidgen closer to him. "But she is out with Reid tonight. Is she trying to make you jealous?"

"I think so."

"You're not sure?"

"No." Adam met Gloria's sympathetic gaze and for a second he felt a tingle and then…nothing.

Gloria blinked and looked away. "For a second there… It's really too bad you're not interested in me. We could be good together. Here." She tossed him the remote control device. "Reid had a satellite dish installed so I'm sure there's some kind of game on. I'm going to find some chips and other junk food."

Adam decided he might as well follow her advice. Gloria really was everything he'd ever imagined he wanted in a woman: smart, sexy, calm, cool and collected. She'd never say anything like "three kisses and we'll be lovers"; she'd never believe in love at first sight. He liked being with her, but all he could get excited about was imagining what Meg and Reid were doing on their date.

He pulled his mind back to Gloria. "Has anyone ever told you you're a beautiful person?"

Gloria looked at him and smiled sadly. "All the time."

A LITTLE AFTER ELEVEN Adam was in his car and headed back toward The Gateway, wondering what exactly he would find there and telling himself yet again that Meg's relationship with Reid was none of his business.

To distract himself, he thought back to Gloria and remembered the photograph in her bedroom from last night. For a second he'd thought he'd recognized one of the faces, but then Gloria had taken the picture out of his hands and he'd moved on to more questions about Reid. Had he missed something?

Lost in his ponderings about the case, he let himself into the dark building. He went to his room, but one look at the lonely cot and he turned away. He wouldn't be getting any sleep until he knew whether or not Meg was back from her date. Not until he knew whether or not she was alone.

He took off his shoes and crept up the stairs, once again thanking his marine surveillance training. He'd served only one term in the army, then refused a promotion in order to return home to look after his family. Usually he was grateful for his military experience; it gave him an edge on the other business writers. He'd never used it for dating surveillance before.

The door to Meg's room was closed. He stopped wondering at himself; checking on her was ridiculous, but he opened the door anyway. Her room was empty. Adam went back downstairs to wait.

He sat in the dark, until he heard a car pull up. Since he'd already gone this far, he couldn't resist peering out through the window to see Meg and Reid stop by the door, talk for a minute, then Reid reach out a hand to cup her chin and hold her face up for his kiss.

Adam felt a peculiar clenching of his gut as he watched them kiss, and then turned away. He sat back down in a chair in the dark and heard Meg's key in the door. She entered and flipped a light switch on.

"Oh," she gasped, seeing him sitting in the chair. "I wasn't expecting you to wait up," she said coolly, her eyes belying her tone by shooting sparks at him.

Adam stretched his legs in front of him. "Just curious about how your date went."

He could see Meg bristle. "That's none of your business."

"Maybe it is," Adam said, standing up.

"You've made it perfectly clear you're not interested.

Luckily for me, Reid still is." Meg brushed past him, but Adam grabbed her arm and pulled her back to him.

At the touch of her skin, Adam felt all the emotions he'd been denying run through him. *Three kisses...* "Maybe you're right. Maybe I do feel something for you, and don't like you kissing Reid Logan. What was that kiss—number two, three? Or are you lovers already?"

Meg stood very still, his hands holding her by the shoulders. "Reid and I aren't lovers." Her words come out softly. She shook her head, a strand of her hair falling over her eyes. "You're confusing me."

Adam laughed, anger, jealousy and confusion filling him. Meg looked at him with her big brown eyes filled with swirling emotions and he wanted to stop hurting her. But more than that, he wanted her. He didn't think he'd be able to live for a second longer if he didn't kiss her, didn't touch her soft skin, didn't smell the sweet scent of her, didn't bury himself in her lovely, sexy body. "*You're* confused," he said with a half laugh, and lowered his lips to hers.

Adam kissed her softly and gently, as if she were a priceless treasure.

He took his time, touching and cherishing her lips. Meg was surprised. She'd been expecting the overwhelming feeling of passion she'd experienced before when he touched her, but instead it was sweet and glorious and magical. She never wanted this moment to stop. She didn't care if he was jealous of Reid, if this is what it took for Adam to kiss her like he wanted to kiss her as if he liked her rather than merely lusted after her. To kiss her like he never wanted to stop.

Adam held her pressed tightly against his body, but his touch on her face was soft. His fingers skimmed down her cheeks, arousing and reassuring her at the same time. His lips followed the path his fingers had taken, and Meg felt hot and weak all over. She had never wanted a man to make love to her as much as she did Adam. She gloried in all the sensations coursing through her body.

Never in her life had she met a man who was so right for her. She brought her lips back to his and kissed him, trying to tell him everything she felt in her heart. Adam returned the embrace, crushing her against him, no longer gentle, more like a man who had lost control. Meg reveled in his possessiveness and met each of his demands with one of her own.

Adam finally broke their kiss, but continued to hold her. "Wow," was all she could say.

"Damn, but you are a good kisser," he said in a bemused voice, stroking her cheek once again. He studied her with eyes darkened by passion. "I want you," he said, giving her the choice.

"Oh yes." She stood on tiptoe, wrapped her arms around his neck, pulling his face back down to hers, and smiled wickedly. "That was kiss number three."

The next thing she knew she lost her balance as Adam scooped her up in his arms and headed up the stairs toward her bedroom. She wrapped her arms around him tightly and giggled.

Then, before she could make much sense of what was going on around her—Adam kept nuzzling her neck and all she felt was heat and need—he tumbled her onto her bed and then was on top of her. Burning flesh pressed against burning flesh. She smelled sweat, male flesh and Adam. Meg opened her eyes to find herself sprawled over Adam. Her legs were nestled between his, her torso lying across his chest. "Now let's work on kisses four through a hundred," Adam said in an amused tone.

She raised her gaze and met his clear eyes. She could feel his hard, wonderful body against her, and he was clearly enjoying having her spread all over him.

Adam laughed and Meg liked the sound of it. He rolled over, raising himself on his arms. "Kisses five, six and seven," he said, his lips brushing against hers. He framed her face between his hands, then outlined her mouth with his tongue, and she tingled everywhere. He broke away, his fingers stroking along her cheeks and then teasingly kissed her again.

"More," she gasped.

"The beautiful lady wants more?" This time he pressed his lips fully against hers, increasing the pressure slightly before retreating again.

Meg stared at him, still surprised by this playful side of him. Once Adam decided to make love to her, she'd rather expected him to throw her down on a bed and ravish her. Straightforward, practical lovemaking from a straightforward, practical hero. Slowly she smiled at him and stretched luxuriantly. With one finger she traced down the bridge of his nose to his lips. He brushed his mouth over her finger, then she pressed the same finger against her own lips, licking it. "Mmm," she said, sighing. "But I would enjoy more kisses…everywhere."

"Everywhere?" he asked, a sly grin crossing his face. "Never let it be said that us heroes didn't satisfy our women." Adam took possession of her mouth and then of her. He held her face again between his hands, angling her mouth just so, deepening their kiss.

Meg lost herself and gloried in it. Her head swam and rational thought fled. All she knew was that she was kissing Adam, touching Adam.

Adam broke the kiss and looked into her eyes. "I got so carried away, I can't believe we're doing this now. You're sure? I mean, to…you know."

"Make love?" She waited for him to correct her and say it was just sex, but he didn't.

"Yes."

"Yes, definitely yes." She unbuttoned the top two buttons of his shirt and pressed her lips against his skin. He tasted solid and male. "Better than great." She ran her tongue down his chest to the top of his jeans, and felt his body tense in anticipation. She raised her head and licked her lips.

"Meg, be careful, you're driving me wild."

"Sounds good," she murmured.

"I want to take it nice and slow."

"Nice and slow? Promises, promises. But if you keep talking, how will we ever get to nice and slow?"

"Shut up." Adam pulled her to him and kissed her hard until she couldn't breathe and couldn't think. When his lips finally left her mouth, she realized her blouse was off—when had he done that?—and he trailed his hot lips down her neck. All she could feel was fire; everywhere Adam touched her burned.

When he reached the lace of her bra, he scraped the edge with his teeth. Meg couldn't help her gasp. "Pretty," he said, his eyes burning as he looked at her. His fingers trailed over the top of her breasts and she felt them swell within the lace confines, her nipples hardening. She was dying for him to touch her.

"Adam, please." Her voice was incredibly breathy.

"Yes." He smiled, looking feral. "You have really pretty underwear. I like it. I like you."

"I know all the best stores in New York, including this wonderful lingerie shop on Fifth." Meg gasped as his knuckles brushed over her nipples. "You like me?"

"Yes."

"I'm glad. I wasn't sure."

"I know. I haven't exactly been forthright when it comes to telling you how I feel about you."

Meg took a deep breath, hating to ruin the wonderful mood she was in—the tingling, couldn't-wait-for-the-next-step mood—but she couldn't stop the words, either. "I was afraid you only saw me as an obligation."

Adam's finger, which had been running along her cleavage, stopped. "I'm not exactly sure how I see you…except maybe naked." He grinned wickedly and his fingers went to the front clasp of the bra, undoing it with one swift motion.

"Good move." She smiled back, suddenly feeling more relaxed. "You must have had a lot of practice."

"A little, but not much lately." His expression grew serious. "I haven't been with a lot of women since Allison, and never without protection. I'm not a love 'em and leave 'em kind of guy."

"I know. I can tell." Suddenly she felt shy. "I'm a little rusty at this. It's been awhile."

"Not since your runaway groom?"

Meg felt her cheeks blush and knew it spread over her chest and breasts. "Not even with him. I think that was one of the mistakes Max and I made. We were going to wait until after we were married."

"Except you didn't get married."

"No." Meg couldn't stand to see the sympathy on Adam's face. Lord, he didn't think she was a loser, did he? Suddenly she was unsure of herself.

As if he knew what she was thinking, what she was afraid of, Adam touched her chin, raising her eyes to his. "Max must have been very stupid not to make love to you when he had the chance."

"Max was in love with someone else."

"Max didn't know a good thing when he had one Luckily I do." Adam brushed her lips with his while his wonderful hands cupped her bare breasts together, his thumbs rubbing over her nipples, sending shock waves clear down to her toes. The man had wonderful hands.

"The first time I kissed you," he whispered into her ear, sending shivers up and down her spine, "I imagined that you would flush from head to toe when you came."

"You did?"

"Yes. Now I'm going to find out."

Then Meg lost track of how things happened. All she could do was experience. As Adam began to make love to her slowly, gently and seriously, more seriously than any man ever had before, Meg became a new person. She'd never known lovemaking could be so consuming. She'd never known it could be so complete. It felt like Adam was reaching her clear to her soul and she wanted to do the same to him.

Adam kissed her; she kissed him. His hands began a desperate exploration of her body, touching and stroking.

His mouth followed, distracted for some time by her breasts. First he skimmed his lips over the curve of them; they felt fuller and sexier than they'd ever felt before. His hands returned to cup the globes together, his tongue flicking from aureole to aureole.

Meg moaned and shifted restlessly on the bed. Adam took the tip of one breast into his mouth while his hand curved around the fullness of her buttock, pulling her against him. Suddenly she was on top, his hands caressing her bottom, Meg feeling the heat of his erection pressed against her.

She cupped his arousal and was glad at her own power over him. "My, you're ready."

"I've been ready to make love to you since I walked into The Gateway on Saturday night. I almost wished I'd been the kind of man you thought I was, so I could."

"Humph. And all this time I thought you didn't want me."

"I was fighting it."

"Despite the fact that your words aren't very complimentary, I'm going to take them as a compliment. And next time don't take so long," Meg exclaimed as she went about discovering Adam's body. He was finely muscled and nicely sensitive as she trailed her fingertips down his chest. Some of his chest hairs had turned gray, and she followed the dark hair as it arrowed down his flat abdomen and lower.

Discovering Adam's body was better than unwrapping a Christmas present.

Finally, with a groan, Adam pulled up her head. "Now," he said simply, his eyes glittering with passion.

"Yes," Meg agreed, and licked her lips. With a strangled sound, Adam captured her mouth, his tongue invading her mouth boldly. His hands encircled her waist. Meg opened her legs, welcoming Adam as he entered her.

"Oh," Meg managed to say as Adam penetrated her. She felt complete. It had never been like this before. Adam began to stroke within her, raising her temperature even further, pushing her closer and closer to the edge where she'd lose all control.

She reached for the other side, clenching herself around Adam, wanting him with her. She cried as the explosion hit her, and then she heard Adam's voice mix with hers as he also climaxed.

Much later, she cherished the solid feel of Adam's body on top of hers. He rolled, pulling her over with him, so that she was on top. "Mmm," she muttered sleepily, more content and satisfied than she'd ever been in her life.

"Tomorrow," Adam said, "we'll work on kisses one hundred through two hundred."

9

MEG WOKE SLOWLY, enveloped by heat. She opened her eyes and realized that she was cradled in Adam's arms. She blinked several times, but the sensation didn't change. She was still in Adam's arms. Hmm. Meg wondered if she dared pinch herself, but didn't want to move in case her pleasant fantasy disappeared. This was one heck of a good dream, she decided. Way better than the one she had of being president of her father's company and going home alone to her cat.

"Are you holding your breath?" Adam asked, his voice a low growl. It sounded so sexy, Meg decided. If this was a fantasy, she didn't want it to end.

"Yes." She spoke the word out loud, and wonder of wonders, Adam didn't disappear.

Instead, he shifted slightly, pulling her more closely against him.

"Why?"

"I didn't want to disturb you in case you woke up, realized that we'd made love and decided to disappear."

"Before you could tie me down or something?"

"Or something," Meg agreed, sitting up to gaze at him. He positively beamed at her and then pulled her on top of himself. She raised herself slightly so she could look into his eyes. "How did you know I was holding my breath? Were you lying here, holding me in your arms, listening to me not breath, thinking how lucky you were?"

"Something like that."

Meg elbowed him. "Which part?"

Adam kissed her. "All of it."

Meg felt hope wash through her, but she didn't want to

reveal too much of herself to Adam, so she stared at his naked chest—and promptly lost her ability to think. Opening her mouth, she said, "I don't know what to say. I'm flummoxed."

Adam pushed a strand of hair out of her eyes. "Flummoxed. You have an interesting vocabulary for a kook first thing in the morning."

"You didn't think I was so kooky last night."

"True."

Meg wished he'd say something else, like he cared about her, or they had had the best sex ever—which in her opinion was exactly what they'd shared. If she'd had sex like that before she'd have had it a lot more often. But at least he wasn't pushing her away. She'd take what she could get right now and build on that. Plus, he had admitted he'd been listening to her breathe. That was kind of romantic.

Because she didn't want to scare him off, she asked, "What are you going to do today?"

"Well, since Abby hasn't returned, I suppose I'll just do some more poking around town."

"Could I help?" Meg realized she was holding her breath again.

"Don't you have to work?"

"Rachel comes into the shop today. She enjoys the store and that way I get a day off. I could ask her to cover for me tomorrow as well. We could investigate, hang out, maybe go on a picnic…" Meg let her words trail off, waiting for him to tell her he preferred to work alone.

"That sounds nice, but shouldn't we wait for Abby?"

"Right, Abby." The truth about Abby had been worrying her for some time. She should tell Adam, but as soon as he got in touch with Abby, he'd be gone. No, she was being selfish, Meg berated herself. Originally she could excuse her actions out of simple desperation, but no longer. "I need to tell you—"

"No, you don't need to tell me anything."

At the look of panic on Adam's face, Meg was sorely

tempted to hit him for real this time. He was scared to death that she was going to tell him she loved him. She opened her mouth, but Adam kissed her and rolled out of bed before she could catch her breath. "Adam," she called after his retreating back.

He stopped at the door, one arm leaning against the frame, not turning to face her. "Don't tell me anything I'm not ready to hear yet."

"You're pretty sure of what I have to say," she commented mildly.

Now he turned to face her and she wished she didn't notice how gorgeous he was. His arms were solid leading to those wonderful shoulders, and then there was the chest and the dark hair narrowing lower to that part of him she had spent such a long time loving last night. Meg pulled her attention back to his face.

"Meg." Adam frowned and brushed a hand through his hair. "Last night was great. Incredible. I'm not going to pretend that I don't feel anything for you, but I have a mission to accomplish before I can think about any kind of—of…"

"*Relationship?*" She offered the word he had so much difficulty saying.

"Exactly." He looked relieved. "I'm going to go take a shower, and then we should go."

"We?" Meg wished her voice hadn't squeaked.

"We," he agreed, and left.

We. She'd settle for working together. For now. It was Adam's way of distracting her from what he was afraid she wanted to talk about—and since she was too chicken to tell him the real truth, she'd settle for it as well.

A fine pair of heroes they made.

"MEG, ADAM. I don't have you listed for a tour." Dana Andrews looked up from her computer screen, pushing back her dirty blond locks.

Meg and Adam stopped inside the small, cramped office that housed operations for Greg's four-wheel company. Meg smiled at Dana. "No, we just stopped by to say hello. I'm showing Adam why I love Sedona and its people so much."

Dana looked puzzled, but quirked her lips in the approximation of a smile. "Are you two getting back together?"

Meg didn't wait for Adam to answer. They'd been asked the question more than once today, and she had the reply down pat. "I'm still considering it. Adam is much more determined."

"Oh, that's nice." Dana surveyed Adam from head to toe, then turned to Meg. "You're lucky to have a man pursuing you so forcefully," she said wistfully.

"Sometimes the fantasy sounds nicer than the reality. How is Greg?"

Dana blushed. "He's out with a group of tourists from Canada. He'll be back this afternoon."

Meg got down to business—distracting Dana away from her computer. "Adam wanted to look at some of Greg's maps, if that's okay."

Dana brushed her hair off her face, looking worried. "I don't know. Greg is pretty guarded about his stuff."

Meg smiled her most sincere, honest smile, the one she'd used when negotiating book deals with ruthless agents. "Maybe you could pull out some maps that he wouldn't mind Adam studying. None with Greg's best routes marked or anything." Meg leaned in confidentially. "I don't want you to think that Adam is trying to steal any of Greg's secrets. He's curious about the landscape and wants to go take some shots. He's something of an amateur photographer, and if he decides to live with me here, well, he'll need something to do."

"I guess that would be okay," Dana answered. She looked back to her computer longingly, but then stood and walked with Meg to Greg's little cubbyhole of an office. She riffled through the mess of papers on the desk and pulled out a map. "Greg has marked his route clearly and there are some good views of the outlooks as well as the desert."

"Thanks, Dana, this is very sweet of you. I really appreciate it. Adam needs to feel he's doing something valuable. I want him to stay here in Sedona so that I can decide about us. But I find that a man needs to feel that he's doing something important—even when he's trying to woo you."

"Yes, well, I'm glad I could be of help." Dana glanced back at the outer office.

Blocking Dana's view of Adam, Meg stepped a little closer to her as if to share girl talk. "How is Greg?"

"Infatuated with a blond Canadian girl on the tour today," Dana said flatly.

"I'm surprised he hasn't noticed what he has in front of him. You really should give him a little encouragement," Meg suggested, glad she was able to broach the topic for once with Dana. Usually the girl was so lost in her own world that they had little conversation together. Meg wished Greg would see Dana for the caring and smart woman she was. He would have to look far and wide to find better than Dana.

Plus, she needed a way to keep Dana occupied in the back office while Adam accessed Dana's computer. Meg knew Dana spent many a late night burning the midnight oil in the office, working on her software programs. Since her computer was already on, Adam would be able to do a quick diagnostic of whatever programs Dana had on her computer. In a few minutes, he should be able to clear Dana or find proof of her involvement in criminal activities.

"Have you ever thought of bangs?" Meg asked impulsively. When in doubt, makeovers always worked.

"What?" Dana asked, pushing back strands of hair that had fallen over her face.

"I don't mean to be rude, or to suggest that men only notice appearances...."

Dana looked down at the papers on the desk. "Greg certainly noticed the blonde today."

"Yes, well, I can't help but notice that you're always brushing your hair off your face. I once edited this book on hairstyles and face types, and you'd look great with bangs. Could I show you?"

Dana nodded hesitantly and Meg picked up the mirror that Greg had in his office. A man as good-looking as Greg had to have a mirror. She gave the mirror to Dana, pulled a brush out of her purse. With a few quick strokes, then holding her palm over Dana's forehead, she showed her what it could look like.

"The bangs focus more attention on your beautiful eyes."

Dana took a pair of scissors off the desk. "Do it. Cut my hair."

"OKAY, WHO'S NEXT? We've been through Dana Andrews and Jason Stavropoulos."

"So far nothing incriminating," Adam said, sounding tired.

"Is this how you usually investigate?" Meg wondered about how he did his job. She'd read several of his articles, learning that he was a good reporter—fair in how he told the story and a talented writer.

"Often. I get a lead, follow it wherever it takes me. Dig around. Maybe find something. Follow my instincts. Meet some interesting people—some innocent, some guilty." He stopped in front of Sedona Retreat, the hotel owned by Michelle and Rachel. "I'd like to try this pair next."

"But they seem so friendly and innocent—although Rachel does love to gossip." Meg sighed. "I guess you have to be suspicious of everyone."

"I have to check out everyone's story. But sometimes my instincts will give me a lead. A sort of sixth sense."

Meg stared at him as he met her gaze, his dark eyes intent. "You mean, you just *know*?"

"Yes," he answered fatalistically. "I can look at a person and know that he or she is going to have the piece of the puzzle that is missing."

"But that's amazing."

"It's kooky, but true."

Meg didn't need to say that was why he was so disturbed by her claim of *knowing* that he was the one for her. Instead she could only stare at him. She felt as if she and Adam were on the brink of something—if only she could think of the right thing to say—when the door to the hotel opened.

Michelle frowned at the two of them. "I saw you standing outside. You might as well come in—I don't have all day to wait for you to knock."

"After you." Adam held the door for Meg, a rueful smile on his face.

She entered, wishing she and Adam could have kept talking. He had really opened up to her for the first time, but the moment was gone.

"Meg has been showing me around town and she's been telling me about your excellent hotel."

"Fifty rooms. We get a lot of corporate business, including five of the top 500 companies as listed in *Fortune Magazine* last year." Michelle dared Adam to contradict her.

"Can I have a tour?"

"I'm pretty busy."

"I'm thinking of writing a piece on the different businesses in Sedona."

"For your paper? The *New York Times?*" Michelle couldn't help the slight softening of her expression.

Adam pressed his advantage. "I usually do more hard-hitting stories for the *Times*, but I occasionally write for a couple of business magazines. Successful businesses combining tourism, small-business smarts and the use of the spiritual sense of Sedona would be a story several magazines would be interested in."

"I see." Michelle considered his words, and they watched the struggle on her face. The businesswoman in her won out. "Come with me." She walked across the lobby to the sitting room. "This is the common area. Notice the picture window with the view."

With her brisk efficiency, Michelle was off on the tour. At the end of half an hour, Adam had to admit Michelle owned and ran a beautiful little hotel. By the end of an hour he was impressed with the conference facilities and the various marketing techniques aimed at attracting new business. But Michelle hadn't left them alone once, although Meg had tried several times to distract her so that he could disappear into her private office. No such luck. Instead he took notes, and Michelle talked faster and faster. Finally he asked her for some literature and her curriculum vitae. "You must have managed some big conference centers before moving to Sedona."

"Yes. Come into my office—I have my work history on the computer."

Adam salivated as Michelle printed out her bio, but he didn't see any way to distract her and get access to the machine's information. Meg shrugged at Adam, sharing his frustration, and picked up one of the pictures on Michelle's desk. "Do you take photos of all your important clients?"

"Some. Others I keep just because they remind me of a fun day when I'm stuck inside going through paperwork." Michelle glanced over at the photo Meg held. "That was taken a couple of years ago at the Liberty L. Gloria had just begun her dude ranch and was asking me a lot of questions about how to entertain guests and basically run the operation."

Adam looked at the picture and froze. The hairs on the back of his neck prickled and he focused in on the face of the man staring back at him. Carlos Mianco, the son of a Venezuelan drug lord. Adam had written an exposé on the connections he'd unearthed between Venezuelan drug runners and certain U.S. government officials.

He concentrated on keeping his excitement out of his voice. "This was one of Gloria's guests?"

Michelle looked at him sharply. "Yes, one of her first. A charming young man. He spent a lot of time by himself. I didn't even know I had caught him in the picture until I'd had it developed."

"Thank you, Ms. Stoneaway, you've been very helpful."

"Call me Michelle." She reached out her hand and shook his firmly, but without crushing it this time. She turned to Meg. "This young man of yours might be okay, after all."

"What did you discover?" Meg asked once they were back at The Gateway. "I saw your face. Michelle might not have noticed anything, but I know you. You learned something." She felt Adam's barely concealed excitement.

"I think Michelle noticed my reaction as well. If there's one thing I'm learning it's not to underestimate the women in this town." To Meg's complete surprise, he brushed a quick kiss across her lips.

He began to pace around the shop. "I recognized the man in the background of the photo because of a story I wrote on legitimate business and drug connections. Carlos Mianco was the heir apparent of his father's cartel until he disappeared about five years ago and was never heard from again. Some law officials thought that he might have been killed by rivals, but no one ever heard of any reprisals, which made an assassination seem unlikely."

Meg clasped her hands together. "You mean he was on Gloria's ranch buying himself a new identity."

"Exactly." Adam smiled with grim satisfaction. That was the curious reaction he'd felt around Gloria—not attraction, but his sixth sense warning him about her. "What we need to do is go out to the Liberty L tonight and find the evidence we need to prove Gloria's guilt."

10

ADAM PARKED HIS JEEP next to an outcrop that effectively hide the vehicle from the Liberty L, wondering how he'd been so foolish and weak as to allow Meg to come with him. He always preferred working alone. He trusted only himself.

But if he hadn't let her come, Meg would have followed him. She'd threatened to do exactly that and he believed she would have. He turned to the frustrating woman. "Stay in the car and call for help if I'm not back in an hour."

Meg got out of the passenger seat. "No."

"Meg, I can't be worried about you while I'm breaking and entering."

"And I'm not going to hide out in the car while you could be in danger."

"There is no danger."

"Then it won't hurt if I come with you."

Adam let out his breath in frustration. "Dammit, Meg, this is serious. It's not some kooky adventure. If you had seen what Kelly looked like..." Trying to scare Meg into staying safely at home, he'd told her about Kelly's injuries and how he believed someone—Reid?—had tried to kill Kelly. Unfortunately, the truth had only made Meg more determined to join him.

She touched his arm. "I'm sorry, Adam. It must have been terrible to see your sister like that. But I'm not going to get hurt—and I'm also not your sister. I only want to come a little closer to the house with you. Then I'll stay back and let you do your work. I just want to be closer in case anything goes wrong." She brushed her lips against his cheek. "You may worry about everyone else, Adam Smith, but I worry about you."

"Then follow me quietly. I'll drop you off by the side of the barn." Adam led the way, still feeling the touch of her lips against his skin and hearing her words. She worried about him.

They followed a path to a fence, easily scaled it and then quietly made their way to the back of the house. "Gloria's bedroom is over there." Adam pointed.

Meg made a funny sound.

"She showed me it during the house tour. Her office is next door. I saw a lot of computers, but stupidly thought she was just an amateur."

"Chauvinist," Meg muttered.

"Sometimes. You stay here. You have my cell phone to call for help."

Meg took the small phone out of her purse. "Right here. I'll be fine. Be careful."

Without really thinking why it was important, Adam pulled her into his arms and crushed his lips against hers. The scent of roses enveloped him as he tasted her sweetness.

Finally he broke away and took off at a run before he could pull her down onto the ground and lose himself in her.

He passed the TV room and saw that the screen was on and two figures sat in the semidarkness. He couldn't make them out, but hoped they were Reid and Gloria. He crept stealthily past to Reid's study. The window wasn't locked, so Adam raised it and climbed in, but didn't waste any time searching the room. He wanted to get to Gloria's office. The hallway was quiet and dark, and he quickly made his way to her quarters. Luckily her bedroom door was open, revealing it to be empty. He passed the white bed, heading toward Gloria's work area.

That door, however, was closed and locked. He pulled a lock pick he kept for exactly such situations out of his back pocket, inserted the smooth metal into the lock, twisted and opened the door. He shut the door behind him and, using his flashlight, turned to Gloria's elaborate computer systems. She had two desktops connected together in a network and another porthole where she could connect a laptop. One other desktop was independent and running. A big letter *E* flashed across the screen, signaling the arrival of E-mail. Adam clicked onto that machine and quickly learned that Gloria ran her business on it. It held E-mail from various clients around the world, her record of invoices and profit projections, personalized schedules for each client. A nicely run, money-making operation, but not what he was looking for.

Instead, Adam turned to the network. There was plenty of capacity to let someone who knew what he or she was doing access almost anything. Gloria must use this system to create her false computer identities. Adam sat down and began trying to access her files. After a frustrating search, he glanced at his watch and saw that twenty minutes had gone by. He had to meet Meg soon, but he'd made no progress in finding the information he needed to prove that Gloria Logan was the mastermind behind the computer forgeries.

It looked like he needed Abigail Milton, after all. Abby was the only one with a direct connection to Gloria and the Liberty L.

"Damn." He switched off the computers and stood, and had turned toward the door to leave when he saw Reid lounging against the door.

"I wasn't expecting you back again so soon, or for you to be so careless," the cowboy said. His voice was cold, his eyes hard as he surveyed Adam. He shook his head. "I never expected you to reveal your hand so easily. In some ways, I was looking forward to a challenge, to a worthy adversary. I guess today's not that day."

Adam stood silently, cursing himself for a fool.

"Let's go back to my study," Reid said. "I'd hate to have to hurt you around such valuable machinery." He pointed a gun at Adam and Adam complied. All he needed to do was stall for a time. If he could delay Reid long enough, Meg would call for help.

The study door was closed and Adam opened it, stepped in and saw his plan go up in smoke. Meg was sitting on a chair, a blond hulk looming over her.

"Oh, I forgot to mention that we had another guest."

"If you let go of Meg, we could still leave and nothing—"

Reid slammed his hand against a wood-paneled wall. "No, you've concluded that I'm one of your suspects. I'm fully aware of how persistent you are once you've seized hold of a story idea. You think I might be a criminal." Reid's lips turned up in an ugly smile. "You're right."

"Adam, I'm sorry," Meg stood and took a step toward Adam, her lovely brown eyes filled with worry for him, but Reid grabbed her arm, pulling her toward himself. He moved the two of them toward the desk and picked up the telephone receiver. "Send Tom into the library. I need some help with our guests."

Adam hadn't expected to walk into a trap. If he could understand Reid's motivation, then he could begin to work on another plan. "I think you're overreacting. I haven't found anything even slightly incriminating about you or the ranch. You aren't even my prime suspect. I much prefer Freddie. Why act now?"

"Freddie? That artiste couldn't begin to have the balls that an operation like mine takes. I'm afraid you and Meg are in a lot of trouble because you couldn't take the hint—your beating, the fire at The Gateway—to leave. I need a guarantee that I'll be safe." Reid pressed the gun against Meg's side. "Consider this my guarantee." Meg flinched and bit her lip, looking at Adam with anxious eyes, but she didn't say anything.

Reid stroked her cheek with a finger, and Meg jerked back. "I really am sorry to involve you in this mess," he said. "But a tenacious reporter like your boyfriend, moreover one with a personal interest in the story, is bound to figure out my involvement sooner or later. There aren't enough people in Sedona for me to hide for a long time. I couldn't afford to take the risk of a third warning that Adam wouldn't pay attention to." Reid looked back at Adam. "Or for you to talk to too many people—who might remember your questions after your disappearance. As it is, you pulled Meg into this. You wouldn't take any of our hints to leave, to drop this investigation. Now both of you are going to pay the consequences."

Reid spoke to Meg with fondness. "I am sorry about this, Meg." He pushed her into a chair, then began to pace over the well-worn wooden flooring. "I know your work, Mr. Smith. Kelly talked about you. How you never give up once a story has caught your attention. She also said you had this funny ability, what you called instinct. How you could trace a story that no one else could. She thought you had some kind of special intuition, but then again, Kelly would think that." He shook his head at the memory, a flash of regret crossing his face. "Even if you had someone else in your sights, like Freddie, I can't take the risk that you wouldn't turn your attention to me. Sooner or later you were bound to consider our operation out here. I'm a cautious man. I like to stop a cancer before its done damage to more than a few cells. Or in good old cowboy terminology, cut you off at the pass."

Adam clenched his fists, looking for the moment he could slam Reid against a wall. This bastard was the man who had hurt his sister. First Adam was going to rescue Meg and get her away from danger. Then he was going to make Reid Logan pay—pay more than the man could even begin to imagine. "Overreaction. You're miscalculating."

"I'm a cautious man," Reid repeated. "I take care of my problems as soon as they appear—and right now you're my problem. How much did Kelly tell you? Did she lead you to me?"

"I have no idea what you're talking about." Adam considered the distance between them. If the man hadn't been keeping Meg in front of him, Adam would make a move now and try to overpower him, but he couldn't risk Meg.

"You're being a fool." Reid crossed the room in three steps and hit Adam with a right hook before he had a chance to move. He fell back, letting the pain wash over him. As he fought to clear his head, he heard the door open and two pairs of heavy footsteps enter the room.

"Put him in a chair," Reid said. Adam felt hands clamp on his shoulders and push him down. He looked up at the large, silent men and recognized them as the ones who had attacked him back in Phoenix. The large blond ox was sporting faded bruises on his Nordic face, Adam was pleased to see. He remembered connecting his fist to the man's face several times. The other man was many inches shorter, but more heavily muscled, as if he worked on developing bulk to counteract his lack of height.

"Reid, what's going on here? Why are you doing this?" Meg asked. She sounded more worried that scared, and Adam realized she was concerned about him. Silly woman, she should be afraid for herself. No matter what, Adam vowed he wasn't going to let anything happen to Meg. Megan Elizabeth Cooper was a woman who needed to be taken care of, to be saved from her own impulsiveness, rashness and emotions. But he wasn't going to be the man who would spend his life protecting her. Adam was going to get them away from Reid and then he was going to deliver her back to her family, who might be able to take care of her. Once she was safe, he was going to get as far away from her as possible.

Reid faced Meg, touching her shiny hair, his expression regretful once more. "I'm sorry, Meg. I do wish Adam hadn't brought you into this. I had such hopes for us. You seemed like such a responsible and sensible woman, with a hint of passion behind that aloof exterior. I was looking forward to igniting that passion. Now…" He shrugged. "I am sorry."

Meg paled, looking scared. Adam wondered if Kelly had looked at Reid with the same fear. He also wondered at Reid's description of Meg. Responsible and sensible? She was the most passionate, impulsive woman he'd ever met.

"Now back to our little problem." Leaving Meg, Reid walked over to Adam and leaned close, his blue eyes cold. "Who sent you here? How did you know? Was it Kelly?"

Rage surged through Adam at the confirmation of his worst fears—that Kelly had been involved with Reid and the forgery ring. But Adam clamped his anger back down. He needed to learn everything he could and then try to figure out some way to rescue himself and Meg. Moreover, no matter what, he had to protect Kelly. She would never be able to face criminal charges or jail, especially not in her present emotional state. "Kelly wouldn't say anything about what happened to her—you scared her very well. I'd spent months trying to track down her last location, who she was involved with. Everything came up blank until I received an anonymous tip."

"I was afraid you'd say that." Before Adam could react, Reid slugged him in the gut and Adam doubled over in the chair, darkness clouding his eyes, pain swamping him. Slowly he worked on regaining his breath, on being able to breathe in on three and out on three. He looked up to see Meg being held back by the smaller thug, concern written across her beautiful face.

"Let go of me," she cried, ineffectually kicking at Tom but the miniature mountain didn't move.

"Be careful," Tom said, "you could hurt yourself." He kept his arms firmly on her shoulders, pressing her down in the chair.

"I'm okay," Adam wheezed. He knew he could live through another beating, but he didn't want her getting hurt. She was too fragile, and he hated the thought of any man's rough hands on her.

"Yes." Reid shook his head sadly, walked over to his desk, picking up a pewter figure of a cowboy on horseback, hefting its weight. "You've already proven you can take a lot and not tell me what I need to know. I'm afraid you've left me no choice." He put the weight back down.

The bastard walked over to Meg and touched her cheek very softly. "I've always thought Meg was a very pretty woman. It would be a shame to destroy her face."

Meg gasped and tried to squirm away from Reid, but the mountain behind her grabbed her arms and held her captive. "I don't know how I could ever have found you attractive," she snapped. "You're nothing but a criminal."

"It's nothing personal, dear Meg. Just business." Reid touched her face gently as she glared at him. "What a shame."

Reid pulled back his arm as Adam cried, "No!" but it was too late; Reid slapped Meg across the face. She didn't scream, but Adam could see the imprint of Reid's hand on her face and tears running down her face. Adam started toward her, but the other thug pointed his gun at him, stopping him in his tracks.

Adam was going to make Reid pay for hurting Meg. No matter how long it took, he was going to make the arrogant cowboy suffer. "You bastard. You enjoyed that."

"No, I didn't. I have a lot of strong feelings for Meg, but I always believe in leading my men by example. Josh will have no compulsion about continuing now—sometimes he can get a little squeamish when it comes to women."

Adam could barely stand to look at Meg. Amazingly, she had stopped crying and had raised her head in defiance. She looked at Adam for only a moment and then concentrated on Reid. Stunned, Adam realized she wasn't going to ask him to reveal what he knew, nor was she foolish enough to beg Reid for pity.

"Talk," Reid ordered.

"I received an anonymous tip," Adam said again, wondering how long he could hold out before he was forced to tell Reid about Abigail.

Meg cried out as something incredibly fast and hard hit her in the stomach and she fell back on the floor, fighting to draw a breath. She heard Adam's angry tone but couldn't make out any words because of the ringing in her ears. When her burning lungs finally let her take in some air, she swallowed huge gasps of it. Josh, the tall blond-haired man who had knocked her down, helped her to her feet. He was gentle as he helped her stand upright, and she ended up clinging to his arm as she waited for her legs to solidify.

"For God's sake," Adam was saying furiously. "I've told you everything I know. Leave her alone! I came to Sedona because of what happened to Kelly, but, having learned the consequences from you, she wouldn't tell me what had happened to her."

"Then why did you check up on the names in your computer? Why did you have a letter from The Gateway when my men found you?"

Adam hesitated, his eyes searching Meg's face. She raised her chin, willing him not to do anything foolish because of her. Adam raked a hand through his hair. "Abigail Milton wrote a friendly letter to my sister and she tried to hide it from me," he lied.

Good for him, thought Meg. His words held just enough of the truth to keep Reid off track.

"I thought it might be just the lead I needed on top of the information I had gathered from my computer investigation. A friend of Kelly's might be able to help me find out what happened to my sister while she was here. Before Abigail's letter, I didn't even know that she had spent time in Sedona. Kelly wouldn't tell me a thing. Unfortunately, Abby hasn't returned from her retreat. That's all I've been waiting for."

Meg tried to concentrate on the men's discussion, but she had a hard time holding steady between bouts of pain. Adam kept answering Reid's questions and, while she wished he would have told her more of the facts of the case, she was glad to learn what she could. More importantly, it seemed like Reid was falling for Adam's elaborate tale.

Reid repeated Adam's story disdainfully. "You received an anonymous tip about illegal immigrants being processed through Sedona and that, along with a friendly letter from Abigail Milton, was enough to bring you here? I don't think so."

"The informant gave names." Adam's voice was angry. "For God's sake, leave Meg alone. I did some checking, and while the identities looked real, further investigation revealed they could be forgeries. I still might not have hurried down to Sedona as quickly as I did, but I seemed to trigger a backdoor trap in the computer networks. I traced someone trying to enter my computer files to find out who I was. Plus I learned that Kelly had been here."

"We did find out who you were," Reid answered. "We hoped you wouldn't pursue the matter any further, but when you landed in Phoenix, my men were supposed to scare you. Unfortunately, we're better at high-tech crimes. I won't make the same mistake again."

"So now you know everything I know," Adam stated.

Meg felt her arm suddenly wrenched behind her back and she couldn't help the cry that escaped her lips. "Dammit," she swore, as a haze of pain clouded her vision again.

"Stop," Adam said again. "You're right, Abigail Milton is the one who tipped me off about your activities. I haven't had a chance to talk to her so I don't know exactly what she knows. Abigail never gave me your name, she only gave me phony identities to investigate."

"Let her go." Reid nodded toward Josh, and Meg felt exquisite relief as the pressure on her arm stopped. She wanted to collapse on the floor and curl into a little ball, but pride and anger made her stiffen her spine and try to pay attention to what was going on between Reid and Adam.

Suddenly the room felt even more dangerous than before as Reid studied Adam. "I think you're telling the truth. You don't like to see a woman suffer."

"No, I don't." His words were clipped, and Meg could

hear another meaning behind them, but didn't know what the two men were talking about. All she knew was that she could hardly breathe because of the tension.

Reid raised the gun that he'd kept by his side throughout the questioning. "In that case, Mr. Smith, if you've told me everything you know, then I don't think we need the pleasure of your company anymore."

"No!" Meg screamed, surprising everyone, including herself, by launching herself in front of Adam. Between Adam and the gun. She gulped. This scene always looked much better on television, when she was part of the audience admiring the spunky, doomed heroine's courage. No, sometimes the heroine lived, she assured herself. At least she hoped so.

She felt Adam's hand clamp on her shoulder as he spun her around to face him. "Idiot," he snarled, and then pulled her behind him. For the first time Meg experienced his full strength and was impressed.

"Reid won't shoot me," she told his back. Adam was being very heroic, but also rather annoying in his assumption that he was the only one who could handle the situation.

"Don't be so sure," he responded, and turned back to Reid.

Reid shook his head, his lips curling in derision. "A fine pair of lovers, each protecting the other. Did you really just meet a few days ago?"

"Yes," Meg answered, trying to break past Adam. He let her move to his side, but kept his arm firmly around her shoulder. "I know where Abby is."

Adam stiffened beside her, but said nothing. She continued, trying to keep her brain a step or two ahead of her mouth. "I'm not sure how she found out what she did about your operations, but I do know that she's read Adam's column in the *Times*. And she dropped some hints about something odd going on. I wasn't really paying any attention, because she was always talking about something. When she kept mentioning strangers, I thought she was talking about extraterrestrials—it's her latest theory. She thinks the reason there are so many alien movies and alien TV shows is because our government has made contact and is trying to get the American people used to the idea of life on other worlds. Same thing with the Mars rock—the one with the possibility of life. Abby was sure that was the next step in the campaign. She considered it proof." Meg smiled ruefully. "So I didn't really pay a lot of attention. Not until now."

"Good," Reid said. "Possible. It sure sounds like Abby. She tried to tell me her alien theory herself just a couple of weeks ago. Now—" he raised his gun again "—I think it's time to finish what I started."

Adam stepped in front of Meg. "Wait," she yelled from behind him. "Adam, for heaven's sake, let me go."

She felt ridiculous jumping up and down behind Adam, trying to get someone's attention. There was no way she was going to let Adam be killed in front of her. She'd waited her whole life for him; she wasn't about to lose him now. "I can call Abby and convince her to come back!"

Her statement silenced the room.

"Let her go," Reid ordered Adam, who reluctantly let go of the wiggling Meg.

Reid considered Meg. "You're willing to betray your friend for him?"

"I'll do whatever it takes to save Adam's life," she answered honestly.

Reid looked at her for a moment and, seeing the truth in her eyes, he nodded. "All right. I want to find out if Abigail Milton is the source. You've just bought your boyfriend some time." Reid paced the room quietly, thinking. At one time, Meg had actually thought this habit of his sexy. She wondered how she could ever have been so foolish. An honorable cowboy, indeed. She couldn't have been more wrong. All of Reid's laconic charm and slow courting of her had been a sham. She was glad she'd never fallen for it completely.

He was so different from Adam. Adam refused to admit he even liked her, in fact insisted he didn't, that she was all wrong for him, but she knew better.

Adam's behaviour showed how much more worthy he was than Reid. He didn't want to incriminate Abby, but he had been horrified by Reid's abuse of her. Adam was a man worthy of her love.

Now all she had to do was prove it to him. And keep them both alive.

Reid stopped pacing. "I'm going to leave you alone here for a few minutes." He smiled sourly. "I have a few details to take care of explaining your sudden departure from our fair town. Luckily, the good folks of Sedona are used to people leaving unexpectedly, so your sudden disappearance won't raise any questions. Especially since your former fiancé—" his lips curled "—has arrived to win you and take you away. Everyone will assume the pair of you have picked up again where you left off." He turned to the shorter man. "Tom, you hide their Jeep." He turned back to Adam, his lips curving upward in amusement. "We knew the second the two of you had arrived, for we have sensors all around the ranch. I let you snoop around to make sure that you really were after our operation and not just being a regular nosy reporter."

He focused on Meg, and she couldn't help the shiver that crawled along her spine. "Then I want you to tell me how to find Abby. I want her here as fast as possible and to learn if that dizzy old broad really is the one who tipped you off. I still don't see how she could have figured out what was going on, but..." He shook his head. "If I've learned anything living here, it's that anything is possible in this crazy place." Reid stroked Meg's cheek with a callused finger. "If you've planned any kind of a trick, I'll kill him."

With that, he was out of the room, Tom following behind, and Meg heard the door being locked. Josh stepped out the balcony door, effectively guarding that escape route. Meg wished Adam would take her in his arms and comfort her, but one look at his stoney face and she knew that wasn't about to happen.

She straightened her spine. No matter what, she wasn't going to let Reid hurt Adam. She was living her dream of adventure. It wouldn't be much of a story to tell her grandchildren if she let the hero die.

11

AFTER REID HAD LEFT the study, Meg dared a look at Adam's furious expression. She regretted lying to Adam about not knowing where Abby was. Well, to be precise, she didn't know *exactly* where Abby was vacationing, but she could contact her.

"I'm sorry I got you involved in this, Meg." Adam scowled, his face dark, and Meg realized that he was blaming himself. Didn't he remember that she had insisted on being part of his investigation? Adam probably thought he should be able to control her behaviour—something he was going to have to learn he never could.

"I'm not sorry. I bullied my way into this—I knew what might happen. You have to believe me when I tell you that I am a responsible adult, fully capable of taking care of myself." She drew a deep breath and met his piercing green eyes. "I wanted to tell you earlier, but it didn't seem like the time and now, I don't know what will happen...." When he didn't say anything, but continued to look at her with those knowing eyes, she screwed up her courage. Somehow facing Reid was easier than facing Adam.

"It's nothing bad," she protested, and then faltered for a moment. "I love you."

Adam seemed to pale, but he didn't flinch or put his hands together in the sign of the cross to ward off evil spirits, so Meg took his overall reaction as positive.

"Meg, I—" The opening door stopped whatever excuses Adam would have offered, and Meg met her future executioners with some relief. She really didn't want Adam to list all the reasons he couldn't love her. Or at least not just at this moment. She needed some time to recover from having told him she loved him. She stopped and considered how she felt: lighter, happier. Being in love, even unrequited love, suited her.

The old Meg would never have believed this, but the new Meg was glad she'd told Adam. She'd never been willing to gamble on Max, but she was with Adam. She was no longer afraid of what she felt—she wanted to live completely, with passion and danger. Even if Adam never loved her, she would never regret telling him.

Reid and his two henchmen were back. Meg wondered once again how she could have found Reid attractive. He stopped in front of her. "No funny stuff. I want Abby."

"Abby is on one of her retreats," she explained, for what felt like the hundredth time.

"All part of her mystical, psychic healing and search for inner self," Reid said scornfully. "With all the kooks in Sedona, I figured no one would ever clue in to something odd happening out here on the ranch. I guess I miscalculated. Just as Adam Smith miscalculated that I wouldn't act quickly against him. A lot of money is at stake. Money I need to make the Liberty L secure for future generations." His face hardened. "No more games. Where is she?"

"I don't know." When Reid slammed his fist against the desk, Meg continued hurriedly. "I don't know where she is exactly, but she took my cellular phone in case of an emergency. I can call her."

"Good. Do it."

Meg stalled for time. She still didn't have the faintest idea how she was going to warn Abby. "What do you want me to say? How do I ask her to cut short her retreat and return without alerting her suspicions?"

One corner of Reid's mouth crooked in an awful smile. "Tell her her store burned down."

That didn't make any sense. "The fire was two nights ago. What if Abby calls someone else and finds out I'm lying?" Oops, too late the words were out of her mouth, when that was exactly the kind of clue she wanted Abby to notice. So much for her plan of trying to give Abby some kind of clever warning in her telephone call.

Reid's voice was as smooth as silk. "Unfortunately, there was a second fire—" he looked at his watch "—about to start any second now. The Gateway will soon be a pile of ashes."

"How despicable." Meg felt sick. She couldn't believe Reid would stoop so low; the store and building were Abby's lifeblood. "Abby loves that store. I do, too."

Reid handed her a portable phone and picked up an extension for himself. "Don't try anything funny—I'll be listening to your conversation. I know your fondness for mysteries and puzzles. You do anything stupid and I'll make him suffer—" he pointed at Adam "—until he wishes he were dead."

With trembling hands, Meg dialed the number of the phone she'd loaned to her friend, wondering whether she wanted Abby to answer it or not. She would be pulling the dear woman into danger, but Meg had no choice.

She counted rings. She could tell Abby to run and hide to save herself, and then she and Adam could fend for themselves. On the tenth ring, Abby answered. "Hello?"

Even in this terrible circumstance, Meg was glad to hear her friend's voice. "Abby, it's me."

"Well of course it's you. It's your phone. I couldn't figure out what that ringing in my knapsack was for the longest time. At first I thought my spirit guide, Althenia, had chosen a new method of communication, and I was beginning to channel when I remembered your phone."

"Oh, Abby, I've missed you."

"What's wrong, Meg?"

Abby always picked up on Meg's distress immediately. In so many ways Abby was the mother Meg had lost at such an early age. Meg had been able to tell Abby all about her misadventures with Max, and how worried she was that she would never find the one great love of her life. Abby had listened and agreed that Meg was right to want to change her life. To start out on her own personal quest.

Now Meg felt tears threaten. "Your store. The Gateway. There was a fire…oh, Abby, it's all gone." Meg's voice broke.

The Gateway had been a good home to her. And it was Abby's dream—a place she had created when she'd been given a second chance after her recovery from cancer. The Gateway literally symbolized Abby's journey and new life.

"Darling, don't cry. Life has taught me it's always possible to rebuild." It was so typical of Abby to comfort Meg, when it was her dream that had been destroyed.

Reid made a slashing motion and Meg hurried to deliver her message. "Your beautiful store, all gone. We need you to come home, Abby."

"What did you say? It sounded like you said something happened to *my* store?"

"Exactly. Your store. Your store has been destroyed. Please…" Meg felt on the verge of tears. "We need you to come home."

"I'll leave at first light. It's a hike of a couple of hours and then a long drive. I'll try to be home tomorrow, but it will be late, maybe after midnight," Abby promised with brisk efficiency, and ended the call in her usual manner with no goodbye.

As the connection broke, Meg realized the enormity of what she'd just done, putting her friend in danger. She shivered and saw Adam watching her. She no longer felt like the heroine of a movie; she was scared and worried. *Please let it work out*, she prayed silently.

She raised her chin and glared at Reid. "There, I did what you asked."

"Yes, you must really love him." Reid nodded at Adam. "I never would have imagined that you could be so passionate about a man. I rather liked your cool reserve, your New York City sophistication." He walked to her and stood close, his blue eyes glittering. Meg refused to move away from him, even when he tipped up her chin with a hand, holding his face far too close to her own.

"It might have been rather fun to discover that passion in bed."

"Take your hands off her," Adam said in a quiet, deadly voice.

Reid stepped away and shrugged. His gaze locked with Adam's steely one. Meg shivered. "Don't worry, I'm not interested anymore," Reid muttered. He paced the room and then finally turned back to them, Adam now standing protectively next to Meg. "I suppose I need the pair of you until Abby shows up and tells me who told her about us. Take them to the TV room," he told Josh. "They can spend the day there. Double security—I don't want them to escape. If they try to get away, shoot."

Meg and Adam were hustled off promptly. She looked back at Reid as she left the office, but he'd already turned on his computer. After threatening to kill people, did he just settle down to a regular day's work?

In the TV room, another massive space that contained a large-screen TV, a wet bar, leather couches and a recliner, Adam turned on her, speaking between clenched teeth. "Abby had a damn cell phone. You could have called her the first night." He took a step toward her and then turned away. "I swear, if Reid wasn't going to kill us, I'd do the job for him. What the hell were you thinking?"

"The first night you were unconscious, as well as the second," she said, knowing her answer was a mistake.

He slumped down in one of the large chairs and buried his face in his hands.

"Adam?"

When he didn't answer, she knelt in front of him and gently placed her hands on his. He ignored her. "Adam, please."

He threw her hands off him, rose and walked to the window. "You knew how to reach Abby at any point during the last five days and yet you never did." He turned on her, his eyes blazing fiercely. "Why not?"

She faltered, then straightened her back. "Because I was afraid that once Abby gave you your answers you'd be gone."

"You were afraid that I'd finish my investigation and leave you. Instead, you thought that an…affair was more important. Your *feelings* for me," he scoffed. "Three kisses. You're in love with me."

The contempt in his words hit her like a slap in the face. Adam had a right to be angry with her, but not to ridicule her feelings. "I do love you," she said quietly. "I'm sorry about how all of this has turned out, but I didn't realize there was so much danger."

Adam's anger deflated as quickly as it had built. His shoulders slumped and he turned away from her. Meg wished she could go to him and wrap her arms tightly around him, but he didn't want her. In a defeated voice, he said, "You're right. I didn't even tell you that the first fire was a warning sign. Or about Kelly. I'm sorry I got so mad. I just feel like a total idiot for walking into this."

"Me, too," Meg agreed, feeling a chasm opening between them. Their lovemaking this morning already felt far away. She let the silence stretch out between them. She had told Adam how she felt. What happened between them now was up to him.

Adam flipped channels idly, almost hoping to get a rise out of Meg. At least fighting with her would keep him from thinking about what a fool he was. He'd blindly walked into a trap without any kind of backup plan in place. Reid could very well kill him, Meg and Abby tomorrow and no one would suspect anything unusual. It would be a week or two before his editor began to worry about him—Adam had disappeared on assignment before. Plus, this time he'd told her that the story was personal, so she would give him even more leeway. Cynthia was good like that.

But he hadn't told anyone what he was working on, because he was afraid of the answers he might find. If his sister was up to her eyeballs in the mess, he'd planned on helping cover up for her. It was what he'd always done for her.

Only he hadn't counted on meeting Megan Cooper. She had knocked him off his feet and he still hadn't recovered. Making love to her had only proved how she had him under her spell. He liked her. He liked her a lot. Too much. She was brave, determined, passionate. Everything he could ever want in a woman.

So he was going to think up some kind of plan to rescue them and then he was going to send Reid Logan to jail for a very long time. And then he was going to say goodbye to Megan Cooper, because if he didn't, his life would continue to be one mess like this after another.

Meg paced the room, the pretty, ruffled pink skirt she'd worn with cowboy boots flaring against her legs as she walked. She might be gorgeous and sexy, but she was all wrong for him. Still, seeing the frown on her face, he was sorry that he had been so rough on her. "Don't worry about Abby, I'll think of something."

"Yes, well…" Meg began. Then Gloria walked in. Today she was dressed in a turquoise shirt and matching flowered skirt. Her shiny blond hair cascaded in soft curls over her shoulders.

She smiled at Adam, her lips, painted a pale pink, curling delicately. A dimple twinkled in one cheek. "Good, you are here. I was afraid Reid might have locked you in our drafty barn."

"No, we're quite comfortable," Meg said, glaring daggers at the woman.

Gloria chose to ignore the sarcasm and Meg altogether. She touched Adam on the back of his hand, letting her slender fingers rest against his darker, leathered skin. It would be so easy to turn his hand over and crush her fingers between his. Instead he linked his fingers with hers. "So you're the mastermind behind this operation."

"Without me, there would be very little profitable activity at the Liberty L," Gloria said proudly. "I thought the name of our ranch was rather prophetic, considering the business I ended up starting. Liberty was what our ancestors fought for. And liberty—an American identity—is what my customers are able to find at the Liberty L."

"You mean purchase," Meg snapped, wishing Adam would let go of Gloria's hand.

Gloria flicked a cool glance at her. "Of course I mean purchase. Nothing is free anymore in this world. Certainly not my services. But where are my manners? Let me ring for some coffee." She squeezed Adam's hand and regretfully turned away from him to buzz the intercom. They waited in silence while Josh arrived with the coffee tray. The blond giant didn't look too pleased at being turned into a houseboy, but he didn't argue, either.

"Delicious coffee," Gloria said with a sigh after taking a sip. "It's sent to me direct from Columbia by a friend who owns a coffee plantation."

Adam was amazed at the woman's coolness. "Aren't you worried about receiving regular shipments from Columbia? The DEA could become very interested in you because of them."

"I prefer the original source as opposed to paying inflated New York prices to have the same coffee shipped to me. Besides, I go into the DEA's computer system and erase the oldest deliveries. I'm not flagged by their programs until I have six deliveries, and I never let my file get over four."

"Tell me how you began creating the computer forgeries."

"I needed some kind of a career." Gloria fluffed her hair as her dimple flashed. "The ranch was losing so much money that we were afraid of going under. Reid wasn't willing to admit the truth, but he was becoming desperate.

"I wasn't sure if I could do it at first, but through my international school contacts I knew people who were willing to pay a great deal of money to have an American identity. Getting into all the systems to be able to create a complete background took me months, but I did it. The first three transactions provided enough money to pay off all of our debts."

"And so your business was born."

"Yes." Gloria nodded sweetly. "It's extremely profitable and yet leaves me with a lot of free time for my studies."

"How nice for you," Meg interjected.

Gloria ignored her words, focusing on Adam. "Reid and I have been conducting our little business enterprise for over five years without any problems, until you came along. Why did you have to pry into our business? Why didn't you take the hint to leave it alone?"

"How did you know Adam was investigating you?" Meg asked.

"I put security checks on all of my newly created identities so I could be alerted whenever anyone looked into one of my people." Gloria smiled her glowing smile. "My people," she said fondly. "In so many ways they're like my babies. Usually, it was banks or car companies who were querying an identity—until the inquiry from the *Times*. At that point I stayed next to my computer waiting for the next log-on. I waited three days for you." She shook her head sadly. "You got careless and I got lucky because you accessed the *Times* main frame from your home. I was able to trace you through their system. Then I tracked you, and learned the minute you booked airline tickets for Phoenix. Unfortunately, you did so almost immediately."

Adam had to admit that Gloria was efficient. "So you arranged to get rid of me."

"Before you learned anything concrete. We weren't sure how you had traced us, so eliminating you quickly seemed like the best idea. I didn't even realize you were Kelly's brother at first. Smith is such a common name, after all. She'd mentioned you, but I'm afraid that I never paid all that much attention to what she said. Kelly was always nattering away about something or other, but nothing was ever that interesting or relevant. Only once I began to do a background check on you—after I had sent out Josh and Tom to stop you—did I learn exactly how personal your involvement was."

Adam leaned back in his chair, clearly fascinated by her explanation. "Unfortunately for you, your men didn't do such a good job."

"No," Gloria agreed, and delicately bit into a cookie. "But we'd never really done anything so...violent. I should have taken that into account. I have now," she added coolly, and Meg shivered. With every word, Gloria's sweet demeanor was disappearing.

She frowned, furrowing her eyebrows together. "It was Abby who sent you our way? Who realized what we were up to?"

"So it seems," Adam said, refusing to admit much.

Gloria scowled briefly, but then her face smoothed back to beauty. "Too bad. Everything was going along so well until you interfered."

"Hardly." Adam couldn't keep the bitterness from his voice.

Gloria studied him for a moment. "You're referring to Kelly. That was an unfortunate coincidence."

When Adam didn't answer, Meg had to ask, "How did Kelly get involved?"

Gloria drank more of her coffee and then put down her cup. "Kelly was before your time in Sedona, Meg. A beautiful, free-spirited girl who fell in love with Reid. And he with her. Only it didn't turn out so well."

Gloria turned cold, hard eyes on Adam. "She didn't tell you anything, did she?"

"No. After the accident, Kelly lost her memory. The last few weeks I've suspected some of it was returning, but she still wouldn't tell me anything. Plus, I believe she truly loved Reid. My sister is very loyal."

"I didn't think she'd talk. I told Reid that, but he wasn't sure. But I saw how much she loved him. Kelly might have been disillusioned by Reid, but she couldn't betray him. And she didn't."

"No, she didn't."

Gloria had moved a little closer to Adam on the couch. Meg stood up, going over to the pile of magazines in the rack next to the fireplace. She discovered several she hadn't read and an issue of *Cosmopolitan* with the excerpt of a book she had edited before her extended sabbatical from Scorpion Books.

She suddenly longed for home and her family. What if she died without ever seeing her father and brother again? Even the office where she had spent so much of her life? She vowed that *when* she and Adam managed to escape, she would return to New York. Ideally, Adam would be part of her new life. But even if not, she would still go home.

But they had to escape. She looked up from her magazines to see Adam and Gloria sitting very close together. Gloria laughed at something he said and arched her lovely neck as she did. Meg wanted to wring that lovely neck. She slammed her magazine shut, but unfortunately, that made little noise.

She stomped around the room, but it had no effect, so she sat back down in a chair far away from the pair and turned to a scandal magazine. She managed to lose herself in the latest gossip, only occasionally raising her head to glare at the back of Gloria's shining curls. The two remained completely oblivious of her.

Finally, Gloria rose, adjusted her dress so that even more skin showed, touched Adam on the shoulder and left without even looking at Meg.

Meg and Adam were taken back to a bedroom and locked in. Once inside, Meg turned to ask Adam if he had any kind of a plan for escape, but he silenced her with a kiss. Then he made slow, determined, passionate love to her and Meg forgot everything.

12

THE NEXT MORNING Meg wondered if Adam's lovemaking had been intended to keep her mind off what would happen once Abby arrived in Sedona. The thought only came to her once she and Adam were back in the recreation room and Meg had turned on the TV in a desperate attempt to distract herself. Abby was due to arrive in town soon and Reid's men would be waiting for her. Then Abby would be in equal danger, all because of Meg. She wished she'd been able to think of some better way to warn Abby than the lame clues she'd dropped in her telephone conversation.

When she thought about their situation, about her wish for adventure, she could hardly believe that they might actually die. It had all happened so quickly. Surely, this couldn't really be the end? The optimistic part of herself refused to believe it, but she was scared.

She also wished that Adam would tell her he cared for her. Perhaps his lovemaking proved his feelings for her. Unfortunately, Meg wasn't convinced.

Gloria swept into the room, today dressed in a shocking pink halter dress and sandals. Meg hated to admit that Gloria looked beautiful, fresh and sexy. She, on the other hand, looked liked she'd been living in the same clothes for the past three days. The discouraging part was that it had only been two days.

Adam looked at Gloria appreciatively, raising one brow. "Very sexy." He made space on the couch so Gloria could sit next to him.

At that moment Meg could have hit him. So what if him seducing Gloria was part of her plan? She had outlined that scenario to Adam last night—but he didn't have to be so good at it. She rather thought Adam also had his own plan, but he wasn't sharing it with her. She wished he would; she wished he believed that they could work as a team. Despite the fact that he'd made love to her as if he treasured her, despite the fact that he'd held her all night long, he was keeping himself removed from her. Oh, she knew she'd thrown him off balance by telling him she was in love with him, but Adam simply refused to believe that they were meant to be.

Meg sighed. With everything that had gone wrong so far, she was beginning to wonder herself.

No, she wasn't. She knew that Adam was the man for her. She was just afraid that she might not be the woman for him. Ever since her abruptly canceled wedding, her luck with romance had been bad, and she feared it was going to stay that way. Okay, she promised herself. Just let them get out of this bad situation alive, and she would leave Adam in peace. But that didn't mean she had to like Gloria. In fact, Meg was beginning to hate the beautiful Gloria.

"We have some new guests coming in this afternoon and I always like to show them all the possibilities," Gloria teased as she twirled around in front of Adam.

"Don't mind me," Meg said. "Just pretend I'm not here."

Gloria shot her an annoyed glance as she sat down next to Adam.

"I'll get some air on the balcony," Meg continued. She stepped out the glass doors and waved at the guard, who stood not more than thirty feet away. Luckily, there was a chair, so she was able to plunk herself down as if she was interested in the scenery. Unfortunately, neither the buildings nor the landscape held any appeal. She wondered briefly about how you hired thugs. Did you advertise in *Thugs Unlimited?* She tried to make out what Gloria and Adam were talking about, but all she was able to hear were Adam's low seductive tones and Gloria's lilt.

Meg couldn't believe she was still jealous. She was the one Adam had made love to. She felt more alive and sensual than she'd ever felt in her life. Even if something terrible happened, she wouldn't have traded a minute with Adam for anything.

All he was doing now was looking for a way to escape. They had discussed it in the middle of the night. Taking Gloria as a hostage seemed to be their only option. Clearly Reid was very fond of his sister.

Meg peered in the window and saw Adam kissing Gloria. Meg turned away, hoping this wouldn't take too long. After a couple of minutes, she couldn't help herself and, waving to the guard outside, went back into the recreation room. Gloria was still plastered against Adam. He looked at Meg as she entered, as if he knew she'd be walking in, and she raised her brows questioningly. Finally Adam separated himself from the blond piranha and looked down at her. "I'm sorry," he said, before he raised his hand, hitting her just above the ear. Gloria crumpled into his arms.

Meg went over to help him hold Gloria upright. "Took you long enough."

"I don't like to hit women. I was trying to work up my nerve."

"As long as that was all you were trying to work up."

Adam picked up the unconscious Gloria. Meg looked around the room for some kind of a weapon, but she didn't think the flimsy magazine rack would be of any use. "What about the guard at the door?" she asked.

Adam put Gloria on the couch. "Open the door, act hysterical and get him in here."

She didn't need to be told twice. In fact, she was rather impressed watching Adam in action. But would the guard fall for this old routine?

She threw open the door and barreled into the thug. It was Josh, the one who had enjoyed hurting her. She hoped Adam hurt him back. "Help," she shouted into his chest. Then she spit out his shirt and raised her head.

"Help," she said again. "It's Gloria. I think she's having a heart attack or something...." She grabbed his hand and tried to pull him into the room. At first Josh didn't budge, until he looked over her shoulder and saw Gloria passed-out on the couch. Putting his hand over the gun in his holster, he moved Meg aside easily and stepped into the room. Meg followed behind, wishing Adam would have told her more of his plan. She'd shared her ideas with him, including that he make Gloria fall for him. He could have shared with her what exactly he planned to do—after all, he was much better at investigating and skullduggery than she was. Normally she read about it or watched it on the screen; she didn't actually live it.

Warily Josh stepped closer to Adam and Gloria, but Adam didn't turn around. "What happened?" Josh demanded.

"We need to get a doctor. She had some kind of seizure."

Josh stepped even closer. "I need to see her before I call any kind of doctor."

In irritation, Adam turned toward Josh and slammed his fist into the man's stomach. Josh doubled over, and Meg, having decided the magazine rack wasn't so flimsy after all, smashed it over the goon's head. The man collapsed face first onto the floor.

"Ouch, that would have hurt," Adam said as he rolled the body over and checked Josh's eyes. "He's out."

"Now what?" Meg asked.

"Now—" Adam took Josh's gun and slung Gloria over his shoulder "—we get out of here." He stepped toward the balcony window and peered out at an angle so that no one outside would be able to see him. "How many men did you spot outside?"

Meg frowned. Most of her attention had been on the action inside the recreation room. "I saw one man by the courtyard."

"No one else?"

"No, that was it." Meg realized how odd that was. Why

would there be only one sentry? Moreover, the man had kept looking toward the road like he was waiting for something.

Adam glanced around the room. "We need some kind of rope so we can bind Gloria—and we'll have to gag her."

Meg grabbed the afghan off the burgundy couch and began to work on the threads she'd unraveled yesterday out of boredom. She stopped and looked at Adam questioningly. "I thought we were taking Gloria with us as a hostage."

"No."

Adam ripped apart the afghan in her hands and used strips to bind Gloria's feet. "Tie her arms behind her."

Meg did as instructed. "Why not?" she asked, when it was clear Adam had no intention of volunteering more information.

"They'd expect us to try to escape by using Gloria. I'm sure by the time we stepped out the balcony door, the lone guard you saw earlier would also be conveniently gone."

"But why? Why would they help us escape?"

Adam checked the tightness of the bindings around Gloria. "Ms. Logan is a strategic thinker. She's been flirting with me to make me try to think of using her as our method of escape. As long as she and Reid help us plan our escape, they can stop us."

"Oh." Meg absorbed this information. "So you pretended to fall in with their plans, but were coming up with a second course of action all the while."

"Exactly." Adam picked up Gloria's limp, bound and gagged body. "Would you open that closet door, please?"

Meg did and Adam deposited Gloria inside. For the first time Meg felt a little sorry for the woman. "I don't think she'll be very comfortable."

"I'm sure her brother will find her soon enough." Adam looked at Meg questioningly. "Well?"

"Yes?" she returned blandly.

"Aren't you going to berate me for having a different plan in mind?"

"One you didn't deign to consult me about?" she asked frostily.

Adam made a slight move with his shoulders that might have been a shrug. "Something like that."

"I certainly wish you had, but now doesn't seem to be the time for a proper discussion about my role in our rescue. What next? Are we going to hide out in the house while everyone searches for us?"

Adam cupped her cheek, his eyes searching hers. "You are the most damnably unusual woman."

Meg smiled. "Thank you. Smart, too."

"Yes." Adam kissed her quickly.

For once, Meg pushed him away. "No time for that."

He grabbed her hand. "You're right. We're going to head outside, as they're expecting us to, and then double back into the first empty room we find. We'll wait for the outcry, and as soon as most of the men are out searching for us, we'll make our getaway."

"Clever," Meg agreed. "To the left of the kitchen is a small room where they keep supplies. I saw Peter take cans from there during our dinner."

"Good. Let's go." Adam took her hand as they stepped out the balcony doors to a courtyard that was completely empty just as Adam had predicted. Sticking close to the side of the building, they headed toward the kitchen door, crouching as they passed the windows. Adam went first, quietly knocking on the door.

"What?" She recognized Tom's voice from inside. "No one's supposed to come this way." Tom opened the door and stepped smack into Adam's fist. Adam hit him twice and the man crumpled. Adam pulled Tom's body into the center of the courtyard, leaving him there as if Tom had come across the escaping fugitives and tried to stop them.

As Adam confiscated the man's revolver, Meg peeked inside the kitchen, which was empty. Nodding at Adam, she entered quietly and made her way past the large ceramic-topped workstation to the supply room. She opened it and stepped inside, with Adam after her.

"Now we wait," he said.

For a second Meg thought about tearing a strip off him for misleading her. Then she realized the truth. "You only figured out what Gloria was up to a few minutes ago—that she was trying to keep us distracted."

"Er, yes. It occurred to me while I was kissing her."

"Well done. I knew you were a clever man, Adam Smith."

"Not as clever as I'd like or we wouldn't have been here, period."

Meg wanted to tease him out of his dark mood. "But then we wouldn't have had such good quality time together."

"There is that," he agreed with a wry grin, putting the guns aside and snaking an arm around her waist and pulling her against him.

Meg loped her arms around his shoulders. "I really don't think we have time to fool around," she said unconvincingly.

Adam pressed his lips against her brow. "There's always time for kissing." At first he kissed her gently, then he deepened the pressure, pulling her to him. Meg felt herself begin to float as all she could do was experience the joy of being in Adam's arms, the texture of his hair under her fingers, the masculine scent of him, the beauty of his kiss.

When the kiss ended, Meg felt as if something had been settled between them. "Adam?" she asked tentatively.

"Yes," he said, answering her unspoken question. "Afterward, we'll—damn, what's that?" he exclaimed at the sound of a commotion outside.

It wasn't footsteps running in pursuit. It was Reid Logan laughing, followed by a woman's voice.

"That's Abby," Meg declared.

"Damn. I was hoping we'd be able to find her before Reid did."

"We could still hide in here while they search for us."

"I don't think so. Reid has what he wants—Abby. He'll force her to tell him what she knows. Then he can kill her. All while we're hiding out in this closet."

"Adam, we have to help Abby. She's been such a good friend to me."

"I know. I suggest we face Reid before he decides to force us out by hurting Abby."

"Of course." Meg was reaching for the door handle, all concern for her own safety gone, when another thought hit her. "Wait. If, when you were kissing Gloria, you figured out she was trying to trick you, what do you think of when you kiss me?"

Adam walked into the harsh light of the kitchen. "When I kiss you, I don't have a rational thought in my head."

ABSOLUTELY NOTHING had gone right for days—why should Adam really have expected his escape plan to work? He should have grabbed Meg and run while they'd had a chance. Run very far away—away from friends and family and all obligations. Found an isolated place where they could be alone, just the two of them. Adam should have followed his namesake in creating their very own private Garden of Eden.

Instead, he'd wanted to be careful. More importantly, he'd wanted to show Meg how clever he could be. To prove to her that he was her hero. For the first time, he truly wanted to take care of someone—to take care of Megan Elizabeth Cooper. Wanted to worship her, to esteem her, to love her.

He'd shown himself exactly how clever he could be. He'd done the most idiotic thing of all: fallen in love with Meg. The woman was brave and beautiful and passionate. Back there, he'd almost admitted the truth to Meg. *Saved by the bad guys*, he thought ruefully. He wasn't going to tell Meg how he felt. If he did say the words, the result would be too messy when the time came to end whatever it was they had together. While Meg surprised him at times, he'd been down that path before. It was fun and exciting but it only led to heartache.

He'd have lots of time to continue his analysis once he and Meg rescued Abby. There was no one in the kitchen, but Adam heard voices in the living room, and they walked down the short hallway to the large room.

Abby was flanked by Josh and another man, while Reid was sitting on the chair. At the sight of Adam and Meg, he rose. "Glad you could make it," he said with a smile. Then he frowned when he saw there were only two of them. "Where's my sister?"

Adam fixed a cool stare on Reid Logan. "She couldn't make it. She claimed a previous appointment."

"Tom, search the house for Gloria. If you hurt her—" Reid clenched his fists, staring at Adam "—you're going to suffer."

Meg didn't care what Reid was threatening them about now. She was so happy to see the silver-haired, sixtyish woman in front of her. "Oh, Abby," she said, her voice almost breaking. She controlled herself. "Abby, I'm so sorry, but I'm so happy to see you."

Abby held open her arms, and ignoring everyone, Meg ran into her embrace. Never mind the danger they were in; it felt so good just seeing her friend. Abby wrapped her firm arms around her and Meg felt better. A heavy hand pulled her away.

"Enough of that," Reid said coldly.

"How did you get here?" Meg asked Abby, undaunted.

Her good friend sighed. "After your call, after what you told me, I rushed. I made it to town this morning and saw what was left of my poor store. Oh my, I did feel such a pain in my heart when I saw the charred ruins that, for a moment, I was afraid I was having a heart attack." Abby pressed a hand against her chest in remembrance. "But I've known loss before and I knew what I was feeling was grief. Then I decided to head over to Michelle and Rachel's, figuring you would be there, but Reid was waiting for me and told me you had spent the night at the ranch. Unfortunately, I believed him and rushed over to make sure you were all right. I knew how responsible you would feel despite the fact that none of it was your fault."

Abby glared at Reid, all five feet two of her radiating anger as she threw her arms about, looking like a furious elf. "I never realized you were such an evil man. I always wondered about you, about how you were able to live such an elaborate life-style, but I truly thought the ranch was doing well. I would never have imagined you to be an arsonist and a kidnapper. Men!" she snapped in conclusion.

"Oh, he's even worse, Abby. I'm afraid he's going to kill us!" Meg exclaimed to her friend, no longer able to suppress her guilt at bringing this dear woman into danger.

The older woman shook her head and smiled sadly at Meg. "I rather think I'm the one who owes you an apology. After all, I'm the one who sent for Mr. Smith. Although, after all this time, I had given up." She turned to Adam inquiringly. "I assume you are the famous writer Adam Smith?"

"Guilty," he agreed. "Not enough postage on your letter. I only read it last week, because my sister Kelly reacted so strangely to it."

"Yes, Kelly, a lovely girl." Abby studied him. "It's almost hard to believe you're related, although I do see some similarity in the eyes. But I think that in personality you are quite different."

"Very," he agreed again.

"Yes, Kelly told me how you always helped her with her problems." Reflexively, Abby blew her bangs out of her eyes. "It might have been better for her if you'd occasionally let her suffer the consequences of her actions. Kelly is actually a very smart girl. Unfortunately, she never had to figure out things for herself—you always did it for her."

Unable to keep still, Abby began to pace, her long tunic

jacket flapping around her. "But after Kelly disappeared so suddenly—and she was so in love with Reid—I began to wonder if my suspicions about Reid and the Liberty L could possibly be correct."

"But Abby, what made you think that something unusual was going on? What led you to Reid?" Meg asked.

Abby looked down and then back up at Adam, her expression rueful. "Sometimes late at night I like to play with my satellite dish and see what I can pick up. I've come across some really incredible game shows. One night I was watching one of the South American shows, something like *America's Most Wanted.* Anyway, what caught my attention was that the man they kept showing a picture of looked so much like one of the guests at the dude ranch. That's why I decided to send you my letter. I couldn't help but think that Reid and Gloria might be involved in something that wasn't aboveboard. Especially since Kelly disappeared without saying goodbye. She's such a warm, loving girl, I couldn't believe she'd leave without saying anything unless something bad had happened. I think I was one of the few friends she'd made in Sedona, and I was the only one she confided in about her relationship with Reid Logan. It's not that Kelly was a secretive girl, but at first she claimed the man she loved guarded his privacy and she wanted to respect his wishes because they were such different people. I think she was trying to prove her worth to him. Then she got quieter and quieter, and I realized that Kelly was scared of something...or someone. Then she disappeared, so I wrote to you."

Abby shook her head, gazing into the distance. "Never for a minute did I connect Adam Smith, intrepid journalist, with Kelly Smith. Instead, it was the forces of the universe, the power of the vortexes, that directed me to ask you for advice. I was merely a vessel following what the spirits were telling me to do."

Abby turned her sharp eyes on him. "So what happened? You figured out it was Reid too late?"

It wasn't really a question, but Adam felt compelled to answer. "You didn't give me a lot to work with."

"That's because I expected you to arrive immediately. Well— " Abby looked around the room "—now we seem to be in a fine mess."

"*You* were the one who figured out that we're selling American identities?" Reid asked incredulously.

Abby whirled around and glared at him. "*Ageism*," she declared with a snort. "Just because I'm over sixty doesn't mean my brain cells have atrophied. I always thought you were an underhanded character, even before I realized that you and Kelly were lovers, that you were the one she feared."

"I've been in Sedona for over four months," Meg interjected, "and no one ever mentioned Kelly to me. Why did no one tell me that Reid had been involved with her? When he started showing interest in me, why didn't you warn me about him?"

"Well, I wasn't sure that he had done anything bad to her," Abby explained. "Besides, you're much more savvy, much less naive than Kelly—I didn't think you'd actually fall for Reid. Did you?"

"No."

"Well, at least that's one good thing." Abby patted Meg's shoulder. "But if you've fallen for Kelly's brother, I'm not sure you've done much better. Kelly told me all about him, and while she clearly hero-worships him, he just as clearly runs the lives of everyone in his family. Total control."

"Oh," said Meg, wondering what she was getting herself into. "But I love him," she admitted to her friend.

"Well, that's too bad, because he's not going to change. He'll always want to be the hero."

"This is no time to be discussing love lives," Reid snapped. He raised his gun and pointed it at Meg. "Now, I want to know who else you told about the forgeries."

Before Adam could stop her, Abby calmly announced, "No one."

"Good," Reid exclaimed in satisfaction. "That makes so many less people to dispose of."

"No one," Abby continued implacably, as if she hadn't just announced a death sentence on the three of them, "unless something happens to me. Then my lawyer will open my safety deposit box and find every piece of information and suspicion I had about you and the beautiful Gloria, with specific instructions to use my estate to investigate you if anything untoward should happen to me."

Reid swore. "Damned interfering, meddling old woman." Adam wished he could kiss Abby.

"Oh, Abby, that was clever," Meg cried enthusiastically. "I was hoping you'd be able to help."

"Fine," said Reid. "You—" he pointed to Josh "—take Abby to her bank and retrieve all the documents."

"No," said Abby.

Reid glared at the silver-haired, pixie-size titan. "I don't think you understand the gravity of the situation. Unless you agree to cooperate—" he gestured with his gun at Meg again "— I'm going to kill her first."

"No," Abby repeated, drawing herself up to her full five-two height. "I don't trust you. As soon as your man tells you he has the information, our lives won't be worth anything. We seem to be at a stalemate."

Pointing at Meg, Reid nodded at Josh. "Shoot her."

13

ADAM STEPPED NEXT TO MEG, blocking Josh's shot, while she gulped, trying to dislodge the big obstacle that had suddenly appeared in her tight, dry throat.

"No," said Abby once again, even more firmly. "Really, you do have such a one-track mind. I care for Meg like my own daughter. Him—" she nodded at Adam "—I don't care so much about, but Meg does. What we'll do is all go to the bank together. In public, I will hand the information over to you and we three will walk out of the bank together. Then I calculate you'll have a couple of hours to clear off the Liberty L, while we try to convince the police to believe us and stop you. If you're fast enough, you might escape."

Reid turned red and shook. "I am not giving up everything we've worked for. The Liberty L is my heritage." He stormed toward Abby, raising his hand as if to hit her, but Abby held her ground.

"I'm not bluffing," she said. "Your only chance to get all the information and escape with your sister is if we do it my way. Otherwise, you might as well kill us all now and run for it. But do you really want a murder charge on top of everything else? My lawyer is very efficient and determined. I'm not sure if I mentioned that he's my son. If he believes you had anything to do with my death, he won't stop until he tracks you down. Plus, Randy works for the IRS, so he knows how to be incredibly persistent."

Reid growled and then nodded his head. "Okay, we'll do it your way. But the first sign of a trick and I'll shoot Meg. Then I'll take great pleasure in eliminating you."

Abby smiled and tucked her hand under Meg's arm. "Come on, dear. Let's finish this."

With Reid leading the way and Josh following behind them, Meg, Abby and Adam trooped outside. Meg felt dizzy; everything was happening so quickly. She took a deep breath, trying to think.

All five of them piled into one Jeep, Meg and Reid in front, Abby and Adam squished in back with the threatening Josh. As the Jeep began to cover the miles back to Sedona, Adam fantasized over the many different ways he would like to hurt Reid. As they hit a series of holes in the dirt road, he bounced closer to Abby and said under his breath, "This is never going to work."

"This is only plan A," Abby muttered back. "Just wait for plan B." She gripped his hand briefly.

The Jeep had covered several more miles of desert when Reid drove around a corner of an outcrop and almost smashed into another Jeep. He swore, slamming on the brakes to avoid the car in front of them. They were all thrown forward as the vehicle bounced and swerved, missing Greg Trenton's four-wheel-drive by inches.

"Damn," Reid swore. "It's a trap."

"Damn right it is," Abby announced cheerfully. "This is plan B."

In the distance, Adam saw two more Jeeps heading toward them from opposite directions and he smiled in grim satisfaction. Realizing that Abby had brought in reinforcements, he looked for his opportunity. Reid had to steer the vehicle with both hands as he increased the speed, so that left only Josh to dispose of. As Josh began to grasp the situation, looking around in confusion at the three Jeeps giving chase, Adam grabbed him by the hair, pulling hard at the roots. Josh yelped with pain. "That was for Meg," Adam said coldly, and then slammed the man's head against the roll bar. "And that was for Kelly." The man made a peculiar sound, his eyes rolled back in his head and he slumped against Abby.

Meg grabbed the steering wheel, trying to wrest control

of the Jeep away from Reid. Abby put a hammerlock around Reid's neck and squeezed hard for all she was worth. The vehicle careened wildly off the desert road into the scrub, hitting cacti. Meg screamed as the Jeep turned on two tires, and had to let go of Reid to grasp the roll bar to avoid falling out. Adam grabbed for Meg to keep her in the speeding car, with Abby still wrapped around Reid's neck.

The car braked furiously and all of them were thrown forward. The Jeep stopped and Adam tried to extract himself from the pile of arms and legs, but he was too late. Reid had his gun out, and he was dragging Meg out of the Jeep. She struggled, her elbows seeking purchase somewhere on Reid's body, her legs kicking wildly.

Adam jumped out and ran after them. Reid saw him charging at them and pointed his gun, but Adam didn't break his stride. He had to get to the cowboy before the man could use Meg as a hostage.

"Adam," Meg cried, her face white as she saw him charging toward Reid without any concern for the gun pointed straight at him.

"Stop, dammit," Reid shouted, aiming the revolver as Adam leaped headfirst, like a football player making a tackle. Adam heard the retort of the gun, felt heat brush by his cheek as the weight of his body pushed Reid and Meg to the ground.

Meg screamed, and in the mess of limbs, Adam reached for her. God, had Reid shot her? he worried. He found Meg and pulled her to him. "Are you all right?" He ran his hands along her sides.

"Oh, Adam, I'm okay." She shook her head in wonder. "You just charged him." Her eyes were wide in that sweet, pale face. Adam opened his mouth, then shut it. Meg was safe—that was all that mattered. He looked up to see Reid getting to his feet, checking for the other Jeeps, which were approaching rapidly.

Reid charged back to his abandoned vehicle and jumped in. "It looks like you tricked me this time, but I'll be back," he threatened as he gunned the engine. "If I was you," he said to Adam, "I'd give thanks for being alive and leave it at that. If you investigate any further you're going to discover how deeply your sister was involved."

With that parting promise, he took off.

Adam let him go, glad the woman in his arms was safe. "I couldn't let him hurt you." It was as close to a declaration as Adam was going to give.

Meg busied herself twisting a button on his chambray shirt. "But he could have shot you."

"I've been shot before."

"You were my hero." She flung her arms around him and kissed him. Her lips trembled under his as he took charge of the kiss, wanting to reassure himself that she was okay. She tasted so sweet, fresh and good. She was everything he could ever want. When they broke apart, she looked at him tremulously and he cupped her face between his hands. "If anything had happened to you…" He couldn't finish, and looked away as he felt a curious kind of moisture at the corner of his eyes.

Meg was quiet for a minute and buried her face in his chest. Finally, she pushed herself away and sat up. "Nothing did. Adam…I…we should check on Abby."

The older woman was having difficulty standing, so Adam gently lowered her to the ground, waiting for their rescuers to arrive. She was pale and had a bump the size of an egg on her forehead.

"Plan B was brilliant," he said to their rescuer, checking her erratic pulse. They needed to get her to a hospital fast. He didn't like how her pulse was racing, how pale she looked or how she seemed to have trouble focusing.

Greg's Jeep pulled up next to them and he jumped out, his blond hair glinting in the sun. "Oh, Greg," Meg cried, throwing herself into his arms, "I'm so happy to see you!"

Greg crushed her against him and Adam tried to quell his feelings of jealousy. He should be feeling grateful, the man had helped rescue them.

"Thank God you're all right, Meg. When Abby told me what she feared, I couldn't believe it. Did he hurt you?"

"Yes, but I'm all right now."

"You can let go of Meg and help me with Abby. She was knocked pretty badly," Adam said.

Greg ran over to Abby, concern all over his face. "Here, let me," the younger man said, but Adam picked up Abby and lay her as gently as possible on the back seat of Greg's Jeep.

The other two Jeeps pulled up alongside. Freddie jumped out of the first vehicle, followed by Ben Holden, one of Greg's cohorts.

"Reid is getting away," Meg said, practically jumping up and down as she pointed at the fleeing car. "Go after him!"

"Are you all right?" Freddie demanded, taking Meg into his arms instead.

Adam was really beginning to dislike how all the men in Sedona felt so comfortable taking his woman into their arms. He pushed the thought away.

"She's right," he said. "You—" he pointed to Greg "—take Meg and Abby back to town and call the police— Meg can tell you all about it. We'll go after Reid. You—" he said to Ben "—circle back to the Liberty L—my hunch is he'll turn up there. Freddie and I will give chase." But even as Adam said the words he knew it was unlikely they would be able to catch up to the cloud of dust.

But Adam knew Reid would head back to the ranch for his sister—the one person he valued more than himself.

Their only real hope was in getting to Gloria before Reid did.

"You LOST THEM?" Meg was so tired she was hardly able to work up any frustration when a disappointed Adam and Ben joined her and Greg at the hospital. The two men were dusty and creased, Ben's shoulders slumped. Adam strode across the hospital room to Abby's bed, took her hand and squeezed gently.

"How are you doing?" he asked Meg, "What did the doctor say?"

Abby pulled his attention back to her. "It was just a bad knock. Luckily, I've got a really hard head. Now tell us what happened."

"We gave a good chase in the desert, but by the time we knew we'd lost Reid and made it back to the Liberty L, everyone was gone. It looks like Gloria recovered consciousness and then made escape plans just in case Reid ran into trouble. As soon as Reid made it back, they left. The other men took off as well—I'm sure we could find them, but they're of no consequence. Reid and Gloria are the only ones I really want. The dude ranch has turned into a damn ghost ranch."

Meg shoved the hair off her face and sighed. Her little adventure wasn't having such a satisfying ending. The bad guys had escaped. Adam met her gaze, his eyes discouraged and worried. He wasn't about to see her as part of his happy ending, either. She straightened her back; no matter how bleak the situation, she'd never been a quitter. "I'm so angry. I can't believe everything that's happened to us—and now Reid and Gloria have managed to escape."

"Don't be so upset, dear." Still looking bruised and fragile, Abby sat up in her hospital bed, reaching for Meg's hand. She was weak, but she refused to let anyone leave her room until she heard the latest update.

Adam admired the woman's pluck, but he didn't understand how Abby had known that a rescue plan was a necessity. "What I'd like to know is how you knew something was wrong. You lied about your schedule and returned to town and hatched a plot with Greg and Freddie. You then performed an elaborate charade, backtracking out of town early in the morning and returning to let Reid find you. How did you know?"

Abby raised a perfectly arched eyebrow. "Why, from Meg's conversation, of course. She dropped such great clues, I would have had to be an imbecile not to understand."

"You did catch my clues!" Meg exclaimed enthusiastically. "I just wasn't sure. I kept thinking of Susan St. James in that *McMillan and Wife* episode. The one where she was kidnapped and every time the kidnappers let her talk to her husband, she dropped innocuous clues."

"That's good," Abby enthused. "I didn't know the reference, but by calling the store *mine* and insisting *we* needed me back, I knew something was wrong."

Greg and Adam looked at each other blankly as the two friends smiled at each other.

Meg clasped Abby's hand and then smiled at the three men. "Abby always insisted the store was as much mine as hers, so I hoped by referring to it as hers she might realize something was wrong."

Abby nodded. "Then when Abby used *we* I knew she wasn't alone."

"She could have misspoken," Adam interjected.

Abby looked at him in surprise. "Of course not. Meg always speaks very precisely. It's because of her former job."

Before Adam could ask what her former job was, Abby yawned. Instead, he filled in the two women on what had happened after they had arrived at the hospital. "The police took my report, and while they forwarded the information to the local airports, I don't hold much hope for capturing our fugitives so easily. I'm sure Gloria would have made up false IDs for both herself and Reid."

"So now what?" asked Meg.

"First, back to Abby knowing something was wrong because you used the wrong pronouns in your conversation." He felt like he'd lost sense of the situation—which, unfortunately, was becoming usual for him. Ever since he'd arrived in Sedona and met Meg. Even worse, he was starting to like the feeling.

Abby straightened up on the pillows, pulling on reserves of energy. "Well, once I understood Meg's message and realized something was terribly wrong, I lied about how long it would take me to return home. I got back to Sedona late last night and contacted Freddie immediately. He told me that an Adam Smith, supposed former fiancé of Meg's, had arrived in town, but I knew immediately who you really were. Then he told me how Meg had had an emergency phone call from her family and the two of you had returned to New York. That's when I knew for sure you were in trouble and Reid was involved. All Freddie and Greg did was agree to wait on the road as part of an ambush if I could get us away from the ranch."

"You were pretty confident of yourself." Adam was almost surprised that he wasn't critical. Having met Abby and seen her in action, he realized an escape plan and ambush would be simple, according to her.

Abby straightened her hospital gown about her shoulders. "It seemed pretty straightforward. I never imagined Reid would get really violent. After all, it is such a white-collar crime."

Meg hugged her. "Oh, Abby, you were a real heroine. You wouldn't believe it, but last Saturday I was in the store wishing for an adventure and Adam barged in. Since then it's been the best time of my life!" Meg glowed at the four of them. *God, she was beautiful* was all Adam could think.

Ben Holden shifted awkwardly. "If there's nothing else I can do…" He blushed when everyone remembered his presence and turned to look at him "…I'm going to leave. My girlfriend's waiting for me." He backed out of the room.

Abby yawned again. "I think we know all we need to know for tonight," Adam suggested.

Meg stood and kissed Abby on the forehead. "You were so wonderful. I'm so sorry about The Gateway."

"I have insurance—good insurance, thanks to my son the lawyer. It's the opportunity for a new beginning."

"Here?" Meg asked.

"Definitely," Abby said firmly, but her voice slurred slightly from the medication kicking in. "Sedona is my home. I hope you find your home soon."

Meg glanced at Adam and then met Abby's steady gaze. "I think I've found it."

Adam didn't query her, although he was sure that he knew what she meant. Instead he ushered Meg and Greg out of Abby's hospital room. In the hallway, Greg stopped, looking too pretty. "Now what?" he asked.

"Now we all get a good night's sleep and decide what we do tomorrow," Adam said discouragingly. "I've made arrangements for Michelle Stoneaway to reserve us a couple of rooms." He wanted Meg all to himself.

"Yeah, right, man. Cool." Greg fidgeted, brushing a blond lock off his forehead. "Don't suppose you want to go for a coffee and, like, talk?"

"No," Adam answered very firmly, tucking Meg's hand over his arm. She leaned against him briefly and he enjoyed the experience. There was that part of him that loved being the man Meg could rely on. He was being an idiot, he told himself, but he didn't let go of her hand.

"Got ya." Greg studied the two of them. "Maybe I'll go over to Dana's. I think Dana would listen. She's really deep, you know."

"It's after eleven," Meg began, but Adam elbowed her in the side.

"*If* Dana is alone." From the startled look on Greg's face, Adam realized the seed he'd planted had taken root. "After all, she's really pretty and smart. A nice combination. I noticed that the first time I met her. If I wasn't trying to win Meg back I might have gone after Dana myself."

"Yeah, she is pretty, isn't she? And nice. Hey, do you think Dana is dating someone?"

"Freddie has told me many times how much he admires Dana," Meg purred.

Greg frowned. "She was helping him with his computer system. Dana is really good with that kind of stuff."

"Oh, no, Freddie set up his own computer system. It's one of his hobbies. He and Dana could discuss artificial intelligence, but Freddie distinctly told me it wasn't Dana's mind that he was interested in."

"Right man, I get it." Greg pondered for a moment and Adam hoped they'd made Greg look at Dana in a new light. Greg sauntered off. Dana was about to be one very surprised, but happy, young woman tonight.

"Do you think Dana and Greg could have something together?" Meg sounded doubtful.

"In Sedona, anything is possible." Adam looked down at her, framing her face between his hands, and kissed her. "If there's anything I've learned, it's that anything is possible in Sedona."

14

"NEW YORK," Meg announced the next morning, when she joined him at the hotel's coffee shop. "We should go to New York."

Adam raised his head from his copy of the New York Times and looked questioningly at Meg. She managed to surprise him over and over again. He realized he'd had her pegged wrong from the beginning. What was important, however, was that she was alive. And beautiful, with sunlight streaming in from the window framing her golden brown hair, enthusiasm and curiosity on her face. He could watch her face all day.

Instead he looked back down at the editorials, but he couldn't focus. Last night, they hadn't discussed anything about the future. He'd been too busy loving her to give a thought about what would happen next.

Adam couldn't forgive himself for having pulled Meg into danger, or forget how scared he'd been that she might be hurt or killed. Damn. He'd managed to keep checked his emotions for her—desire, frustration and admiration—until they'd registered into the hotel for the evening.

As he'd signed them into one room, Meg had looked questioningly at him but hadn't said a word. He'd expected her to make some crack about sharing a bed—he half expected her to declare that if they slept together three times they'd get married—when she didn't, he knew she'd been affected by their ordeal as well.

He let Meg into the room and closed the door behind them, staring at the wood paneling, wondering exactly what he should do. He turned back to face Meg who stood uncertainly next to the bed, biting her lip. He knew exactly what he wanted to do and in three strides was beside her and wrapped his arms around her.

She buried her face against his shoulder. "I was so scared. I thought they might kill you or Abby or me or…"

"It's okay now," he whispered against her hair and framed her face between his two big hands, tipping her head back a little so he could kiss her forehead. Only that wasn't nearly enough, so he kissed closed both her eyes and trailed his lips down to one corner of her mouth.

That had been all the talking they'd done as they both seemed to want to lose themselves in each other. To forget about the past and the future. To hold and love each other through the night.

The first time had been fast. He hadn't even gotten all of Meg's clothes off before he was in her, making her cry out and dig her fingernails into his back.

After he'd found his senses once again, he'd taken his time. Kissing and loving every beautiful inch of her, letting her know by his actions how he felt. Meg had been so responsive and attuned to him. Making love to any other woman had never been like it was with Meg.

Afterward Meg had wrapped her body around him and kissed him so sweetly he thought his heart might break. Sweetly. Like she'd been saying goodbye. He looked at her sharply. Is that what she'd been telling him last night? That she, too, realized they had no future together?

The idea hit Adam like a punch in the gut, hurting him more than any of his previous injuries. No, this wasn't the time to worry about his feelings for Meg. He'd get them under control soon enough.

Instead, he pulled himself back to what Meg had said. "Why New York?"

"Isn't that where your sister lives?"

"In Queens with my mother." He was beginning to follow Meg's logic, and he didn't like the way she was thinking. "Why?"

"Because I think Reid plans to use her against you."

A chill shivered through his body. "Why would he do that?"

"Because he knows you. Kelly told him how persistent you are whenever you're on a story."

Adam didn't want to believe Meg might be right. "He and Gloria could be out of the country by now. They had no reason to stay, or to go after Kelly. Reid let Kelly go once," he argued logically, but felt sick to his stomach. His damn nerves were telling him that Meg was right. Reid was going to use Kelly as leverage.

His damn instincts were also telling him he was making a mistake saying goodbye to Meg. It was only lust, he tried to tell himself, but he knew he was lying.

"Reid and Gloria are greedy," Meg answered, picking up her coffee spoon and tapping it against the table. "You interrupted them before they were in business for long. Knowing the little I do about Gloria and Reid, I'm sure they're not willing to leave and live in exile. I imagine them relocating somewhere in this country and beginning the whole scam again under new identities. Their only problem is you. You could take it upon yourself to keep your eyes and ears open, look for something unusual. A clue that would lead you straight to them." Meg gave a couple of hard taps and then smiled crookedly at her own actions. "Funny, I thought I'd stopped this habit of mine. I guess the stress of the last few days has brought it back."

She smiled weakly at him and Adam realized that Meg, too, was contemplating the end of them. That's why the unusual habit of hers had resurfaced. Suddenly he was furious that she didn't believe it was even worth trying—but he stopped himself. Meg was only concluding what he had kept insisting. After all, he didn't believe in happy endings. He refused to tell her how he felt about her.

"That's why they want to make sure that you're silent." Meg returned to their original topic. "And Kelly is their best, most direct route."

Adam digested her words and had to admit they made

a lot of sense. If Reid managed to use Kelly successfully as leverage against him, he would stop any investigation. Then Reid and Gloria could start business fresh. Their operation had only been up and running for two years, and while they had surely netted a hefty profit, there was a lot more to be made. From his other stories, he'd learned that the hard step for any criminal was first crossing that line into illegal territory. Afterward it was difficult to get out.

"Tell me about Kelly," Meg suggested.

Adam sat back in his chair, crossing one jean-clad leg over the other. He might as well tell Meg everything. She deserved it. "Kelly is beautiful, wonderful, sensitive and caring and doesn't know the first thing about taking care of herself. My job has been to look after her."

"Ever since your father died?"

"Yes."

Meg tapped her spoon against the side of her cup and then grabbed the utensil with her other hand. "You look after your mother and brother as well?"

"Yes. I admit I'm probably overprotective now, but I've learned from hard experience that I need to be. Dad died shortly after losing his company, then my mother lost all of her savings and her insurance in a pyramid scheme. Walter, my brother, turned into a juvenile delinquent, while Kelly drifted from dream to dream and man to man."

Meg kept a neutral expression as he told his family's story, but he could read a faint bit of criticism.

"If the men Kelly picked hadn't been so impossible," Adam continued, "I would have been happy for her. I would have been happy for anyone in my family who managed to find some joy for themselves after the devastation of my father's death, but it never happened."

Meg reach across the tabletop and clasped his hand. With shock, he saw that her eyes were glazed with tears. "Maybe you were the one who missed your father most."

Adam looked at her and worked past the lump in his throat. "I think so. I really loved him and admired him.

When Dad was around, our family worked. My mother was always impulsive and flighty, but together they made a nice team. It was afterward that I realized how foolish she could be. Within six months of his death, she had lost every penny she had to live on."

"Oh, how awful." Meg got out of her chair, wrapping her arms around him. Reflexively, he held her to him and felt better.

"By the time I began to get her life in order, Walter was out of control. It wasn't so difficult to help him straighten out. I had been ignoring him during my own grief, but he was the one I really focused on for the next year."

"And then Kelly became a problem?"

"Yes. Although it was just small things. She finished college and had no focus, just all kinds of crazy dreams. I got her a job in an advertising agency, but soon she was having an affair with her married boss. When that affair ended badly she lost her job. Then she started to drift. She tried running her own catering business, but that lasted less than two years.

"One day she claimed she needed to experience new things, an adventure—" Meg winced "—in order to discover herself. The only way to do this, apparently, was through travel. My mother received a postcard from her every once in a while. The last one we received was a picture of the Grand Canyon.

"Kelly was in a coma for two weeks before she came back to us. And she's never told me a word of what happened to her."

"It must have been very difficult for you," Meg said as she rubbed her face into his chest. Adam enjoyed her touch. She was warm and loving and beautiful—everything he could ever want in a woman. But he was making a mistake.

"Your wife was similar?" Meg asked his chest.

When he didn't say anything, she raised her head, searching for the answer in his face. An answer he could see she was afraid to learn.

"Exactly the same. I repeat the same problem."

"And you think you're making the same mistake with me?"

Adam remained silent, but he didn't deny her words. He was making the same mistake, but he couldn't regret it. Meg was spirited and beautiful and wonderful.

If only she wasn't going to break his heart.

"I TOLD YOU I COULD GET us a good flight into New York," Meg said as they deplaned at LaGuardia. In a strange way Adam felt that the closer they got to New York, the further he felt Meg moving away from him. Moreover, he had to restrain himself from pulling her into his arms and kissing her until she agreed to stay with him. At first she'd chattered excitedly about seeing her brother, his new wife and her father, but as the miles distanced them from Arizona, she grew quieter. Twice she'd begun tapping her swizzle stick against the food tray. The second time, she'd thrown it away in disgust.

Passing the luggage carousel, Meg weaved her way through the crowd of anxious passengers who were wondering if their luggage had decided to arrive in New York with them. "This way." She walked through the airport quickly, her carry-on luggage slung over her shoulder. Her slim, jean-clad legs gathered the appreciation of several men, and Adam was forced to glare at all of them.

Meg clearly was a New Yorker. He'd almost doubted her claim to Long Island roots, but her expert maneuvering of LaGuardia made its familiarity to her very clear. "Let's ignore the taxi line," she said of the queue snaking along the street. Instead she headed toward the limousines. "We have an account." She scanned the line and waved at someone, after which a car started to make its way toward them.

"Quick, while none of the officials are looking." Meg took off at a run, heading forward as the limo sped past them and the LaGuardia officials who carefully regulated the New York taxis, then Meg grabbed the door handle and threw herself and her bag into the moving car, and Adam followed suit.

The man behind the wheel accelerated, weaving expertly through the traffic. Once he'd gotten them into the outside fast lane—fast by New York standards—he grinned into the rearview mirror and tipped his hat. "Miss Cooper, how delightful to see you this afternoon. I was not expecting you."

Meg leaned forward and smiled broadly. "Graham, my favorite driver. Now I know I'm really home. I can't believe my luck at having found you!"

The man grinned, checking out Meg and Adam in his rearview mirror. "But I had no idea you were coming back to town. No one has mentioned a word, and they've all talked about you a lot. I was so sorry to hear about your very sad nuptials."

"Fourteen months and one week ago, Graham. My life has changed since then. I'd like you to meet the new man in my life, Adam Smith."

"Ah." Graham nodded as he cut off three cars. "I was sure you would be back. Very nice to meet you, Mr. Smith. Any friend of Meg's can always get a ride from me." He took a hand off the wheel that Adam wished he wouldn't, rifled through paperwork on the seat next to him, took his eyes off the road and then handed a card back to Adam. Adam grasped it quickly, wanting Graham to return his attention to his driving.

Meg and Graham continued a gossip session. Adam studied the Manhattan skyline as it came closer and closer. He wasn't used to the variety of emotions he was experiencing. He liked having Meg with him. He was worried about his sister. He was accustomed to the latter but was disconcerted by the first.

He had to admit that Meg could be correct. Reid might have decided to use Kelly against him. What would happen to his sister? Reid had almost destroyed her once, yet

Adam knew how biddable his sister was. Could she possibly stand up against Reid's tactics? Deep down Adam doubted it. His sister could be manipulated so easily. That was why he'd had to protect her for so long.

"East Fifty-fifth Street," Meg suddenly announced. Adam turned to her, surprised she was giving Graham his address. "I'll drop you off at your apartment. You try to contact Kelly. I'll go to my place and you can phone me as soon as you've found out anything. You will phone me?" she said suddenly, studying him intently.

"Yes." He accepted her number, written on the back of her airline ticket.

The car pulled in front of his apartment. "Meg…"

"Phone me as soon as you learn anything," she said again, but she didn't look at him. She was fiddling with something in her purse. He slid a hand under her chin and raised her face to his. Her brown eyes were filled with concern, her face pale.

"Meg, I…" he began, but didn't know how to continue. They had agreed that they would separate, each returning to his and her regular New York life. Actually, Meg had insisted, claiming she wanted to see her family and check on her old job. Suddenly Adam had a bad feeling about letting her leave him. Maybe he should just go into the apartment with her and make love to her until they both forgot everything except each other.

She broke away from him and gathered her bag, holding it against her chest as if for protection. She looked back at him. "Please, call me. I deserve to be in on the end of this."

"Yes," he agreed, wondering what exactly he was promising. That the end of the investigation was going to be the end of them?

ADAM SLEPT UNCOMFORTABLY, waking early, feeling disgruntled. He took his time showering, then got dressed, made coffee and read the paper, checking his watch. He was meeting Meg at eight. It was Monday, just over a week since he'd met Megan Cooper and begun to fear for his own sanity.

They were meeting for breakfast at the Plaza, Meg's suggestion. As a Long Island heiress, she was used to spending money, so the exclusive hotel's restaurant, usually frequented by New York business and entertainment elite, suited Megan Elizabeth Cooper, he reminded himself yet again, trying not to remember how much he had missed her since they'd separated. He'd only missed her because they had spent almost every second together since they'd met. Had it really been only nine days since he'd met her? He felt like he'd gone through a lifetime with her and was already regretting when it would end.

Nevertheless, he left his apartment too early and was seated in the restaurant by quarter to eight. He ordered coffee and waited, watching New York's elite make deals, schmooze and breakfast.

A very attractive brunette dressed in a killer black suit with a short skirt and high heels entered the restaurant. Adam casually surveyed her, admiring her figure and her confident, hip-swaying walk as he looked past her toward the door, anxiously awaiting Meg. He wiped his sweaty palms on the cloth napkin. He was behaving like a ridiculous schoolboy with a crush on the head cheerleader.

The brunette headed in the general direction of his table. She waved to the publisher of the *New York Star* and stopped to talk to the editor of a women's magazine. The editor motioned for her to sit down, but the woman indicated she had a previous engagement. Adam rechecked his watch. He was still early. It was only ten to eight.

He noticed a pair of very attractive, slim female legs stop at his table. Slowly, appreciatively, he perused the long legs, short skirt and slim hips, past the nicely tailored jacket waist and very nicely curved breasts to…"Meg?"

He couldn't keep the surprise out of his voice as the maître d' seated her. She looked like a successful, capable New York businesswoman.

"Of course," she said, unfolding her napkin. "Close your mouth. You shouldn't be so surprised that I own a designer suit. I told you I was from New York."

"You told me you were from a rich family in Long Island."

"I also told you I was a successful career woman. In Manhattan. You didn't believe me. You assumed because I was willing to be different, because I was searching for adventure, I had to be some kind of a hippie. I'm not."

"Who are you?" he spluttered.

Meg took her time, as if enjoying his discomfort. "I'm the editorial director of Scorpion Books. Or at least I was until my sabbatical. You never know how things change, especially in publishing, when you're away. And yes—" she shook her head sadly "—I do work for my father's company. But I'm a good editor, really good. I've had a lot of offers from our competition and a lot of books on the *New York Times* list, not that I really consider that a good indicator of worth. Nevertheless, I could get a position with any publisher in New York. But I like my family's company. I like what we're trying to do. Not all family is a weight around your neck."

"Point taken," he agreed, but he was still stunned by the appearance of the new Megan Cooper. It was more than the clothes, it was her natural confidence in an atmosphere he admired.

"Don't be fooled," she added mischievously, as if reading his mind. "I'm still nuts."

"I missed you last night." Adam reached for her hand and kissed it.

Meg blushed and pulled her hand away, looking confused. "I did, too. Did you talk to your sister?"

"No." According to his mother, Kelly hadn't come home last night. She had called saying she was okay, but hadn't offered any further information. Adam hadn't wanted to worry his mother by telling her that he was afraid she was with Reid. Would Kelly have really gone with Reid voluntarily? Was she still in love with him even after what he'd done to her? Or was Reid coercing her?

"Do you have any ideas?"

"Yes." Then, unable to help himself, he asked, "Do you always look like this in New York?"

"Always," Meg said blandly. "I am editorial director. In fact, I believe we bid on your last book. You profiled ten successful leaders."

"Scorpion made an offer."

"It was a good book. But you wanted too much money."

"I don't come cheap." He grinned at her.

She smiled a killer smile back, and he suddenly imagined her as a very ruthless negotiator.

"Good thing I have a powerful agent," he added.

"Your agent was dreaming. Most of them do. Never mind all that. What are we going to do about Kelly?"

"My mother hasn't seen her since Saturday; she left the house by herself for the first time. Then there was her call last night. Kelly claimed she was with friends, but my mother wasn't so sure. She thought Kelly's voice sounded strained."

Meg tapped her spoon against her coffee cup. "So Kelly disappeared right around the time Reid Logan could have arrived in town."

"Exactly."

"What about your friends at the *Times*? Did they come up with anything?" Adam had spent last night talking to all his contacts.

"I managed to get more background on Reid, but nothing on what he might be doing right now."

"So what should we do?"

The waiter arrived at their table. Meg smiled at him. "The usual please, Stuart," she said.

Adam ordered pancakes while she considered her options. She was worried not only because she didn't know what else to do, but because of how admiringly Adam was staring at her. He liked the old Megan Elizabeth Cooper, supersuccessful New York editor.

But that was no longer her. Meg could still walk the walk and talk the talk, and she intended to do something about her career with Scorpion, but Adam had to understand the new Megan Elizabeth Cooper was the person she was meant to be. It had taken her thirty-three years to figure out that truth.

They ate and Meg considered. Adam had spent the night working his leads, so he hadn't been able to come to her. At least that's how she'd reassured herself last night. Or was it that he already wanted to end their affair? She wanted so much more. Would she be willing to settle for an affair, no matter how passionate and wonderful it would be while it lasted. And afterward? How would she mend her heart? Now that she'd found her man, would she be able to leave him? How was she going to live without him?

The political editor of the *Times* made his way over to their table and kissed Meg on the cheek. "Oh, hello, Adam. I didn't see you," he said. "Don't tell me you're lucky enough to have sold your book to Meg?"

Meg smiled at the rotund, dapper man. "Thomas, always a delight. You do realize that I'm still waiting for a new book from you. Even a nice collection of essays would make Daddy happy at this point."

"Soon," Thomas promised. "When did you finally get back into town?"

"Just last night."

"And Adam already cornered you for breakfast. He must be desperate to sell that manuscript."

"Our relationship is purely personal," Adam muttered between clenched teeth, glaring at Thomas's hand on Meg's shoulder.

"Lucky man," Thomas said. He kissed Meg's cheek again, whispering, "I've never seen Adam so jealous."

Once Thomas was gone, Adam threw down his napkin. "Come on, let's get out of here."

Along the street Meg didn't have to hurry to catch up with his long-legged stride, since her Manhattan walk was just as quick. She tried to tell him what she was feeling. "When the right book comes across my desk, I just get this funny inkling that it's going to be a hit." Adam made a peculiar sound—probably one of derision, Meg figured, but she continued anyway. "It's very much like the feeling I experienced when you first threatened your way into The Gateway. I just knew you were the man for me."

"You're crazy."

Meg decided to ignore his sarcasm; Adam was worried about his sister. "Where are we going?"

"To the office. I figure Reid may try to leave a message for me there."

"Good idea. Call me when he does. This—" she pointed at a tall, gray building "—is the headquarters of Scorpion. I want to go in and say hello to my father. Tell him I'm back." Meg touched Adam's arm. "Promise you won't do anything without me."

"I'll let you know what I'm up to," Adam hedged.

"No." Meg was firm; she wanted to help Adam. "Like I said before, I deserve to be in on the end of this—and you could use the help. I've been invaluable to you so far." She grinned at him, daring him to disagree.

"That's true." Adam was glad for the excuse to spend more time with her. He wanted to pull her into his arms and kiss her, but he wasn't sure about this new, different Meg.

"I'm going to work. My father may have kept my old job for me." When she turned away, he was unsure whether or not he should kiss her. The Meg from Sedona would have thrown her arms around him and kissed him. He missed that.

"You like the New York Meg, don't you?" Meg smiled sadly. "Let me know the second you hear something about your sister. I feel responsible." She pecked him on the cheek and left.

Adam had never felt so alone in all his life.

15

"YOU'RE BACK!" Peter Cooper took off his telephone head-set, threw out his arms to his daughter, and she hurtled into them.

"I missed you so much." Meg felt so safe and loved in her father's arms that tears pricked at her eyes. She blinked them away, smelling the reassuring scent of her father's tweed jacket and something else...some kind of spicy fragrance. She recognized Jill's perfume and smiled. She was glad her father and Jill, a senior editor with Scorpion, had found each other.

Her father kissed the top of her head. "If you missed me so much, you could have come home a lot sooner," he said gruffly, and cleared his throat. "Let me look at my little girl." He held her at arm's length, but clutched both of her hands as if afraid she would disappear.

Meg gently disengaged herself from him. "I'm not going anywhere, Daddy. I've come home."

"Thank goodness for that. Did you find what you were looking for?"

"Sort of. I figured out some important things about myself. I learned to take more risks."

"You took risks every day here at work."

"Personal risks. I met all kinds of new and interesting people—people I would never have made any time for before. I'm going to try to keep that up." Meg blushed, looking down at her feet and then back to her father. "I met a man."

Her father stilled and then sat behind his big desk. "Tell me about him."

"He's incredibly responsible. He looks after his family

and is always determined to do the right thing." Her father noticeably relaxed. "I met him when he broke into the store I was managing and threatened me with a gun."

"What?" Her father leaped to his feet.

"Relax, Daddy. You were starting to like Adam too much and you've never even met him. Remember, you liked Max almost more than I did."

"I still like Max, even if he treated you very badly."

"No, Max did me a favor. He forced me to really live. To find out what I've been missing. To not make all the safe choices."

"And this is where your young man comes in?"

"I don't think he's so young—definitely forties. But he is very handsome. He's also incredibly stubborn and uncompromising. I have a horrible time making him see things my way." Meg and her father chuckled together, each knowing Meg's desire for control. "Unfortunately, I don't think he's in love with me."

"You love him?"

"Desperately." Meg sighed, her hand smoothing down the black skirt. "I'm not even sure if he likes me very much."

"I'm sure you're wrong, dear. How could he possibly not like you?" her father spluttered.

Meg walked over to her father and perched on his desk, shaking her head. "You're my father, so you have a biased opinion. Adam thinks I'm impetuous, impulsive and flighty. That I can't take care of myself."

Peter Cooper frowned, taking her hand. "How could he ever get such a wrong impression of you? What have you been doing, Megan?"

So Meg told him. She told him all about her travels, about Abigail Milton and the letter Abigail had sent Adam, and almost everything after that. He was her father, after all—Meg couldn't tell him *everything*. Peter Cooper raised his brows and exclaimed periodically, but let Meg finish her story. "You do love him," he said at last.

Meg nodded and the two sat in silence for a few minutes. There was little her father could tell her that she hadn't already worked out for herself, but it was nice to feel his support. Finally she asked, ''Did you keep my office or did you let some eager editorial assistant take over?''

''I had to fight off the hordes, but as the president and your father, I was able to keep it for you. Let's go take a look and I'll show you how the fall list is shaping up.'' The elder Cooper walked her back to her old office, talking excitedly about the books they had acquired since Meg had gone on sabbatical.

Meg loved being back at Scorpion Books. Every hallway and every framed cover was like an old friend, as were her colleagues. Her father left her at her door to return to his office and make some phone calls.

Sarah Tepper still had the office next to Meg, her nameplate still bearing her maiden name, despite that Sarah now had an enormous rock on her left hand.

''Girlfriend, that is a major piece of change my brother put on your hand,'' Meg teased, leaning in the doorway.

''I'm worth every penny,'' Sarah said, without raising her head from the cover she was proofing. ''We even eloped, since you weren't anywhere to be found to invite you to the wedding. Jay was as annoyed with you as I was.'' Then she raised her head and smiled. ''But I also understood.'' Sarah got up, walked over to Meg and embraced her. ''Girlfriend, it's good to have you home.''

ADAM'S BOYHOOD HOME was exactly how Meg had imagined it: a small two-storey in Queens. For decor, his mother favored a lot of pastels and yellows and doilies. Adam shifted uncomfortably on an imitation Regency chair. He didn't like meeting Kelly and Reid at his mother's house, but that was what the letter delivered by courier late this afternoon had insisted upon. Reid had also demanded his mother be there—knowing Adam wouldn't do anything to put his mother in danger.

He clenched his fists, wishing it was Reid's neck he was squeezing between his fingers. The man was a complete scoundrel to use her as a shield.

"I'm really sorry about this, Mother," he declared again. He was also sorry that he'd had to bring Meg along, but the note had insisted upon her presence, too. He'd really messed up the investigation of this case. Now all the women he cared about were in danger. At least that's how he'd phrased it as he'd driven Meg out to Queens.

Meg would have hugged the fact that he cared about her to herself, except for the tone of grim resignation in his voice.

Mrs. Smith patted her son on his knee. "Don't worry about me, dear. The tea leaves said I would be in for some fortuitous changes in the near future. And Madame Zordova hinted that some dangerous men might be entering my life, but that it would all work out well."

"Madame Zordova?" Meg asked, absolutely delighted with Adam's mother. Mrs. Smith had a cloud of white curls, sparkling blue eyes and was wearing a pink dress, pink lipstick, pink clip-on earrings with matching necklace and bracelet. Her shoes were pink with black polka dots. After this was all over, Meg intended to ask Caroline Smith where she had found them. Meg had a dress the shoes would match perfectly.

"She's my personal psychic. I tried those people on the phone, but they were a sad disappointment. I don't like to speak ill of anyone, but, well, I do believe that the person I spoke to was nothing but a charlatan. Madame Zordova is a treasure. She's the one who told me I should buy the poodle, and I've never been so happy with anything. Isn't that right, Sweetums?" she asked the poodle that was trying to steal a cookie off of Adam's plate. Meg was quite sure that Caroline changed the poodle's bow daily to match her outfit.

"Of course, when she talked about the dangerous men, I thought she had foretold of the purse snatcher, but now

I see she was seeing much further into the future." Caroline gave Sweetums one of her own cookies.

"You never told me about any purse snatcher." Adam sat up straight, frowning at his mother. "This is a dangerous neighborhood. I wish you'd listen to me and move to those condos in Virginia."

Caroline pursed her mouth. "Like they don't have criminals in Virginia. I'm not going to move from the house your father and I worked so hard for. Where I raised my children and spent the happiest days of my life. Here Sweetums—come have another cookie." Caroline pulled the dog into her lap and fussed with the bow. When she looked back to her son, her eyes were suspiciously bright. "This is the house where I lived with my husband. I didn't tell you about the purse snatching because I knew you would overreact, and besides, it all turned out well. I simply blew on my emergency whistle, which I always keep around my neck, and Sergio, the dry cleaner's son, ran right after the juvenile delinquent and caught him. That's why I like this neighborhood. All my friends live here. It's where your father and I lived. I am not moving!"

Adam remained silent, but Meg suspected he'd pick over this topic again with his mother. The poor woman. Meg sympathized with her. Adam did have an annoying habit of believing he knew what was best for everyone.

"Who is this man who is meeting you here?"

Adam stood and began to pace, his presence filling up the small room. "Who he is doesn't matter. As soon as he arrives, I want you to go to the kitchen and stay there. No matter what, don't come out."

Caroline Smith put down her tea cup very firmly. "I most certainly will not hide out in my own kitchen like some common criminal."

"Mother, I don't want you in any danger."

"And I don't want anyone hurting my little boy. What kind of a mother would I be if I left you and this lovely girl alone with a group of hooligans? Now what is it that you're not telling me?"

Adam remained silent, pacing around the coffee table, over the ottoman and around the nesting side tables.

"It's Kelly. Somehow she's involved in this. Oh, I knew something awful happened to her," Caroline said, her voice rising. She stopped and took a deep breath. "Don't look so surprised, Adam. I'm not the blithering idiot you seem convinced I am."

"Mother, I've never thought any such thing."

"Yes, you do. I can see it on your face." Caroline turned to Meg. "When my husband died I was devastated—I just couldn't imagine a life without my George. After George had lost the business, he became obsessed with regaining it. He had a hard time imagining a good life where he wasn't a business success, so he tried all kinds of get-rich-quick schemes. After his heart attack, after he was gone, I learned he'd invested what was left of our savings on some biotech stocks. He gambled and we lost everything. Luckily, the house was paid off and I have my small pension from teaching. Plus, I do some tutoring on the side, so I make do."

"Mother, I...I didn't know." Adam sat next to her and took her hands between his own.

As Caroline squeezed her son's hands, Meg could see the similarity between them: the same steady, concerned eyes, a firmness around the mouth. "I couldn't tell you the truth, Adam. You were hurting enough already, so I lied and said that I had lost the money on a pyramid scheme."

"You lied to me?"

"I wanted to protect you. The problem was that it worked a little too well. You took on all the responsibility for the family. At first I was happy to let you take over, because I was trying to come to terms with my life without George. It took a long time." Caroline removed her hands from her son's, found a lace handkerchief and blew her nose. "I don't want to hurt you, Son, especially after how good you've been to me, but it's time we all began to stand up for ourselves. Including Kelly.

"I know all the problems she's been through—and how much worry she's caused you—but whatever it is, I am going to help her. I am her mother."

A key being inserted into the front door stopped whatever Adam might have said in reply. As the door slowly opened, Meg found herself holding her breath, hoping her plan worked. Would Kelly expect her brother to rescue her yet again?

The first person to enter was Kelly, a waiflike blond with a heart-shaped face. She was very thin, with shadows under her eyes, her T-shirt and leggings emphasizing her slight build. Following her was Reid, who looked even more the cowboy surrounded by all the chintz and lace in the living room. Gloria glided in looking splendid in blue capri pants and a matching blue sweater set.

"Well, well," Reid said with a chuckle, "the family's all here."

"Just like you demanded," Adam said, stopping his pacing, clenching his fists by his sides. "What are you offering?"

Reid grabbed Kelly's arm and pulled her into the center of the room. "I'm offering you Kelly's freedom. Tell them, Kelly. Tell your darling brother how you liked to help us with our little venture."

Kelly had been busy staring at the floor, but now she raised her sad face and in a quiet voice said, "Reid told me about the guests at the ranch. About the identities Gloria created for some of them." She scuffed her boot against the hardwood floor. "I was kind of jealous because Reid was so proud of his sister, so I wanted to help. I wanted to do something to prove that I could be smart and brave, too, so I offered to act as a courier. I picked up documents from Washington and New York several times."

"Why didn't you tell me?" Adam asked.

"After the accident, I didn't remember. Not for weeks.

And then only bits and pieces…nothing more until I saw that letter from Abby." She gave a weak smile. "That's when I began to get scared. To wonder if my accident really had been an accident. I didn't want you involved in the mess that I had made by helping Reid."

"And I have the signed receipts," Reid added grimly. He looked at Kelly with an expression that Meg couldn't make out. It almost looked like…regret.

Reid loosened his hold on Kelly's arm. "So the deal is very simple. You hand over all your information on me and you promise to drop the investigation." He smiled bitterly. "I trust your word. Gloria and I will disappear under our new identities, and you get to keep your sister out of jail. If you try to find us, I will send the FBI all my information on Kelly and she'll go to jail as an accomplice, while Gloria and I will still be free."

Meg looked at Adam, wondering what his response would be, but was unable to read his hard face. He had spent a lifetime looking after his little sister; would he be able to stop now? If Meg were in his situation and her own brother was in trouble, wouldn't she do everything she could to protect him? Hadn't she covered as much as possible for Jay when he was a prime suspect in the embezzlement at Scorpion?

Kelly looked at her brother, fear filling her eyes, her lower lip trembling. "Adam, I'm so sorry."

Adam opened his arms and Kelly rushed forward. He crushed his sister to him. "Don't worry," he said, brushing her hair off her face. "I'm not going to let anything happen to you." Kelly nodded.

"No, Adam, don't do it," Meg said loudly, too loudly for her own ears. She could hardly believe what she was going to say, but she had to. "Don't make the decision for Kelly. Let her decide."

"Foolish sentimentalist," Gloria sneered at her. "Do you think Kelly wants to take the rap for something she did because she was in love with my brother?"

Kelly broke away from Adam and stared at Meg. "Who are you?"

"My name is Megan Elizabeth Cooper. I'm in love with your brother."

"Oh." Kelly studied her mother, who was sitting quietly on her chair, and then looked at Reid. Meg watched in amazement as Kelly's face showed all her emotions: fear, worry, love. "You know, I really loved you a lot."

Reid took a step toward Kelly and then checked himself when he saw Adam move forward, his fists raised. "I loved you, too. I'm sorry you lost interest in our little business."

"It was wrong! It may have taken me a long time to realize it, but what you and Gloria and I were doing began to eat away at me. I had to leave before I started hating you."

"What happened at the end, Kelly? How did you get hurt?" Meg asked.

Reid turned to his sister. "You hurt Kelly. Why?"

Gloria narrowed her eyes. "Joshua went a little too far in delivering my message to her."

"You were responsible," Adam said to Gloria. "All this time I thought it was Reid."

"If I had known…" Reid glared at his sister. Then he turned to Kelly. "What happened?"

"I told Gloria I was leaving. I asked her to give you my message that…that I loved you, but I couldn't agree with what you were doing any longer. I was afraid you would try to convince me to stay and I didn't trust myself to say no to you.

"But then I had a car accident, halfway home. I got scared because my brakes failed and you had just had them checked out for me a few days earlier. I thought you had tampered with the brakes, that you were trying to kill me."

"I never wanted to hurt you," Reid said sincerely. "I loved you very much."

Gloria took her brother's arm, bringing his attention

back to her. "We needed the insurance. Joshua was just supposed to scare Kelly a little, so that she would know what would happen if she told anyone about our profitable operation."

"But how did you get back home after the accident?" Meg asked. "Adam said you were really badly hurt."

"I was, but I didn't know how much at the time. My only thought was that I had to get home, that Adam could make everything right for me, just like he always does."

Kelly stepped away from both Adam and Reid, standing alone in the center of the room. She bit her bottom lip, then took a deep breath, looking at her brother. "That was the same thought I had this evening, after Reid told me you had followed my tracks to Arizona and that he was now going use me to get you off his back. I wanted to get home and let my big brother fix my problem. I'm really sorry, Adam, but I was scared of going to jail."

"You're not going to jail," he said firmly.

But Kelly straightened and looked around the room. "No, I'm not going to hurt you anymore. It's time I learned to take responsibility for my own life." She smiled at Meg. "You're right. I'm making the choice. Take all your evidence to the police and I'll testify in court about everything I know."

"Good for you," Meg exclaimed.

"Kelly…" Adam began, but fell silent when he saw the gun Gloria had aimed at his sister.

"You silly girl," she hissed at Kelly. "I am not going to let you ruin us."

Adam was sure he saw the finger actually moving on the trigger, and he was preparing to jump and knock his sister out of the way when a voice behind Gloria said, "Freeze. It's the police. Put down your weapon." A short stocky man had entered the hallway from the kitchen, holding up a badge and aiming a gun at Gloria.

Gloria looked behind her and seemed to calculate her chances for a minute.

"Put down your gun," Reid told his sister. "You're not helping the situation."

Gloria lowered her gun and the policeman took it out of her hands. "Call my station and ask for backup," he said to Meg.

"You can't hold us," Reid said. "You don't have proof of anything."

"I saw with my very own eyes this lovely woman threaten to kill Ms. Smith. And I do believe the pair of you have held Ms. Smith captive for the past twenty-four hours. We call that kidnapping in this town. By the time we've processed all the paperwork on you, I'm sure the FBI will have had a chance to review Mr. Smith's files on you and decide on new charges." The police officer smiled grimly at his two suspects.

"Who are you?" Adam demanded, not believing what was going on.

"Doug Hatfield. I usually work homicide, but Meg asked for a special favor tonight."

Caroline Smith rose and went to her daughter. "Yes, dear, the charming police lieutenant was in our kitchen, waiting for a good time to arrest your criminals."

"What if Kelly hadn't agreed to cooperate?" Adam demanded.

"Well, that was a bit tricky," Doug Hatfield acknowledged. "Meg was hoping that she could talk your sister around, so we agreed that I would wait in the kitchen and only come out if your sister agreed to do what was right. She did." The police officer nodded at Kelly. "You're a brave young woman."

Adam felt his legs about to collapse under him so he sat down on a chair and watched the activity around him. Meg was on the phone as Doug Hatfield handcuffed both Gloria and Reid. Caroline Smith pulled her daughter over to the sofa and sat next to her, holding her hands comfortingly. Finally Adam turned to the policeman and asked, "How do you know Meg?"

"She's my editor," Doug Hatfield said proudly.

_____ **16** _____

"I STILL CAN'T BELIEVE you did that."

Adam stepped closer to Meg, clenching and unclenching his fists, and she had to fight to stand her ground. She'd expected Adam to be annoyed about her backup plan, but he was coldly furious, which scared her. She raised her chin, meeting his dark green, angry eyes. "I was doing the only responsible thing. You would have behaved exactly the same if it had been my brother."

"No, I wouldn't," Adam said.

"You're lying. You wouldn't have wanted to see me throw away all my principles to protect someone I loved. I couldn't let you do that, either. I know you, Adam Smith. You would have hated yourself."

Adam ignored her words and looked around her apartment instead. "Nice," he said sarcastically, and Meg sighed. Winning Adam over to her point of view wasn't going to be easy. Meg was certain, though, that deep down Adam knew she was right—he just didn't like to admit it. Didn't like to admit that by babying his sister all these years, he hadn't done her much of a favor at all.

He stalked over to her window with the spectacular view of Central Park. Meg had inherited her apartment from her mother's side of the family. It was far too big for only one person, but she liked having the space for entertaining. She'd set up one of the rooms as her office, a convenient place to keep the ever-growing pile of manuscripts.

She'd never done as much entertaining as she'd meant to—mostly she'd hosted a couple of book launches—but now she vowed she was going to take the time to entertain. No matter what Adam decided about them, she was going to change her old New York life. She was going to remember the lessons she'd learned in Sedona.

To distract herself, she picked up a pillow, turning it round and round in her hands. "You would have done the same if it was my brother, Jay," Meg insisted. "I know because I did for years. I always made excuses for him and covered for him—until he met Sarah Tepper. He learned to stand up for himself when he finally fell in love. But until then I was holding him back. Always wanting the best for him, I hurt him."

"What if Kelly hadn't agreed to testify? Your police lieutenant would still have had to arrest her." Adam kept his back to her, but she heard the anguish in his voice.

Meg longed to go over to him and wrap her arms around him, but she felt a chasm growing larger and larger between them. She hugged herself. "Not necessarily. Doug was doing this as a favor to me. I was hoping that he'd be willing to break the rules and just forget he'd spent an evening in your mother's kitchen if you had gone along with Reid's deal."

"It was a big risk," Adam grumbled, turning to face her. He looked tired. "You should have told me what you were planning."

"If it hadn't worked, you would never have known about it. No one would have except your mother."

"Humph. You should have told me."

Meg decided to ignore his grumbles and that bleak expression on his face. She needed to do something, so she walked toward her kitchen. "I'm going to make coffee. I could offer you something stronger, if you like."

"What? No, coffee is fine." Adam turned back to the window.

Meg brewed the coffee, pulled out a tray and two of her favorite cups. When she caught herself tapping an overture against the sugar bowl with her coffee spoon, she vowed to see a hypnotist and stop the habit. It had only returned once she'd feared that Adam didn't want to be with her. When the coffee was ready, she carried the tray into the living room, where a defeated Adam was sitting in one of her white-and-beige-striped wing chairs.

Had she done that to him? He thought loving her would be that terrible? Meg took a deep breath and stepped forward. No matter what, she wasn't going to make him unhappy. But she also knew she wasn't the woman he wanted.

She handed him a cup and sat in her favorite chair across from him. Wrapping her hands around her own mug, she enjoyed the heat and aroma of the coffee. Finally, when she could stand the suspense no longer, she asked, "What now?"

He sipped his coffee and then looked at her levelly. "It looks like we've reached the end of your adventure."

"I mean about us."

"Yes, I know." He stretched his legs in front of him. "I must admit I rather like this new you."

Meg's heart sank. "You mean the successful, capable businesswoman."

"Yes."

"I'm no longer that old Meg Cooper. I liked my search for adventure. It brought me you."

"Three kisses and we'll be lovers."

Meg blushed. "I'd never said anything like that before. Taken a chance like that. Been so bold or so brave."

Adam got out of his chair and crossed the room, pulling her to her feet, keeping her hands crushed between his. "Meg, we could have something. I care for you."

"Do you love me?"

Adam didn't say anything, and Meg felt a sinking sensation in her stomach. Adam still didn't trust his feelings for her. She was doomed. "Oh, Adam!" She stroked his face, brushing his hair off his forehead. "I love you, more than I thought possible." He pulled her tightly against him and kissed her until she was dizzy. The room spun away from her and she realized Adam had swept her up in his arms.

"Which way to the bedroom?" Adam nuzzled her neck, his breath hot against her skin.

"Adam, stop. We need to talk."

He stopped but didn't put her down. "Why do women always want to talk just when things are getting interesting?"

"Why do men always insist that sex is the answer to all problems?" Adam loosened his grip on her and let her slide to the floor. Once her feet touched ground, he let go of her completely, and Meg felt bereft.

"Adam, I want you to be happy. I don't want to be a burden or an obligation to you."

"Trust me, I don't see you as a burden. I find you, however, very, very appealing." He stepped forward and Meg backed up a step. She raised a hand to his chest to halt him and had to stop herself from clutching the material of his shirt and pulling him close to her.

"Three kisses," he reminded her.

"Yes, but Adam, you don't believe in the three kisses. In love."

"Of course I believe in it. It's brought me nothing but trouble all my life."

"That's what I mean! You see love as something bad. All the time you say you care for me, all the time you love me in bed, you're thinking about the end. About how we'll hurt each other."

"Well, I have to admit I did at first. I thought you fell into the pattern I've been repeating all my life. I believed you were like Allison and Kelly. But I've learned that you're not. You're a successful woman more than able to take care of herself."

Meg waited for him to say that he loved her spirit of adventure, her desire for change, but when he didn't she knew she'd lost him. "Oh, Adam. I told you I was perfectly capable of taking care of myself."

Adam frowned at her. "I see it now." He took her hand. "Let's go to bed."

"No, you only see my old New York self. That's no

longer the real me. The real me is the woman you met in Sedona. The woman who, after taking one look at you, knew you were her life mate. Who said and believed in things like three kisses." She hung her head. "That's the woman I am."

He grabbed her by the arms. "No, you're not. That was just a—a vacation We could be something together."

Meg still waited, hoping for him to tell her he loved her. "I love you," she said again. Adam opened his mouth, but still didn't say anything. "Oh," she said weakly, finally accepting that he would never want to love her. "Maybe you should go."

"Meg, please. We should…"

"Date? I know, Adam. I know you're the man I want to spend my life with—my whole life. I have no doubt. But you do."

"I do," he admitted, looking as if he wanted to say more.

"Goodbye," she said again, feeling such a sharp pain in her heart that she didn't know if she could stop herself from calling out to Adam when he left. Instead, she turned her back to him, hoping that when she was strong enough to face him, he would be gone.

He was. The man of her dreams had left her life.

ADAM RETURNED to his old life, the life he'd enjoyed before he'd been ambushed by Megan Elizabeth Cooper. Except it was no good. His job was still interesting; he managed to cover several big stories and his editor nominated one of his pieces for an award.

Kelly received a suspended sentence and a job offer from Abigail Milton to return to Sedona and manage the rebuilt The Gateway. She took the offer, and her letters home were filled with news about Sedona residents— news he looked forward to hearing. Freddie's name came up more than anyone else's and Caroline Smith had asked what Adam would think of Freddie as a son-in-law. As much as he hated to admit it, Adam thought Freddie might make an excellent husband for Kelly.

Determinedly, Adam had asked out three very wonderful women, women who were the type he thought should be part of his life: Beverly, a lawyer; Charlene, an investment banker; and Maureen, a children's librarian. Unfortunately, he'd been bored by the first two. Beverly had spent far too much time talking about her career and the political moves she had to make within her firm to make partnership. Meg had never once talked about her career when they'd been together. Charlene had kept offering him financial advice and encouraging him to diversify his portfolio. She had spoken ominously about how much money they would need for retirement, and how much university education for their children would cost. Her sense of gloom and doom was so different from Meg's optimism and determination—even when someone was pointing a gun at her.

Maureen, however, was perfect. She was attractive and liked to talk about ideas. She understood and appreciated his passion for writing and discovering the truth. She cared for children, but she wasn't obsessed by her biological clock. They had had a nice dinner date, followed by an evening at the symphony. It turned out they shared a passion for music.

One Sunday they walked across the Brooklyn Bridge and meandered along the waterfront, passing the vendors. Maureen picked up a hat, red felt with a bright pink rose, and tried it on. "What do you think? Too silly for a children's librarian?"

Adam looked up at her animated face, and for a second she reminded him so much of Meg that he had to take in a deep breath.

"You don't like it?" Maureen asked. "I thought it looked rather nice on me."

"It looks great on you. I was just thinking of something else." Adam nodded at the vendor. "She'll take it." He pulled out his wallet.

Maureen frowned at him, but she waited for him to pay before looping her arm through his. "Let's walk farther along the river."

Arm in arm they strolled, stopping to watch the sun set. Adam wondered what the hell was wrong with him. Maureen was the perfect woman for him. Bright, charming, funny, levelheaded. Everything he'd always thought he wanted. And what did he feel for Maureen? Nothing. A big fat zero. He'd met the perfect woman and all he could think about was that she wasn't Meg. His senses didn't go on alert when she entered the room. He didn't keep thinking about her. When something good or bad happened to him he didn't long to tell Maureen; he longed to tell Meg.

"Adam, we need to talk," Maureen said, still looking out at the river.

"Most conversations that begin with those words never end very well."

"I like you an awful lot, Adam. So much so that I didn't object when you paid for my hat before I'd decided I really wanted it. You do have a habit of deciding what is best for other people."

"I've been told it's a bad habit of mind. Sorry."

"Told by the woman you're dating me to forget?" Maureen turned to him and smiled wistfully. "It's pretty easy to tell that you're pining for another woman. You compare everything I do to her."

"I do not. Well, maybe sometimes." He took Maureen's hands between his. "There was someone, but she was all wrong for me. You're the kind of woman I want—" He felt something solid jab into his back and Maureen gasped.

"Nice and steady, now," the young kid's voice behind him said. "Alls I want is your money. And that sharp ring your lady is wearing."

Adam raised his hands, cursing the fact that he and Maureen had turned a corner along the river so that no one else could see them. Maureen paled, her hands shaking as she pulled the ring off her finger.

"My wallet's in my right-hand pocket. I'm going to turn around and give it to you." Adam spoke the words slowly and confidently, and turned around slowly so as not to frighten their young assailant.

The kid didn't look much more than seventeen, but Adam knew anyone could be dangerous. Adam reached into his pocket and pulled out his wallet. The young punk grabbed it and then turned to Maureen.

"I want that ring."

Tears were streaming down Maureen's face as she held out her ring. "It belonged to my grandmother. She didn't have a lot to leave behind, but she gave me this on my seventeenth birthday."

Adam moved in front of Maureen, blocking her from the kid. The boy looked at him with great surprise. He tucked Adam's wallet into the front of his jacket, looking up and down the street nervously. "Hey, man. Stand still."

Adam held up his hands again, making eye contact. The way sweat broke out on their assailant's face gave him hope that the kid was fairly new to his life of crime and Adam would be able to get him and Maureen away without being hurt. "My date wants to keep her ring. You can have all of our money—I even have a really nice watch, a Rolex." Adam unclasped it from his wrist and held it out.

The kid looked around, confused. "Man, you're weird."

"I don't want any trouble. My date just wants to keep her ring."

"I say what goes."

"Of course. You're absolutely in charge." Adam waited as the kid shifted his weight from foot to foot, then lowered the gun and held out his hand.

"Give me the watch."

Adam tossed it to him and with a shake of his head the kid ran off.

Maureen grabbed him by the arm. "Don't go after him! He had a gun."

Adam wrapped his arms around her. "Don't worry. He's gone."

"Adam, I was so scared." She shook, her teeth chattering.

"I know. But it's okay now." He rubbed her back. "I've been mugged three times."

"Five, this makes my fifth mugging," she muttered into his jacket, and then stepped back. "I swore if I was mugged one more time I was going to move back to Wisconsin."

"Are you?"

"No. Despite everything, I like New York." She gave him a wobbly smile. "Come on, I want you to take me home. That was more than enough adventure for one night."

Adam took her arm and they walked until they found a taxi and settled in for the drive to Maureen's apartment. All the while, ever since she'd said the word *adventure*, and even before, when he'd wondered if he might be killed, he thought of Meg.

Try as he might, he could no longer pretend. He could no longer ignore the truth. He loved Meg. He'd known for a long time but he just hadn't wanted to admit it. Or rather, he hadn't been willing to admit it to her. He'd just thought his love for her might go away. That he would be able to cure himself of Meg if he gave himself enough time. It had been three months and not one iota of feeling had changed.

Meg had ruined other women for him.

Truth to tell, he didn't want any other women. He wanted Megan Elizabeth Cooper.

Every fear he'd had was just that: fear. He was a coward when it came to love. Sure, he'd had a bad marriage, but that didn't mean anything when it came to Meg. He and Meg were different from him and Allison. No, what had frightened him had been how carried away he became around Meg. He lost his balance, his tightly held, rational grip on the rest of the world, when he was with her. When he was with Meg, he was more alive than he'd ever been in his life.

At Maureen's apartment he walked her up the steps of the brownstone. She fiddled in her bag for her keys, then after she'd found them, she kept her head bent for some time. "Adam, I don't think I can see you anymore."

"Why not?" Even though he'd been trying to think of some graceful way to say goodbye to her, he was still disconcerted.

Maureen sighed and looked up at him sadly. "Because of tonight. I'm grateful you rescued my grandmother's ring, but…you were foolhardy. Or maybe you were just being a hero, but I can't live like that. Worrying that you would do something else crazy like that. I want a much safer, calmer life." She smiled regretfully. "You're a great guy, Adam Smith. But you're not the man for me."

MEG WALKED INTO her apartment, kicking off her shoes the second she stepped over the threshold, dropping her manuscript bag and rubbing her toes. On one foot she hopped over to her couch and collapsed. Staring up the ceiling, she wondered if she was tired enough to go straight to bed.

And dream about Adam? No, it would be better to read a manuscript and watch infomercials on television until she fell asleep on the couch. She'd had to stop watching her favorite old movies because most of them were love stories and depressed her. She'd thought she'd been upset when Max had betrayed her. Now she knew her pain at that time had only been hurt pride. She wasn't sure she'd ever lose her feelings for Adam.

The worst of it was that she wasn't even mad at him. She just couldn't make him love her.

"Tough day?" asked a deep voice from somewhere near her window.

She jumped off the couch, clutching her arms over her chest. Was she beginning to hallucinate? "What are you doing here?" Her voice squeaked.

So much for cool and sophisticated. She'd told herself over and over again that when she met Adam again she wouldn't let her face betray all of her emotions. It wasn't working. Her heart began to pound heavily and she felt heat creep into her cheeks.

Adam stepped into the light, dressed all in black—the same black jeans and leather jacket he'd worn the first evening. He looked pale and there were deep lines around his mouth. "I've come to kidnap you."

"Kidnap me? Don't be ridiculous." A little bubble of hope began to grow within her, but she quashed it down. It had been over three months since he'd left her. For the first few days she'd had to drag herself out of bed and try to get on with her life. What was Adam thinking now? "How are you going to kidnap me?"

"I have a gun." He took a menacing step toward her.

Meg held her ground and raised her chin. "No, you don't."

Adam stopped and scowled at her. "Meg, don't be ridiculous."

"If you're going to kidnap me you have to show me your gun." She crossed her arms. "Otherwise, it's not a real adventure. How can I possibly trust you if you haven't come prepared to kidnap me properly?"

Adam's lips twitched, but he suppressed his smile. "I can't believe you. You haven't seen me in months."

"Three months, two weeks and four days." Meg held her ground.

"You are the most impossible woman. When I planned this, I thought you'd fly into my arms and tell me you loved me…." He looked at her hopefully, but Meg only continued to wait. "Right. I'm here to tell you, to tell you…" Adam took a deep breath, looking nervous

"…and you want to see my gun," he finished in a disbelieving tone.

"I insist on seeing your gun. Otherwise you can't kidnap me. It's not how it's done. I want to know you're serious. That you're interested in more than a brief fling. What do you want to tell me?"

In irritation, Adam reached behind him and produced the same gun he had first pointed at her the night they met.

Meg smiled. Her toes tingled and the bands of logic and reason she'd wrapped tightly around her heart started to loosen. "What do you want to tell me?"

"I love you."

"How long have you known that?"

"You're supposed to say you love me back."

"I said that before. Now I want to know how long you've known."

"I've known from the first time you kissed me."

"The first time!"

Adam moved in on her with a wicked gleam in his eyes and Meg retreated. "The second kiss made me crazy with lust for you."

"And then?"

"The third kiss convinced me I'd never be happier than if you would agree to spend the rest of your life with me."

"But—but you don't want to be with me."

Adam grimaced. "I tried it without you. I even dated some very suitable women. They all bored me. I couldn't stop comparing them to you."

Meg quashed the quick rise of jealousy at the thought of him with other women. Then she wanted to throw herself into his arms, but she had to make sure. "But I'm the Megan Cooper from Sedona. I like trusting my instincts and taking chances."

"I know exactly who you are." Adam smiled, his green eyes boring into her soul. Deliberately he walked across the room to her sofa and sat down. Then he pointed the Smith and Wesson .45 at her. "Come here."

She looked at him in amazement as he put the gun aside and leaned back against the sofa. Surely he didn't think he could just walk back into her life—or break into her apartment—and she'd welcome him back. Unable to help herself, she took a step closer.

His arm shot out and he captured her wrist and pulled. With a muffled cry, she tumbled on top of him. Adam shifted slightly, letting her fall between his legs. Then he smiled at her.

"Let me up," she said, but his legs and the hand still holding her arm held her prisoner.

"I caught you. I'm keeping you."

"Are you?"

He ran his free hand down her shoulder along her back, and then down her legs to the hem of her skirt. Every area he touched tingled, and she delighted in the feel of her breasts and stomach pressed against him. He began to raise the hem of her skirt very slowly, running his fingers along her bare leg, and she gasped as she felt herself respond to him.

"Adam, what are you doing?"

"You owe me."

"What do you want?"

"I want you," he said as both his hands stroked from her shoulders to her knees. He pressed his hips up slowly and rhythmically into her waiting juncture, and she could feel how ready he was for her seduction. He increased the slight movement of his hips and she couldn't help but press herself against him. His eyes smoldered with burning passion as he kept looking at her, waiting for her response.

Two could play at this game.

She raised herself up on her arms so that she was looking down at Adam and then moved her body a little higher. "Kiss my breasts," she said in a throaty, brazen voice. Adam's eyes widened in surprise and then he pulled up her blouse and touched her with his lips through the lace of her bra. "More," she begged. "Undo my bra." With fumbling fingers he obeyed and then held her breasts as he laved and kissed them. He used his teeth on her nipples and she welcomed the edge of pain.

She reached between them, undid his belt and lowered his zipper, then slipped her hand inside. First she cupped his hardness, feeling the power in her hand, and then she freed his erection. She kept her hand on him, stroking until he moaned between her breasts.

Meg wanted him now. She wished she could be naked, but all she could do was pull down her panties. As soon as they were off she took him inside her and sighed in relief. His hands went to her hips immediately and they began a fast rhythm, not touching anywhere else, not talking. Meg closed her eyes in sheer bliss, but then she opened them again, wanting to watch Adam's face.

He was looking at her and she smiled, feeling powerful, like a female goddess. They moved together in strong sure strokes, faster and harder until Meg felt the beginning of her orgasm. A small exclamation escaped her lips and Adam drove himself into her twice more before she felt his release. She stayed with him all the way, riding out their storm together until she collapsed on his chest.

They lay together for several minutes, her arms around his neck, him cradling her to his chest. He brushed his lips against her ear. "Damn, that was good."

"Yes."

"You are the woman for me." Adam brushed her hair off her face and kissed her forehead. Gently he helped her stand up and straighten her clothes. She watched him, mesmerized, as he walked back to her window and picked up one of her travel bags. "Put your shoes back on, unless you want to be kidnapped barefoot."

"Adam, you're crazy. Did you really break into my apartment?"

"Yes, you've turned me into a desperate man, Megan Elizabeth Cooper. I can't live without you, so I'm taking you."

Meg couldn't help the grin that split her face. "Where are you taking me? I should change."

"Oh, no you don't. I like this New York City look of yours, your short skirt and high heels. I'm looking forward to stripping them off you. It's one of my personal fantasies. As long as my Meg from Sedona is wearing them."

Meg laughed and ran to Adam. He caught her as she wrapped her legs around his waist and kissed him. Her senses reeled as she breathed in the smell of Adam, tasted him, felt him. He cupped one hand under her bottom and dragged the other through her hair, angling her lips so he could take their kiss deeper.

"Enough of that for now," Adam finally gasped, putting her back down.

Meg pouted. "Why do men always say that just as it's getting interesting?"

"Come on." Adam took her hand. "Let's go. By the time we get to three kisses I plan to have you naked and in a bed where we can take forever saying hello again."

Meg put on her shoes. "Okay. But where are we going?"

Adam looked at her with love on his face. "Megan Cooper, I love you and I want to spend the rest of my days with you. Together, we're going to have a lifetime of adventures!"

_____ Epilogue _____

MEG STEPPED THROUGH the church doors, blinking for one moment at the contrast between the bright sunlight and the dimmer vestibule. She grinned and had to restrain herself from skipping down the aisle to her groom. The man she'd waited all her life to marry. Their life together would be the greatest adventure of all.

Her father squeezed her arm. "Ready?" he asked.

"Raring to go," she said with a smile. She stretched up and kissed him on the cheek. "Thank you for agreeing to have the wedding here. Sedona means so much to me and Adam and our new friends."

Her two attendants began the walk down the aisle, first Kelly, who was sporting a brand-new engagement ring from Freddie. The ring he had made for her this time truly was one-of-a-kind. Then Abigail followed, grinning broadly at her friends as she passed them along the aisle.

"I only want my daughter to be happy. When you and Adam disappeared six months ago, I was beginning to fear the pair of you had eloped."

"No, I wanted a proper romantic wedding with all my friends and family." Meg smiled at everyone as she and her father began their studied walk. Jason winked at her and held Michelle's hand, and Meg glowed. Love was making her positively giddy. She wanted everyone to be as happy as she.

Adam had been perfectly willing to marry her at any point during their travels, but Meg had insisted that she wanted a proper church wedding. She'd agreed, however, that they could have their honeymoon first. And she had enjoyed their perfectly splendid adventure. She and

Adam decided they would travel together across the country with no particular agenda. Even including the time they came across the poor lost child they'd restored to her parents and the time they'd foiled the bank robbers, the adventure had been fabulous. After six months, they agreed it was time to return to their more regular lives, confident that even the most mundane existence would still be good because they were together. Two weeks ago they had arrived back in Sedona, and Meg had declared that this was where they would be married.

She had called her friend Emma Delaney Thorne, Max's wife, and insisted that the bridal consultant owed her big and had to plan her a wedding in less than two weeks. Emma had groaned but agreed. After all, she did owe Meg a wedding.

Meg reached the front of the church and took her place next to Adam, the place she belonged for the rest of her life. Adam grinned rather foolishly at her, his eyes a little too bright, and Meg knew exactly what he was feeling. They were truly blessed at having found each other.

She, Megan Elizabeth Cooper, the adventurous bride, was marrying the man she hadn't even known she was dreaming of. She couldn't have wished for a better ending. Or for a better hero.

HARLEQUIN®

Temptation

He's strong. He's sexy.
He's up for grabs!

Harlequin Temptation and
Texas Men magazine present:

1998 Mail Order Men

#691 THE LONE WOLF
by Sandy Steen—July 1998

#695 SINGLE IN THE SADDLE
by Vicki Lewis Thompson—August 1998

#699 SINGLE SHERIFF SEEKS...
by Jo Leigh—September 1998

#703 STILL HITCHED, COWBOY
by Leandra Logan—October 1998

#707 TALL, DARK AND RECKLESS
by Lyn Ellis—November 1998

#711 MR. DECEMBER
by Heather MacAllister—December 1998

Mail Order Men—
Satisfaction Guaranteed!

Available wherever Harlequin books are sold.

HARLEQUIN®

Makes any time special ™

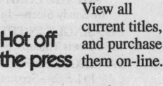

What do you want for Christmas?

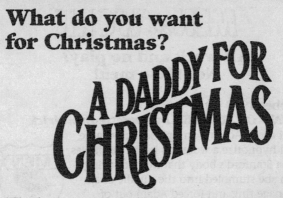

A DADDY FOR CHRISTMAS

'Tis the season for wishes and dreams that come true. This November, follow three handsome but lonely Scrooges as they learn to believe in the magic of the season when they meet the *right* family, in *A Daddy for Christmas*.

MERRY CHRISTMAS, BABY
by Pamela Browning

THE NUTCRACKER PRINCE
by Rebecca Winters

THE BABY AND THE BODYGUARD
by Jule McBride

Available November 1998
wherever Harlequin and Silhouette books are sold.

HARLEQUIN®
Makes any time special ™

Silhouette®

Look us up on-line at: http://www.romance.net

PHBR1198

MEN at WORK

All work and no play?
Not these men!

October 1998
SOUND OF SUMMER by Annette Broadrick

Secret agent Adam Conroy's seductive gaze
could hypnotize a woman's heart. But it was
Selena Stanford's body that needed saving—
when she stumbled into the middle of an
espionage ring and forced Adam out of
hiding....

November 1998
GLASS HOUSES by Anne Stuart

Billionaire Michael Dubrovnik never lost a
negotiation—until Laura de Kelsey Winston
changed the boardroom rules. He might
acquire her business...but a kiss would cost
him his heart....

December 1998
FIT TO BE TIED by Joan Johnston

Matthew Benson had a way with words
and women—but he refused to be tied
down. Could Jennifer Smith get him to
retract his scathing review of her art by
trying another tactic: tying him *up?*

Available at your favorite retail outlet!

MEN AT WORK™

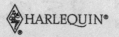 

Temptation®

COMING NEXT MONTH

#709 A PRIVATE EYEFUL Ruth Jean Dale
Hero for Hire
None of Samantha Spade's team of bodyguards had *ever* met
their boss, so when she summoned Nicholas Charles, he was
intrigued. And then annoyed. His assignment was to sit
poolside in a luxury resort, waiting for something to happen.
What happened was Corinne Leblanc—a prime suspect for
something, with a body that demanded his undivided
attention....

#710 THE REBEL'S RETURN Gina Wilkins
Southern Scandals
The prodigal son has come home for Christmas.... Fifteen years ago,
young hell-raiser Lucas McBride was run out of town, accused
of a crime he didn't commit. Now he's back to settle the score—
and reclaim the girl he'd made a woman.

#711 MR. DECEMBER Heather MacAllister
Mail Order Men
Lexi Jordan only wants one thing for Christmas: a man! And
who better than sexy Spencer Price, *Texas Men*'s Mr. December
himself. But one look at the gorgeous scientist has Lexi making a
different kind of wish list—one that keeps Spencer in her bed
well into the New Year....

#712 THE RIGHT MAN IN MONTANA Kristine Rolofson
Boots & Booties
Help wanted: Wife. When Sylvie Smith read the want ad, she was
desperate. So she applied to a very sexy but *very* confused
cowboy. It turned out that Joe Brockett's orphaned nieces and
nephew had concocted this scheme to find a mommy for
Christmas. But Sylvie couldn't stop thinking how great it would
be to welcome Christmas morning as this man's wife....